They were getting close and someone didn't like it.

"Joy, there's a piece of paper under your windshield wiper."

"Yeah, I see it." Her eyes arrowed and I saw the determined earnestness in her expression.

She pulled the note free very carefully, then opened it. It was a white piece of paper folded in half. I could see there were words on it.

Joy looked around us and then unlocked the driver's door. "Let's get in the car."

I slid into my seat, then turned to look at her.

"Well?" I asked, not liking the fact that she wasn't telling me what the note said. "What does it say?" My heart was racing.

"Here," she said, handing me the note.

I opened the paper, then read the words out loud, "Drop your questioning and chasing around. Let old bones rest."

Old Bones

A Neighbor's Mystery

by

Rita Schulz

Published by 53rd Street Publishing
Head office: Gibsons, British Columbia Canada
http://www.53rdstreetpublishing.com

Dedication

For Russ. First one.

Old Bones
A Neighbor's Mystery
Rita Schulz

Published by 53rd Street Publishing
Copyright 2017 Rita Schulz
All rights reserved

Cover art © Ferdericb | Dreamstime.com
Cover designed by R. Edgewood
Cover design and layout copyright 2017 by 53rd Street Publishing
ISBN: 978-1-927621-57-8

53rd Street Publishing
Head office: Gibsons B.C. Canada
www.53rdsteetpublishing.com

Chapter One
Old Bones and New Neighbors

"THEY'VE FOUND A BODY at the empty lot," said Manda, standing on my front cement porch letting cold air into the house. She was my dear friend and neighbor and had a wide grin on her face.

Manda's dark brown eyes were twinkling as she patted her head to make sure her long, black-and-silver hair was secure in its braided ponytail. She was an active, petite, older Indian woman in her early seventies with enough energy to put me—I'm a healthy fifty-five-year-old—to shame.

My eyes opened wide in surprise as I heard the news. I was shocked. Not possible. I looked at her to see if she was pulling a practical joke on me. She knows I write mystery books as well as other genres, but my current project happens to be a mystery novel.

"There may be bones, but I think it must be an animal, a cow or a horse, something like that," I said as I swung open the oak front door to let Manda enter and hopefully to keep some of the warm air inside too.

Manda shook her head. Her warm, fudge-brown eyes looked straight into mine, and while I saw excitement, I didn't see any guile. "No, it's human; and you know what that means."

I moved aside and let her into the little foyer of our home.

Just think, a murder in our neck of the woods?

I stopped short at that thought. Manda said that they found a body, then some bones and now she was saying that it was human.

1

Interesting. There was nothing about a murder, at least not yet.

"Old bones?" I asked her, opening the hall closet.

"Human, old bones," Manda added, her voice filled with authority.

I nodded and smiled at her.

This had never happened in our quiet Vancouver neighborhood, as far as I remember, and I've lived here my entire life.

I was having trouble with my latest book. I'm a storyteller, a full-time fiction writer looking for a good story. My latest deadline was coming up fast. It was mid-March now and my book was due at my editor by the end of May, the same time as my birthday.

That meant the best present for me this year would be to finish this book and turn it in as soon as possible, hopefully before the deadline.

Bones. A body? This might be exactly what the doctor ordered. A nice, simple, local mystery that I could ramp up and turn into a book.

"Excellent," I said, smiling at Manda. "Let's check it out, shall we? Come in; it's cold out there. I'll get my jacket. It's time to take Buddy out anyway," I said as I stepped back from the open door.

"It is cold. I can't believe it's the middle of March. Usually it doesn't get like this after January," she said as she stepped into the warm front hallway.

I closed the heavy oak front door, painted sage green, behind us. We went to the hall closet to get my heavy navy-blue parka and Buddy's leash.

"Where's Lucky?" I asked as I snapped Buddy's leash to his collar. Lucky was Manda and Dillon's chubby beagle, who really needed his walks.

"He was sleeping in his bed by the heater in our bedroom. You know, doing his job keeping Dillon company," she said with a chuckle.

Like Manda, her husband Dillon was in his early seventies. They had emigrated from India a long time ago. After arriving in Canada, Dillon had earned his teaching certificate and taught school at John Oliver Secondary School for many years. They had lived in the South Vancouver community since they came to Canada. Manda worked at the local drug store on Fraser for a very long time too. They had retired at the same time and were a very close couple.

The foyer of our house is a small area between the front door and the door which led to the seldom-used attic. Tom, my husband, and I placed a tall Parsons bench in front of it for people to hang their coats and to sit on when putting on their shoes.

On the left side of the foyer was the hallway that went toward the back of the house and the extra large kitchen and small bathroom. The three upstairs bedrooms were on the left too starting with the master closest to the front of the house.

On the right side of the foyer behind a beveled glass French door was the living room, with cheery red couches and lots of wood.

I was putting on Buddy's leash after pulling on my coat when there was another knock on the door. I looked at Manda, who looked back at me, her eyes curious, and shrugged.

I stepped forward, opened the front door, and saw Betty, another neighbor, from down the street. I motioned for her to come into the hallway, which was getting very crowded with the three of us, especially since they were wearing thick, heavy winter parkas.

"I see your new neighbors have arrived, Heather," said Betty as she entered the foyer and closed the door behind her.

I quickly took a peek over her shoulder before the door was shut to see a large moving truck.

"I hadn't noticed. I guess they just arrived," I said as I herded everyone to the door.

The noise in our home was deafening. Although there were only three ladies in the hallway, we were all talking and laughing, asking about the body and at the same time trying to find out about Manda's trip to India. She had been gone for two months and had just returned.

"Come on ladies, let's get going so that we can come back sooner. I'll make us a nice pot of tea and I have biscuits," I said, taking charge of the situation and ushering everyone out into the cold March day.

We knew we had to hurry. If we didn't get to the empty lot soon, all the good vantage points would be taken. Two of us being shortish ladies, we were very aware of the importance of being early to get a good viewpoint or we wouldn't see anything interesting.

Soon we were all shivering in spite of our warm coats. The only one not affected was Buddy, my little red cairn terrier, who was too busy sniffing and marking every tree and bush to notice the cold.

I usually enjoyed my daily walks with Buddy, so I wasn't sure if I was shivering from the cold or excitement at the thought of seeing a dead body in our little quiet neighborhood.

I wondered if it was someone from the neighborhood, or if the body had been just dumped here. And how long had the body been there? Going over the basic who, what, where, when, and how in my mind, I wondered if and when we were going to get any answers.

I told myself it was pointless, speculating without more information, but my mind had gone off on a tangent and was asking all sorts of questions. Most of all, I was wondering if I'd be able to use any of this information for my newest book.

I wanted a good story. That's what my readers wanted and what I enjoyed writing, but that was also my worst problem: coming up with a good story.

It seemed everything that I'd come up with lately had already been done a dozen times or more and seemed deadly dull to me.

As Manda and Betty walked down the front stairs, I turned to lock the door behind us; then I remembered that I didn't need to, Tom was home.

My husband had taken this week off to work on one of his projects. He was a writer too, but he still had a day job, at least for now. His three loves are me, writing, and golf.

He planned to go in to the office next week and then take holidays until his birthday in May, when he would be turning fifty-five years old. He'd always planned on retiring at fifty-five. I guess it was past the planning stage since he had already submitted his resignation letter and management had accepted. His retirement was a done deal as far as he was concerned. I wasn't so sure.

One more week and then we would both be home writing full time.

I retired last year at fifty-five after working for the Bank of Nova Scotia for thirty-five years. I ended up as the Senior Loans Manager in the training branch at Forty-Ninth and Fraser, close to home. And Tom had worked for the Canada Border Services Agency, the old Canada Customs, as a Senior Compliance Verification Officer. He only had thirty-four years in, but since he meets the age requirement, he won't have any penalty so his pension should be fine.

I was startled to hear a female voice yelling just as a golden retriever puppy came bounding from around the moving van. The young dog ran over to where Buddy and I were standing. I stopped walking so that the two dogs could say hello to each other.

Old Bones

"Kirby, get your funny face back right here, right now," said a young-looking woman, probably in her late thirties, with a bright purple toque pulled down low over all her hair and the tips of her ears, and a hot pink-and-purple striped scarf wrapped round her neck. She had a heart-shaped face with a small nose and inquisitive, bright blue eyes. She jogged around the corner of the van, running after her escaped pet. She wore a friendly grin on her face as she slowly ran toward us.

I reached over to let the young golden sniff my hand as the dog wagged his tail and smiled at me. I gently, slowly reached for his collar. The metal chain collar was new and had a strap that was a lovely shade of bright green against his dark red-brown fur. It was a Martingale collar, the kind that I favored for Buddy. Only, for the golden, it was the extra-large size. He was a big boy, but from the way he was acting, probably only about two and a half years old.

"I gather he belongs to you?" I said as I held on to the dog's collar until the young woman came over to my friends and me.

Since we were all owners or previous owners of different kinds and sizes of dogs, Kirby didn't spook any of us.

"Hi, my name is Joy Kendal. Thank you so much for holding Kirby," she said as she took a firm hold of his collar and smiled at our little group. We all introduced ourselves.

"Nice dog, how old?" asked Manda. Kirby had come over to her to sniff the edge of her coat, his tail wagging all the time as if taking great delight in this new game of chase he had discovered.

"Yes, he's a year and a half old, a really wonderful dog, but the move hasn't left much time for his daily walks in the last few weeks."

Joy took off one of her matching purple gloves to shake hands all around.

She pulled her toque off since it had slipped down over her eyes.

Her hair was cut in a nice shoulder-length bob and was a lovely rich red color, natural too, judging from her red eyebrows and a sprinkle of freckles over her nose and cheeks.

She seemed to be a warm, intelligent person.

"If you'd like, we could help you with walking Kirby this week while you get settled," I heard myself say as I smiled back at Joy.

I felt my heart clench in my chest. What was I doing? I had enough on my plate with my normal schedule, a book due in the next four weeks, a Spring Tea at the church I was organizing for the end of May and Tom's impending retirement would take some adjustment for both of us, too. I couldn't possibly take on another task, especially with a dog the size of Kirby. He was probably about ninety pounds and stood up to my hip.

"Thanks, that would be wonderful. We would really appreciate it, at least for a few days until we can at least get the big stuff inside," said Joy, beaming at me.

"Don't worry, we could all take turns during the day. He's a big dog, but he's leash trained so it shouldn't be a problem," piped up Betty.

Betty and her husband George used to have a dog too, but Ruby had passed away a year ago. Since Betty worked shift work and her husband worked very early hours at a bakery, they didn't feel that they could do another dog justice—especially a puppy.

"I know that George used to run with Ruby; do you think that he could do the same with Kirby? That would really help use up some of that energy he has," I suggested to Betty.

Just then I saw Kirby lunge forward and pull out of Joy's hand, then with head and tail high, start running next door to our house.

I was really starting to feel the cold seeping through my jacket.

Old Bones

I glanced down at Buddy since I knew we had to get moving, and started walking down the street toward the empty lot.

"Goodbye Joy. Nice to meet up, and you too, Kirby!" I called as we started walking quickly down the street.

I looked up when I heard the sound of a car motor and saw our garage door start to open. Our garage was in back of the house and we had our own little driveway on the side from the road next to the house. It made for a long, narrow house, but it was built a long time ago and we hadn't made any large changes.

I saw the escaped Kirby stop at the rose bush next to the driveway at the corner of the house and sniff at the scents he found there. At the same time I saw our blue Volvo station wagon slowly going backward down the driveway toward our garage.

I knew there was no way Tom would be able to see the dog. The animal was completely in his blind spot, so I started yelling and waving my arms as I stepped onto the driveway with Buddy in tow.

Tom didn't see me either and kept on backing up.

Joy ran after me, heading for Kirby.

Our car was now headed toward both Joy and Kirby. Tom wasn't going fast, but if they got under the wheel, it would still do a lot of damage to a person and probably kill a dog.

I hoped Kirby would stay at the bush until Joy got there. Just as Joy came up to his shoulder, I could hear her speaking to him and he sat as she commanded. Joy calmly walked toward him.

Tom was looking toward the road but now Joy was hunched over talking softly to Kirby, reaching out her hand to take his collar; there was no way Tom would see them.

I watched Kirby. He sat on the ground but kept his eyes on Joy.

As she opened the clip on the leash, he shot forward away from her, trying to get across our driveway before Tom and the car got there.

I could see that it was going to be close. I screamed, hoping that Tom would hear me, but with the motor running, the car windows closed, and the radio on, I doubted he could.

I watched Joy as she realized that the car was bearing down on both of them. They had only a few seconds to either move out of the way or get hit.

I was startled when I heard someone screaming down the block. That got Kirby's attention and, rather than sitting and waiting for Joy, he took off at a full run down the block toward the empty house at the end of the street.

Tom's car came to a halt next to me and he rolled down the driver's side window. "What's going on?" he asked as he saw our little group and Joy chasing her dog at a full run down the street.

"Hi, honey," I said. "They've found a dead body at the empty lot and we're all going to check it out. We just met our new neighbor Joy and her golden retriever Kirby. He's running around playing tag with her, so be careful." I explained this all as simply as I could.

"A dead body, you say. I was just going inside for a coffee. I think I'll join you instead," Tom said as he pulled the car further up our driveway and parked it in front of the garage.

"Did you lock up?" I didn't know that he was out when I left the house and was surprised to see him coming home in the car. I could see this was going to take a little getting used to, having him home during the day. Which I knew, but it's all the little things that you take for granted that throw you off. We were going to have to discuss this.

"No, you were home," he said as he started walking down the street with us.

"I thought you had a coffee date with Pastor Brian this afternoon?" I asked.

"You are correct, my dear," he said as he turned around and headed back into the house.

"I don't understand." I paused; if he didn't want to tell me, I wasn't going to interrogate him. "How's Brian?" But I could still ask a few questions.

I waited for a reply, which didn't come, then started to hum to myself as I hurried after Manda and Betty.

I really needed this story for my book and I heard about it first. What if Tom used this idea for his own book? I felt a little... not jealousy exactly, but perhaps there was a little competition between my husband and myself. I surprised myself; this had never happened before. Tom and I wrote differently, and usually different genres. The stories that interested him I enjoyed reading, but weren't my style of writing.

I can't say I liked the feeling I was having. I didn't want to compete with anyone, especially not my husband. And especially not since he was retiring soon and we'd both be working and living in the same house. That sounded like trouble to me.

I pushed these thoughts to the back of my mind to ruminate on them later. Right now I needed help in finding a good story and getting as much detail as I could from the scene in the empty lot. I hoped I'd be able to ask questions of the police and get some interesting answers.

"It might help if you get a leash," Tom called out as he passed me at a slow jog. Kirby, with Joy following, came trotting past me; only this time they were headed up Fifty-Third toward Fraser.

I closed my eyes and then opened them.

This was now getting serious. Someone had to catch and control that dog.

Fraser was a very busy main street and I knew that Kirby would have to be caught or he might end up under the wheels of a car or bus.

I knew I couldn't go after him; I hadn't done any jogging ever. Even in school, when I tried I always ended up with a stitch in my side and finished the laps by power walking.

I looked around to see who of my friends would be able to help Joy and my eyes fell on Tom.

"Tom. Stop for a minute. Please help Joy catch her dog. He's headed up to Fraser," I called to him.

Luckily he heard me and turned around. He saw the problem immediately and started running back toward Joy and Kirby, seemingly as fast as his fifty-five-year-old legs could carry him.

"His name is Kirby and her name is Joy," I added as he passed me.

I watched my husband with admiration. Even though he was fifty-five years old and for the last ten years had been fighting his weight, he had gotten serious about getting in shape in the last year and dropped fifty pounds through diet and exercise. As he told me, he was getting ready to be a very active retiree.

I had been really glad when he finally took his health seriously. I had always been a little on the plump side myself but had dropped weight in the last two years, too, under the doctor's instruction. Cutting way back on the sweets was number one. Then I started more walking. I enjoyed swimming, too, but not jogging. I always felt it was too hard on the body although I admired people who could do it.

I watched as Tom ran onto the boulevard from our side street. I could tell that he had decided to try and head the dog off.

Old Bones

I watched, not knowing what to do. We lived half a block from Fraser, and Kirby and Joy had already covered half the remaining distance so Tom didn't have much time. He had to get ahead of the dog, then run toward him without spooking him too much.

"Joy! Stop chasing him," I called out to her. "Run toward me and maybe he'll follow you."

I didn't know if she heard me since at first she didn't stop. Then I saw her nod and begin to slow her pace. She stopped and called to Kirby. "Kirby, come on, find me!" She stared to walk backward toward me.

Kirby noticed Joy was no longer running after him and stopped by a tall cherry tree on the boulevard for a sniff. Then he looked at Joy, who was laughing and slapping her thigh.

I watched as Tom got closer and closer to the dog and hoped that Kirby wouldn't notice him.

I saw Kirby's head go up as Joy started to turn away from him.

"That's it Joy, keep going!" I shouted.

That did the trick. Kirby started running after her.

I quickly turned and started down the street too, with Buddy in tow, hoping that Kirby might stop to say hi to Buddy and I could grab Kirby's collar.

Joy came up to me and passed me as she walked quickly, not looking back at the dog.

"Come on, Kirby, you mangy little mutt," she said in a light, friendly tone as she passed.

She arched her eyebrows and her hand in a mock salute to me as she smiled and shook her head.

It was cold and her breath was coming out in small puffs of fog. The ground was white with frost, something we normally didn't have this time of year.

I shivered again and tried to get deeper in my parka, looking for more warmth.

"He's coming toward you. He's following you. Keep going," I said, letting Joy know what was going on and to encourage her.

There were at least five to six blocks before we hit another main street so I thought that we had ample time to catch Kirby.

I started to power walk and Tom soon caught up with Buddy and me.

Manda and Betty were already by the empty house and were gathered with the rest of the people talking and milling around a small backhoe that the workers had been using to push the dirt out of the way for the foundation of a double garage.

I noticed two black, unmarked police cars parked on the side of the street and two more white-and-blue police cars blocking the street from any traffic that might come down, with their emergency lights flashing.

By this time Joy and Kirby were across the street, Joy leading the way and Kirby stopping to explore every once in a while.

Joy's face was flushed and she was walking slower. I could tell that she was getting tired and worried.

I had an idea.

I walked up to the black, unmarked police car and noticed that it was empty. I didn't know any dogs that didn't like car rides and had used it a few times to catch Buddy. I turned to look at Kirby and smiled.

"Kirby, come. Car ride," I called out as I stepped up to the police car and opened a passenger door.

Thankfully it was unlocked.

Buddy immediately ran over and jumped into the back seat.

Old Bones

Kirby stopped and looked toward the car, his tail slowly wagging and his head cocked to one side as if he was thinking the situation over.

The wind started to increase. The air was getting colder although it was just late morning.

I looked at Buddy and he seemed to be very happy he was out of the cold and off the frozen sidewalk.

"Come on, you silly big puppy. Kirby, let's go for a car ride," I yelled out in my most cheerful voice. I clapped my hands together and then bent down and opened my arms wide.

Kirby took one look at me, his eyes as bright as a shiny new penny, then he started to run toward me. I laughed and watched him come running at full speed toward me and the police car. What a beautiful dog he was, a very happy puppy.

Kirby ran up to me and barely stopped as he jumped into the open back door of the car.

"Good dog," I said before I slammed the door closed on Buddy and Kirby.

I turned to look at him. He filled up almost the entire back seat. That's when I realized that Buddy wasn't in the car.

No Buddy.

"Hey, lady, is that your dog? What's he doing in my cruiser?" said a tall blond man wearing blue jeans and a puffy navy-blue bomber jacket as he walked to the black car.

"Heather. Heather!" I heard Manda calling me. Her voice was getting louder and louder. Finally she was yelling.

Great. I quickly prioritized the calls. Police first. Then the friend, then Buddy. Hopefully Manda has Buddy.

"Lady, I asked you if that's your dog and why you put him in my police car?"

"Ah, hello, officer. No, it's not my dog. He ran away from my new neighbor, Joy, and he's been leading us on a crazy chase," I said, looking for Joy to give some validity to my statement.

"Ryan, is that you?" asked Joy as she approached us.

"Aunt Joy? I might have known it was Kirby," said the tall blond officer with a grin.

"Good thinking, Heather. One thing that Kirby loves is going for a car ride," said Joy, smiling. "Oh, by the way, Heather…" Her voice trailed off when she obviously couldn't remember my full name. She indicated the blond police officer with a nod of her head.

"Ross, my name is Heather Ross," I said, helping her out.

Her cheeks flushed slightly. "Yes. Heather Ross, may I introduce my nephew, Ryan Falcon. He's the pride and joy of the family. He just made detective."

Joy opened the back door of the car and told Kirby to sit as she blocked the door with her body. He sat and she clipped the leash onto his collar.

"Excuse me, Detective Falcon. There's a dog digging in your crime scene and I think it's got one of the bones," said one of the uniformed officers.

I realized I had been hearing all kinds of noise in the background and finally stopped to identify them. There were people laughing and others yelling. Some were even whistling and calling.

I stopped, took a deep breath, closed my eyes as I turned toward the empty lot, then slowly opened them.

I saw a dozen of my neighbors about one hundred feet away from me, all bundled up in heavy coats. Half were looking at a hole dug in the lot they were working in, the other half were looking at me.

I smiled at them.

15

Old Bones

Yep, I could hear Manda and Betty calling, "Buddy. Buddy! Come here."

I knew Buddy wouldn't come to them. Unless, of course, they had a cookie; then it might be worth his while to obey them. He was a cairn terrier after all, and that's a special breed of dog; or maybe it was just Buddy that was so special.

"Excuse me, Detective Falcon. I'll be right back," I said. I strode to where a shallow pit had been dug and the body had been found.

And there he was. My Buddy. I could see his back and tail through a cloud of dirt as he frantically tried to free a bone the size of his body.

Okay, here comes the test. All those years of obedience training—will they pay off? I reached into my coat pocket and pulled out a small plastic bag containing liver training treats. Like American Express, I never leave home without them.

Somehow I had to get Buddy to come to me. He had his leash attached to his collar so I knew if I could get him close I could either pick it up or step on it to grab it.

I got myself ready. I knew I only had one chance. Buddy learned quickly. He was smart and sneaky. I lifted my head, chin up, squared my shoulders, and stood as tall as I could manage. I told myself when I call Buddy, he will come.

"Buddy, come." I ordered in my best no-nonsense voice. Then I whistled.

Buddy stopped digging and looked up, his ears up and alert. He looked at me standing by the sidewalk next to a tall cherry tree.

I whistled again and held up a treat so he could see.

It worked. Buddy came running right toward me, his little pink tongue sticking out and his eyes bright.

He moved as fast as his little legs could go. At that moment I was so proud of him and all the hard work we had done together.

He ran right up to me and sat down in front of me. I nodded to him, leaned down and picked up his leash, then gave him his treat.

"Good boy, Buddy. You're the best," I said as he sat and watched me.

There was never a doubt in my mind he would come for me, especially when a treat was involved.

I had made it a point in training him to always give him a treat when I whistled. I didn't use the whistle very often. Usually only in an important I-need-you-to-come-right-now situation. And it paid off.

As the trainer at the Community Center said, "This is nothing to fool around with. You need a command he knows you will honor, and also a release word he knows is from you. It's a matter of trust and not just obedience."

"Mrs. Ross?"

I turned toward the voice to discover Ryan Falcon standing behind me. Now it was my turn to apologize for using his car as a dog trap. I sure hope Joy will help me explain it to him.

I looked up, way up, and tried to meet his eyes. Which was a little difficult since he was more than a foot taller than me.

I smiled at the young police detective. "Please call me Heather. It's really a pleasure to meet you." I held my hand out for him to shake.

Joy appeared with a soft grin on her face as she stood next to Ryan and watched as I introduced myself.

Out of the corner of my eye I could see that Joy had a firm grip on Kirby's collar.

I stood with my hand extended, looking into Ryan Falcon's deep azure eyes. His mouth was set in a stern, straight line and I could see his jaw was clenched.

Okay, this was starting to get embarrassing. I guess his parents didn't teach him proper manners. Or he was really so angry at me he wouldn't shake my hand.

I wondered if Buddy or Kirby made a mess in his car.

Oh dear. My mouth went dry and my stomach clenched as I started to drop my hand to my side. Okay, I decided I was going to have to change tactics and take a look at the inside of the car to determine how bad the damage was.

Suddenly, Falcon smiled and reached for my hand. He firmly grasped it and gave it three warm, friendly shakes.

"Almost had you, didn't I?" he said as his eyes lit up with amusement.

"Oh, come on now," I started to laugh with him and shook my head at his abrupt change in attitude.

"Admit it, Heather, he's a pretty good actor," said Joy as she joined in the fun with a big smile that started at her lips and ended in her eyes. "You ought to see him do the good cop, bad cop routine. He has 'em really sweating."

"Thanks all the same, but I think I'll forgo that little pleasure," I said with a chuckle. I turned back to gaze into the pit and remembered the reason we were all gathered here.

"Buddy didn't disturb any evidence did he?"

"No, the coroner had just left with the remains when the littler guy jumping in," said Ryan. "I think he was pulling on an old tree root that still had the smell of the bones on it. Thank goodness Buddy's timing was just a little bit off and nothing was damaged," added Ryan.

I nodded my head as all three of us, with the two dogs in tow, went close to the shallow pit.

Actually there were two shallow pits, a large one probably for the main house and another one probably for a double garage. The smaller one, for the garage, was where the old bones had been found.

Joy stood next to me and looked intently at what might be a crime scene. I pulled out the camera I had shoved in my pocket before we left and started to take pictures of the pit. I zoomed in for some close-ups, then I took pictures of the house and the lot as well as the street and the boulevard.

I could use my imagination and put the bones in the hole for my story. Even if I didn't use this lot for the novel I was working on, I could use it for another one in the future.

"What do you think happened?" Joy asked me.

"I don't know. I understand from the gossip they are very old bones. So I guess they've been here for a while," I said.

"I better get back to the station, Aunt Joy," said Ryan. "You won't be needing the car to catch any more dogs this morning will you, Heather?" He grinned at me and my cheeks grew warm.

"No, thanks. I think I'm good for now." I nodded to him. He turned away and got into his unmarked car, started the engine, and drove away.

"I wonder," said Joy softly.

"Manda," I called to my neighbor when I spotted her standing with Betty on the other side of the hole.

Manda smiled at me, then said something to Betty, who nodded, and they made their way toward me around the police tape.

"Okay, what did you guys see? I need all the details," I asked, scanning their serious expressions.

"Well, there is obviously a mystery here. Someone has been killed. I don't think this was the site of a family gravesite. If so, it would be odd to only have one body in it.

Old Bones

It really all depends on how old the body is, and if they can tell if the person died of natural causes or not," said Manda, starting the conversation.

"Would they call all of these police if they didn't expect it to be a murder?" I asked.

I looked at the police officers as they took down most of the yellow crime scene tape, except for the immediate site of the garage, and then all got into their vehicles and left.

"Unfortunately, these old crimes don't usually get solved. People and witnesses have since died or moved away. It's really hard to solve," said Joy as we started to walk home together.

I nodded at Joy's reasoning. It was quite logical. But now I had a real problem. I would need to solve the crime before I could use it in my book.

"Nothing I like better than a good, old-fashioned murder mystery. Don't you?" she said as she tugged Kirby's leash to encourage him to follow her.

"Funny you mention that. I'm a mystery writer and yes, there is nothing I like better than a good murder mystery. Especially one that hasn't been solved or told yet," I explained.

"Ah, then you must be a writer looking for a good story. Good thing, because I love a good puzzle and I'm very good at solving them," said Joy with confidence in her voice.

"Really?" I said my hopes rising a little.

Perhaps this would be a very good friendship after all. I'm naturally curious and ask questions, and she likes to solve puzzles. It was a match made in heaven.

"Well, what do you say? Shall we investigate our first little mystery?" Joy grinned at me.

"I do hope it is a murder," I said. "It would be perfect for my next book. If that would be all right with you?"

"Excellent. I know just where we can start, too. I'll have my sister and her husband and the rest of their brood over for dinner this Saturday. Would you and your husband like to come over as well?"

I thought this was a strange turn of topics until I realized that she must be talking about Police Detective Ryan's parents.

"That sounds like a wonderful idea." I nodded.

I planned to get detailed maps of the neighborhood, maybe one from the library going back about fifty and then thirty years, to see what the area had looked like.

I could get old telephone books too, which would give me the names of the people living in the area, then sort out the relationships. It was quite common for people immigrating to settle in family groups close to each other.

Once I got the maps and telephone books, I'd have enough to start the first chapter of my new book.

My book would be a fiction, of course, but based on reality. That way I could make stuff up once I got all the bones of the story down.

"What can we bring?' I asked Joy as we started walking up the street with the dogs and the rest of my friends.

I knew all my old friends would really enjoy Joy. I had a very strong feeling she would fit in fine with the rest of us. We each had special skills besides walking dogs and gardening.

"A green salad would be lovely. By then, Ryan should have the coroner's report, too. That will give us a really good place to start," Joy said as she turned and went into her house.

Joy's new house was a thirty-year-old Vancouver Special.

Old Bones

It had a level entrance; two floors with a tiny deck out front and a good-sized one in the back; and there were three bedrooms up and one full bath, and an en suite and walk-in closet in the master bedroom. The downstairs had a huge family room, a bathroom, a room for a guest bedroom, and an office. There was major renovation done by the last owner; that's why it had a walk-in closet and an en suite, but they had sacrificed the hall closet. The basement would need a complete overhaul.

I had been invited by their real estate person and gone to the open house. The new pitch was, "do you have anyone, friends or family, that would like this house and this neighborhood? This is your chance to have some say on who your neighbors are."

Everyone I know is retiring and that house is way too big for two people; it is over twenty-five hundred square feet.

It was okay, but the outside had cream-colored vinyl siding downstairs and faux red brick upstairs, and the useless deck drove me crazy. Either tear it off or do something with it.

I was stressed about the book I had to write. There was a tension knot between my shoulders. I rotated my shoulders, loosening them. I knew I would be just fine, that I would meet my book deadline. I had a very strong positive feeling about Joy. I wondered what she did for a living? I hadn't had a chance to ask her.

I thought I'd ask her over to my place for a cup of tea tomorrow afternoon.

Then I smiled to myself as my imagination took flight. Now I wasn't just working on this new book but a whole series of books. A whole village. No wonder my poor little subconscious and I were tired.

I pulled back my imagination before I got too carried away. I know, too late; but I cleared my mind and focused.

First write this book and make it the best I could. Then work on the second one.

Do one thing at a time.

But the idea did appeal to me. A series of mystery books that take place in a neighborhood in Vancouver and the outlying area; it really inspired me.

Another thought occurred to me. I wondered if my current neighbors knew anything about this murder? Some of them had lived on this street for a very long time—some even had family, now passed, that had lived here, too.

"Tea. Heather, where are you? Zoning out again?" asked Manda as she and Betty came up our front stairs with me. "How is that new book you're working on?"

"Yes, tea, of course. Let's hear about Manda's trip to India." I asked as I opened the door and offered my friends a tight-lipped smile.

We usually had tea at my place after our walks; it had become part of our routine.

"Do you have pictures?" Betty asked as we all came into the foyer.

Tom had forgotten to lock the door anyway. Oh, well, I guess we're going to have to work on our communication skills a little more even after all these years of marriage.

I made mental notes to talk to Tom about the dinner invitation and to invite Joy for tea. Yes, there were definitely going to be interesting times ahead. I could hardly wait.

Chapter Two
Barbeque in early March

SATURDAY DAWNED COLD and clear. They were predicting snow, and there were some years we did get a little bit of very soft snow—nothing that amounted to anything or even stuck to the grass, roads, or sidewalks—this late in the year. Occasionally it was just enough to interfere with the buds on the trees.

The early cherry blossoms had been out since the warm spell a week ago and then it got cold again. The daffodils and crocuses were all starting to shoot up and in some places were blooming. I noticed that my hyacinths were up and starting to open and the new variety of peach daffodils had started to form buds.

I had my large, clear glass bowl with me and Tom carried a variety of salad dressings. I had made a salad with fresh spinach, hard-boiled eggs, crispy bacon, and sliced mushrooms. It was a hearty salad, one of our favorites.

There were times in the summer when it was too warm to cook and Tom had to get to bed early since he got up at five thirty and started work at seven o'clock. Those were the times I would make a big salad and pick up some fresh buns or full-grain bread at the BreakTime coffee shop and bakery.

BreakTime is where I sometimes go for coffee and maybe a treat with my friends. It is the only privately owned and run bakery in the neighborhood. They have seating outside and in nice weather we walk there with the dogs. In nasty weather the dogs stay home and we all car pool.

There is a running battle between us whether it was a bakery first, then a coffee shop second or the other way around. It had originally been a bakery, but when the new owners bought it, they kept the baker on—and his recipes—so they still have the original European bread and baking. Every now and then they add a new cookie, dessert bar, or cake, but the bread and the glazed doughnuts are what we had grown up with when it was called the Fraser Bakery.

Today as Tom and I headed for Joy's house I made sure I was carrying my larger purse with a notebook so I could quickly jot down information.

"Come on, Tom," I said as I hurried him along.

I really didn't want to be late. I didn't know if Joy, like some people, was a real stickler about latecomers. I know I always like to be at least five to ten minutes early. Even if I just wait in the car and freshen my hair and makeup, it is better than arriving late. Tom, on the other hand, was never in a rush and quite often was a few minutes late.

I think the only time he was ever on time or early for something was for our wedding, and that's only because his best man, Bruce, had strict instructions from me that Tom had better be early. And he was, much to my very pleasant surprise.

I also wasn't sure what to wear today to Joy's house. I hadn't been this nervous about anything for a very long time.

I wanted to make a good impression with Joy. She seemed like a nice woman and someone I could get to like and hopefully even work well with.

Why should I care? I didn't have to worry about what people said. I wasn't trying to climb a corporate ladder. I don't know, but I did care.

Old Bones

I was comfortably retired and working at my writing and gardening. But I don't know, there was a possibility of something there, something more. At least that's what my intuition said. I guess I'd see. I picked up my still warm tuna casserole and held it in both hands as Tom opened the door for me.

We walked one door to the east, up the stairs, and I reached out my hand to Joy's doorbell and rang it. I heard barking. A deep-throated loud barking, and I knew Kirby was at home. The door opened and there stood a lovely woman with shoulder-length red hair and green eyes. She was wearing a deep, avocado-green sweater over blue jeans and running shoes.

Good, the dress was going to be casual, and the black Dockers and light gray sweater I was wearing would do just fine. I was wearing my New Balance black leather shoes with the solid soles. They were a shoe, but looked like an ankle boot. Versatile footwear.

"Hi, I'm Heather, one of the neighbors." I indicated Tom with a slight nod of my head. "This is my husband, Tom." I saw the broad head of Kirby poking between the door jam and the side of this woman's hip.

"Hi. I'm Grace, Joy's sister. Here, let me take that for you," she said as she stepped to the side and took the bowl from me. "Come on in. Everyone is in the kitchen. Surprise, surprise," she said as she turned to go into the house.

"Okay, pup, let's go," I said to Kirby as I nudged him forward with my hip, making room for Tom, who was following closely behind me as we closed the door after entering.

I wasn't going to take any chances, not after that silly dog led Joy on that wild-goose chase this morning.

Tom and I followed the sound of laughter and the smells of coffee and cinnamon into the kitchen.

There were about a dozen people gathered in the expansive area, milling around, telling stories, and laughing as they had fresh coffee and homemade cinnamon buns oozing with cream cheese icing.

My stomach started to rumble. I sure hope no one heard it.

The kitchen was very large and there was a smaller family room off to one side with a fireplace; on the other side was a small kitchen table. The kitchen had a nice island and updated stainless steel appliances.

It was well laid out and very functional, something that I would really like to do at our house. Tom and I were planning to redo our kitchen this summer with some of the severance money he would get from the government.

I looked around and noticed Ryan amongst the guests. He was deep in conversation with an older gray-haired gentleman who also had the look of a police officer about him. Only he appeared to be a long-time veteran officer, probably in his early fifties, he looked familiar.

"Oh, Heather, I'm so glad you've come," said Joy as she approached Tom and me. "Thanks for the salad, it looks wonderful."

"Our pleasure," I said as I handed her my famous tuna casserole.

I looked around at the seemingly happy, boisterous group. "It seems that you've got quite a crowd." The energy in the room was positive and I enjoyed taking it all in.

"After we eat we'll get Ryan alone and talk to him about the old bones. His partner Nigel is here too. Come on and meet them." She led the way around the room and did the introductions to her guests.

All I can remember is the names of her two sisters. Hope, the elder sister, was tall, slender, blonde, and married to an accountant, Bob. They were Ryan's parents.

Old Bones

Then there was Grace. Joy's younger sister was the baby of the family, recently separated from her husband of six years. Grace had the same red hair as Joy, but instead of blue eyes, hers were green.

And of course Edgar, Joy's husband. Funny, I wouldn't have pictured Joy with someone like Edgar. He was on the short side, about five feet eight, with light brown hair that was combed over to one side.

His chin was weak and his eyes had a soft look with an underlying uncertainty. But you can never tell about people and there was that saying about not judging a book by its cover.

Dinner was quickly served, buffet style, with dishes set out in the dining room and living room.

Joy had extended her table and it was set for the main meal: fresh vegetable and pasta salads, some hearty casseroles, and other hot dishes. On the island there was a wonderful assortment of fresh fruit and sweets. The fruit included some of my favorites: pineapple, strawberries, and grapes. Oh my, did I see cheesecake?

I was very tempted to bypass the main and go right to the desserts except someone had brought mouth-watering barbequed chicken. Barbequed chicken is one of my favorite foods in the entire world and a real treat, especially in March.

"Okay, who brought the barbequed chicken and how did you make it in the middle of winter?" I just couldn't resist myself as I speared a piece of chicken breast and plopped it onto my plate.

Then I spied potato salad and realized there was a theme running through this meal. Usually I am pretty quick on the uptake and I found this very delightful. Imagine, a picnic in winter.

"I hope you don't mind, but I cannot tell a lie; it was I," mumbled Ryan through a mouthful of potato salad.

28

He swallowed, then explained, "Nigel has an outside gas barbeque he can use all year since it's partially covered and has a gas heater next to it so the chef doesn't freeze important parts of his body off. When I grow up, I want to have one just like it." He grinned as his partner.

Nigel put down his fork, reached over, smacked Ryan gently across the head. Nigel's deep brown eyes were twinkling with the enjoyment of the moment.

Nigel's hair was the darker ginger color that red hair goes when a person gets older. He was wearing a deep green tee shirt and dark blue jeans. I guessed him to be in his late fifties.

When he laughed it was more of a growl, deep in his throat with kind of a throaty wolf finish. It was very unique.

I put down my fork. My mouth had gone dry but I managed to swallow. I picked up my cup of lemon water and took a sip. My stomach had done a flip and my heart was beating double time. My knees felt like they had turned to jelly and were going to buckle under me.

I scanned around the kitchen, my eyes not able to focus now. Everything appeared indistinct, somehow vague or hazy. I took in a deep breath to steady myself.

My mind must be playing tricks on me.

I looked at Nigel and realized that while it was a thirty-year-old memory—my memory—it was still accurate.

I still remembered the smell of him as we danced. His arms wrapped firmly yet gently around my waist as our bodies moved together; we swayed to the beat of a live band playing, "Three times a Lady."

I had fallen for Nigel Wallace that night, and when he kissed me I had thought he had feelings for me, too.

It had been a blind date, my one and only blind date.

Old Bones

My girlfriend from high school had suggested we all go out together. At the time, Nigel had just broken up with his long-time girlfriend.

Apparently he really liked me, at least according to my girlfriend's fiancé, and was going to call me. Only his old girlfriend called him first and they had gotten back together. I had heard that they had gotten married, had two children and she had passed away a few years ago.

I smiled to myself. It was a bittersweet memory and one I was sure only I would remember.

I glanced over at Tom and he seemed to sense me looking at him because he turned toward me and winked. I smiled at him and lifted my glass, toasting him with my water. He grinned, nodded, then toasted me back with his glass.

I loved Tom Ross. When we first met I only liked him, but as our friendship grew, I fell deeply in love with this man that I eventually married.

All I can say is that it was a good thing I was available when Tom had come along.

"How long have Ryan and Nigel been partners?" I asked Joy when she walked by me in the living room.

"About one year. Ryan was so lucky to have gotten Nigel as a partner. Nigel's previous partner had just retired and I understand he can retire himself in about another two or three years. All I know is that he's a really good guy and great to work with. I better put some coffee and tea on," she said as she turned to put the kettle on.

I walked through the house and realized it was already a home. I don't know how Joy had done it, but in just a few days it had gone from boxes stacked up in every corner to a warm, comfortable home.

She even had pictures up on the walls and plants in places that looked like they had been there and thriving for a long time.

The doorbell rang and Kirby started to bark. I saw Joy in the kitchen and her sisters helping her. None of them appeared to react to the doorbell since they were engrossed in preparing platters of food.

"Heather, can you get that? And don't forget about Kirby," Joy called from the kitchen.

I went to open the front door after making sure I had gotten a firm hold of Kirby's collar.

I swung open the door to find two more of my neighbors. "Hi, Catherine and Beverly." I was really glad to see Catherine Braun. She was a woman in her early eighties who had recently lost Peter, her husband of over forty years.

She and Peter had lived in a house across from the elementary school and they had attended the Mennonite Brethren Church on the corner of Forty-Ninth and Main.

The young people from our church and theirs sometimes got together for special events.

I'd have to make a point in going over to visit her.

I knew Beverly Frissell quite well; she taught the Dog Obedience Club at the community center. I took Buddy to her refresher course every spring.

I was glad to see Catherine and Beverly were friends.

I wasn't sure what to do. I was really enjoying myself, but at the same time I wanted to get home. I also wanted to find out if the fellows had any information on the old bones that were found. If it had been up to me, I would just have Ryan and Nigel over for coffee and then ask them. I've always liked the straightforward approach; but since it wasn't my home or my guests, I knew I had to wait and let Joy take the lead.

Old Bones

"Okay, Heather, why don't we go into the living room and talk to Ryan. Nigel is almost getting ready to leave, so now would be a good time," said Joy as she walked up to me.

I looked in the kitchen and Tom was talking to one of our other neighbors. It was nice to see Joy had invited Manda and Dillon as well as Betty and George.

"Sounds like a plan to me," I said, letting a small smile curl the corners of my mouth. I quickly followed her as she led me into the living room.

Nigel and Ryan were still in the living room when Joy and I joined them.

"Nigel, thank you so much for coming today," said Joy in a cheery voice.

"It was a real pleasure meeting you," I said, looking at Nigel.

"Ryan, you be careful of these two lovely ladies. See you tomorrow," said Nigel. He had a smile on his face and a twinkle in his eyes as he walked down the hall to the doorway.

I could tell Nigel had meant what he said in a nice way, but also he was giving Ryan a bit of a warning. I wasn't sure if I felt flattered or a little embarrassed. I felt that Nigel was a very smart man and I was sure he'd already spoken to Ryan about me.

Now it was up to Joy and me to see how much information we could get out of Ryan.

"Ryan, let's sit down," Joy suggested, indicating the two leather sofas beside each other in one corner of the room "I'm curious about the old bones that were found at the empty lot a couple of days ago. Did you get any information about them?" Joy asked once we were settled on the deep, dark brown leather sofas.

"Okay, Aunt Joy, you don't waste any time, do you?"

"We were just curious and thought maybe since we live here we may be able to help in some way?" I looked between Ryan and Joy.

"Well, yes," he said. "I'm sure you know what was released to the press."

I looked at Joy and we both slowly shook our heads. I hadn't had the news on today.

"Okay, if it hasn't come out yet, it will tomorrow. So I'm not really giving you any information you wouldn't be getting along with everyone else. You'll just have it a little earlier."

I watched Ryan and listened carefully to what he was saying. The minute we were finished I would make my notes. Then later I would put down questions that came to me, no matter how silly they seemed. I've found that sometimes the only real question is why? And if you know all the answers to the Why question, then you will have all the other answers, too.

"As far as we can tell, the body is that of a young woman in her early twenties. It seems that she had been buried there for about fifty years and yes, before you ask, she was struck across the back of the head. It was a fatal blow. It crushed her skull," said Ryan, his voice and eyes serious. As he spoke he watched his hands as if he might find an answer there or at least some questions.

"Do you think it could have been an accident?" I asked, watching Ryan's eyes to see if I could get any more information: did he look away or directly at us, maybe he was telling the truth or hiding something.

"Our coroner says not. Apparently the angle isn't right for an accident," he said very tentatively, obviously afraid to reveal too much about a potential case.

I watched him and nodded at each response to show him I was listening.

Old Bones

It seemed to me that he wasn't telling us everything he knew. I know this is a common technique in new investigations, to help weed out the real suspects opposed to the common variety crank.

"Is there anything else?" asked Joy very gently.

"No. We went back into our database where a lot of the old missing person files were entered a few years ago, but there was no match to anything around the time we estimate the death took place. So it's going to be a really old, cold file."

"Any identifying marks? I guess not after all that time," said Joy, answering her own question.

"How about jewelry?" I asked, not wanting to sound too pushy, but Ryan had really not given us very much to go on.

Ryan shook his head and didn't say anything more. He looked out the large picture window as if seeking guidance from an unseen source.

"We're going to be in contact with the family that lived there, but so far it seems the parents have died and so have their two children. The children left families and we will be interviewing them, but it seems that all the people who would have known something are gone. Which leaves us very little to go on."

Neither Joy nor I said anything; we just waited for him to continue. We didn't want to stop the flow of information. We just nodded and looked at him, hopefully supporting him.

I thought the situation was incredibly sad. A young woman's life was deliberately ended and no one would pay the price for the crime. That was just wrong.

I didn't know how much time our busy police department could put into solving a case like this one. Not with all the crime and the different task forces that were so common nowadays.

"How much time did they give you on this case, Ryan?" asked Joy.

"Not much. We're going to appeal to the population in the papers and ask if anyone knows of someone that disappeared during that time frame living in the area to please come forward, but usually in a case like this…" he shrugged, his voice trailing off as he looked at both of us with doubtful eyes.

"If either of you two ladies come up with anything, come to me or Nigel. Okay? And I mean anything." His tone became serious and his expression hardened. "I can tell you're both really interested in the case but I want you to keep clear of it. This isn't an amateur investigation like on television or in the movies. This isn't pretend." He arched one eyebrow. "We're trained for this kind of thing and it's our job to follow up on the leads, not yours." He finished with a smile as if to take some of the sting out of the words.

I looked at Joy and she grinned sheepishly at me. We both looked at Ryan, then nodded in unison. It seemed we were in perfect agreement.

Ryan stood and said his goodbyes to his family and kissed his mother. He's a good lad.

We'd check on the leads we had and the ones we would have, then when we were ready, we'd let Ryan know. After all, we didn't want to waste his valuable time.

Joy and I stood, accompanied him to the door, and waved as he left.

"Tomorrow morning?" I asked Joy out of the corner of my mouth as I was waving at Ryan with a smile on my face.

"No, I have an early shift tomorrow, but I'll be free by two o'clock," she said.

"How about three?"

"That would work great," she said as she closed the screen door and shivered.

"What do you do?"

"I'm a hairdresser," said Joy. She grinned at me and checked out my haircut. "Cute," she said with approval.

I nodded. "I'll meet you at my house. I've got some old maps from the library, and I've requested others from the land title office. They should be ready to be picked up tomorrow morning. I'll get them and then we can go over them tomorrow."

"Good idea. And we can have a strategy meeting Monday. Since you don't work and I do, we can divide up some of the work. What do you think?" asked Joy

"Sure. I've taken notes on what I have so far and questions that have come to me," said Heather

"Great, that will give me enough time to pick up the information, get home, and put the kettle on."

I was surprised to see it was early evening already and getting dark. Tom and I had to get home to feed Buddy. I guess I wouldn't have to make dinner tonight since we had lunch late and had been nibbling on goodies all afternoon.

"Come on, Tom, let's go and remind Buddy that we love him and haven't deserted him after all."

"Good plan," said Tom with a nod. "Tomorrow's Monday and there's nothing on the schedule, so we can sleep in a little." We said our thank-yous to Joy and Edgar, then left the house to walk home.

We walked around by the sidewalk to our front door, rather than taking a shortcut over the lawn and through the shrubs on the side of both yards.

"Oh, I forgot to ask you. How was your coffee date with Pastor Brian?" I asked Tom.

"Funny you should ask. Angela Kay was there today. I know it's not one of her regular work days for the office, but I think she was helping the Decorating Committee. I asked her about the body that was found."

"Yes," I said after a few minutes of silence, trying to encourage him to continue.

"Wait until we're inside," said Tom as he got out his house key, slipped it into the lock, and opened the front door.

"You remembered to lock it," I said, teasing him.

He frowned at me. "Do you want to hear what I found out or not?"

"Sorry, Tom. Yes, I very much want to hear about your conversation with Angela." I took his coat and slipped mine off my shoulders, then hung them both in the hall closet. Something he usually did for me, so it was kind of a peace offering for teasing him.

"Angela said she didn't remember anything about it at all."

I looked at Tom in surprise. I had expected something a little more than that. And then I remembered Angela Kay's maiden name had been Braun. Her family had once lived one block down on the other side from South Hill Elementary School, which is across the street, kitty-corner from the old empty lot.

Sometimes it was hard to keep track of who lived where, a lot of the family's who had cousins and sisters and brothers who lived together in the same house for a while. They worked until they could afford their own place.

I know that across the street we had the Gertz's and the Gardners's living together for about six years. The mothers were sisters and their grandmother lived with them too.

Old Bones

So at the time she would have been somewhere in the neighborhood of fifteen years old when I had been about seven.

I had grown up in the neighborhood. My parents had come over from England and my father was a landscaper. My parents, John and Isabel Wright, had bought the house about fifty years ago. Tom and I decided to move into my parents' old house two years ago when Dad passed away. Mom had predeceased him by five years.

My one brother, Spencer, lives in Burnaby, one of the suburbs of Vancouver, and had no interest in moving into the family home. He had three children and a large dog, and his large home reflected the room he and his family needed.

The old house on Fifty-Third is a total of two thousand square feet, one thousand on each floor. It had three small bedrooms, a bathroom, a cozy front room, and a huge kitchen on the main. For some reason there was no dining room off the front room, which was common for the homes built in that era.

Most builders had incorporated the dining room and the kitchen together. Which meant we could have a huge kitchen table in the kitchen, which my parents did. Our house was wonderful growing up because all our friends knew they were more than welcome at our home, and Mom always made great after-school snacks. So a few times a week we had a gaggle of kids gathered around our kitchen table, eating and doing homework and talking up a storm.

These days for Tom and me, the house and yard are big enough. We put a small, oblong oak table in the kitchen. The table had two large leaves in it so it could open up to create a bigger table like we had when the kids were growing up. Then we put an apartment sized loveseat recliner and our television into the same room, so it was convenient having the kitchen, the table, and a small family room all in one large space.

Rita Schulz

Seeing that our two children were grown and they and their families lived in Calgary and Toronto—much to my disappointment—we had all the room the two of us needed.

I would love to have a master bedroom with a beautiful en suite bathroom and a walk-in closet, but the configuration of the house just didn't work unless we knocked the house down and built again. This wasn't in the cards. We were retiring early and didn't need or want a huge mortgage, so it was retire early or bathroom. We had to choose. The early retirement won out, hands down.

We have grandchildren that we very seldom see. But thank goodness for computers and Skype, I manage to keep track of everyone, especially the grandkids.

While my parents' house is cozy, it is plenty to keep clean. Of the three upstairs bedrooms, one I use as my office, another we keep as a guest room, and the third is our bedroom. We also have an entire finished basement downstairs, which is half below ground but has high ceilings. There is a one bedroom apartment with its own three-piece bathroom, a large laundry room with a two-piece bathroom, and a room that had been designed as a studio apartment.

Tom uses the studio apartment as his office; that way we are still in the same house but our offices are on separate floors.

We haven't had an opportunity to decide what to do with the one bedroom apartment yet. I'm leaning toward making it into a guest bedroom and then the upstairs extra bedroom we could make into a walk-in closet and dressing room. Which would take care of where to put our clothes since the house has tiny closets.

We'll see. There is no rush, after all.

Chapter Three
Old Maps and Old Houses

THE NEXT MORNING EVERYTHING went as planned. Joy and I met as agreed and started to bring everything in from the car when Tom entered the kitchen.

"What do we have here?" asked Tom as he poured himself a cup of coffee from his French coffee press and added a splash of milk to it before taking a sip. A look of satisfaction crossed his face and he sighed.

"Nothing like the first cup of good coffee in the morning," he said to us.

"To answer your question, we have a bunch of old maps and stuff," I said to Tom before turning my attention back to my cohort in crime-solving. "Joy, could you please help me and give the table a pull. Once we get it apart, I'll get the extra leaf so we can spread our stuff and open up some of these maps."

Joy gripped one end of the table and I gripped the other and we pulled simultaneously. The table came apart easily.

"I could have given you a hand, Heather," said Tom with his coffee in hand.

"I know, sweetie, but you were enjoying your first coffee of the day. Besides, it's not a big deal to open up this table. I've done it a lot of times myself. If we're going to use you, it will be for bigger and better things than taking the table apart," I said with a playful wink at him.

I left the kitchen and returned with more maps and documents. Soon Joy and I were studying old street maps, comparing the layout with the land title registry information.

This way we would have the address back in the day and the names of the people who lived there then and now.

"Did you get any more information from Ryan?" I asked Joy.

"You mean after he left?" Joy looked at me, her eyes quizzical. "What do you think I did, call him and talk to him again or that I called Nigel?"

I winked at her. "Both. What did he say and what did Nigel say?"

She grinned as she confessed. "Okay, I did call Ryan, just in case there was something he forgot and wanted tell his dear old aunt that he may not have felt free enough to share with a stranger. I called Nigel, too.

"Basically they both said the same thing. They only had a minimum amount of time to solve this case or it would go into the Cold Case files and wind up in storage. Actually it sounded like their captain wanted to dump it already."

I sighed. That's what I had expected, which meant we had to work as fast as we could. On a fifty-year-old case, the odds of solving in were slim, and the people who would really know anything may have died or forgotten things since a lot of time had passed already.

I watched Joy as she sorted through the maps. I was impressed by the way she grabbed the cups, sugar holder, and other things to weigh down the map corners to keep them flat.

"I've got the names and the address correlated," I said as I opened my little notebook and showed her my neat entries.

She quickly compared the address and the information from the land titles office and nodded in agreement.

Then she went back to studying the map again.

Old Bones

"Why do people call it the empty lot?" Joy finally asked.

I thought for a few seconds before responding, trying to recall the history of the neighborhood as best I could. "There was a large house and a double garage on that lot when I was very little. I remember the garage even had an apartment built on top of it, and a very long set of stairs that went from the ground all the way up to a little landing and door. Strange I hadn't thought about them at all." I poured myself another cup of tea. I was surprised I still had the memory of those days long ago.

"Very good, Heather. I see it here as you describe it," Joy said, shifting her gaze to the map again.

I watched as she traced her finger along the back alleys that ran down all the streets in that part of town.

"So you don't think we ought to give up on it?" I suggested.

"Don't be silly. If it's going to be solved, then we're just the people to do it. Of course, we will call in Ryan and Nigel to give them the credit. Right?"

I looked around to discover Tom had gone off to work during our discussion. It dawned on me this would be his last week downtown. Then our world would change forever. I was really looking forward to the idea of seeing more of him, and at the same time scared that we would have a different relationship. We were now used to me taking care of the home, shopping, and cooking. We had already decided how we were going to divide up the chores and what our priorities would be, that was easy. But it was the not knowing what it would be like. Would we be happy, both working from home, writing as our main jobs and as hobbies, him golfing, me painting? I knew that it was the unknown that I was afraid of; we'd have to see what would happen.

"Yes, of course. We will give them the credit. But I can still use the ideas for my new book, right?"

Joy smiled and nodded.

"After all, people use old cases all the time as inspiration to write their own stories. I just wanted to make sure you're good with that." I wanted to make completely sure Joy knew why I was doing this.

"I understand, Heather. You'll be using the story, information, and details for your new novel. I also understand that you may take and change information for the purposes of your story. Also that this is your story and I am not involved in the writing of your fictional work. Do you want me to sign something to that effect?" asked Joy.

"Actually, that is a good idea." I quickly pulled open my notebook and jotted down the date and the case of the old bones found in the empty lot in Vancouver. And I wrote I would be writing a novel about the mysterious situation and that Joy Kendal had no input on the work and no ownership of said work. I gave it to her to sign.

"Looks good," she said. "Let's sign and date it. I don't think we need witnesses. Also, if I decided to write my own stories about this I can, right?"

"Be my guest," I smiled mischievously at her. "You can't copyright ideas."

This was the clincher for me: I needed the story and the offshoot ideas that would come from it for my writing. As it is, I was going to have to do research and detective work, then squeeze in the writing at other times.

A good old surge of adrenaline coursed through me. I was excited. I always got this way when the deadline was short and I had to get it done.

I could hardly wait to get started, but I wasn't sure of our working relationship so I wasn't going to treat this as a done deal just yet.

"I think it would be best to talk to people that lived around here during the time of the murder. Especially if they are around the same age as the victim," said Joy.

"Yes, it would be really good if we could at least get a name for her. I feel awkward calling her The Victim," I said. "It feels so impersonal. How about we call her Jane Doe for now?" I noted down the name on a fresh piece of paper.

"Good," Joy agreed. "Let's visit the people you have listed in your notes that still live around here. We can both start on that this afternoon." Joy walked around the kitchen. "Do you think we should call each person first or just drop in on them?"

I realized that Joy was pacing. I had read about people doing that but never really seen anyone do it before.

"I do have a few phone numbers for the people I know. I have Angela Kay, she's the church secretary and lived in the area when she was growing up, and of course Manda and Dillon Singh, my neighbors to the east, and Beverly and George Chong, who live next to them," I said as I made some more notes.

"Should we go together to interview people or do them separately?" Joy asked.

"I think we should go together, at least in the beginning," I said, "and see how it goes. I know most of the people around here so they may be more comfortable with me," I felt it would work, and also I could introduce Joy to the people in the neighborhood we were going to interview. It would help her get to know everyone faster.

Joy nodded in agreement.

I scanned my notes. I still had three people listed, other than the neighbors I knew well, who lived within a few blocks and might know something or have heard something.

"Okay, then we can do a couple of each. Let's start with Catherine Braun. They lived the closest, across the street from the empty lot and the school," suggested Joy.

We finished off our tea and coffee and grabbed our jackets from the hall closet. Buddy ran to beat us to the door, his nails clicking as he went. He wasn't too happy when I told him to stay.

I reminded Joy that the two sisters Catherine Braun and Sloan Rempel had been at her home the other day for the housewarming. She told me they had brought over a large azalea plant and a chocolate cake.

I filled her in with some of their history.

Catherine had just lost her husband Peter who, along with his only brother Otto, had grown up in the neighborhood. Catherine and Sloan were in their mid- to late-seventies. Catherine had worked at home while Sloan had never married and had a good job at the Royal Bank.

When Sloan's parents passed away, she had stayed in the family house and rented her basement suite out.

I recalled another time there had been a really nice woman we called Andy, short for Andorra, that had rented the apartment. She was always smiling. Her round face and big, dark brown eyes and hair made you feel warm and welcome. She was about ten years older than I was, but I had been in my teens. Andy and I had been friends for a lot of years until she moved to North Vancouver and then I had lost touch with her.

It was really surprising all the funny little details and memories this case was stirring up in my mind. Old friends and lost loves.

I should jot down some of the ideas—they would make good fodder for short stories.

Old Bones

We approached Catherine Braun's house and it was like traveling back in time.

It was a tall, three-story house with a long driveway that ran down the front side of the house rather than from the back alley. The house must be at least seventy-five years old and even had dormer windows. The window on the top floor facing the main street, not the side street, had a really neat little balcony with two little glass doors that swung open to let in a breeze in the warm summer months.

I had always wanted to take a look at the inside of the Braun's' house. I remember being a young girl and watching with fascination as they built what must be a huge deck on top of the garage next to the house. It had a railing that ran all around the top of the garage and I could always see planters with evergreen in the winter, and flowers, tomatoes, and other veggies in the summer. I know there must be herbs for the kitchen too, from the wonderful smells coming from the house at dinnertime.

I always imagined that from the deck you would be able to see over everyone's roofs and be able to see the Fraser River and maybe even Vancouver Island.

They had a lot of stained glass windows, it seemed as if in every room. I fantasized as a child seeing streams of golden sunlight making the house come alive with different bright pictures that were painted in light on the walls and the floors and furniture. I looked up as Joy and I walked up to the house. It was a lovely day, the sun was shining, and the stained glass would be at its best. I was going to be in luck.

I had always been fond of stained glass windows and I wondered if this house was the seed of the idea of how pretty stained glass windows are when I was a very young child. Between this house and the lovely stained glass windows at our church.

46

I learned to appreciate stained glass. I vividly recall the red, blue, green, and yellow light making intricate patterns on the church floor and on the wooden pews.

We knocked on the door and it opened within seconds. It was as if we were expected.

***

I stood on the wooden landing, gazing at the tall wood and glass door. It had old lace curtains hanging in front of the glass so that people couldn't look inside the house.

The door swung open about a foot, then stopped.

I smiled uncertainly at Joy. I wasn't quite sure whether to laugh and push the door open or more properly wait to be invited in.

A thump of a heavy cane striking a wood floor made me jump inside. The door started to open farther.

"Come in quickly. You know better than to stand there and let my cat Mizzy out," Catherine chastised us as she quickly rushed us into the house and closed the door behind us with a loud, echoing thud.

There were dust motes swimming in the rays of colored sunshine that streamed through the stained glass windows, chasing each other around the vestibule.

It was a beautiful sight. I paused to look around the vestibule slowly. It was like being in the middle of a kaleidoscope, all different colors and patterns.

From the vestibule you could see into the large living room and dining room. Everything was made of polished, gleaming oak from the floors to the paneling to the staircase leading to the upper floor.

Old Bones

The air smelled of lemon wax and lavender with a trace of mothballs. It was a homey smell.

I looked down to see a lovely longhaired tortoiseshell cat. It gracefully padded up to Joy, delicately sniffed her pant legs, then came over to me and I received a similar treatment.

"Hello, Mrs. Braun, uh, I mean Catherine. I don't know if you know if you remember me or not, but I'm Heather Ross."

"Good grief." Catherine emitted a hoarse chuckle. "Of course I know you. Don't you remember coming over to visit with your mother?"

"Yes, of course I do. This is Joy Kendal, she's just moved into the neighborhood."

I felt a rush of memories. My mother and I would often visit our neighbors; it was something I remember fondly. I felt a warm flush come over me at the memories of spending time with my mother.

"Come into the kitchen," Catherine said as she turned away to lead the way down the hall. "Would you ladies like a cup of tea? I think I have a nice lemon pound cake you must try as well," she said as she motioned toward the wooden ladder chairs surrounding the round kitchen table that was covered with a blue-and-yellow tablecloth.

Catherine Braun was a short woman in her midseventies, with thick, steel-gray hair cut in a short bob. An easy cut to take care of but one you would have to get touched up often. She moved quickly and easily over the gleaming oak floors and I realized the cane I had heard was for the cat, to stop it from running away. She had left it by the front door in a square brass umbrella stand.

As we entered the kitchen, I was at a loss; nothing looked familiar. They had obviously gutted the kitchen and installed modern appliances, cabinets, and flooring.

The large south-facing window that had looked over the backyard had been converted from a plain flat window to a bay style.

To my delight there were all kinds of different herbs growing in the south-facing window. The entire window was covered in different shades of green. Smells coming from several pots of lavender, basil, and rosemary were fragrant and the smells filled my nose and mouth. These plants are very hard to grow inside, but here they were all thriving.

"You have a wonderful green thumb, Catherine, how did you get your herbs to do so well over winter?" I asked her.

The words were out before I really remembered why we were here and it wasn't to talk about plants.

Joy looked out of the window at the backyard. She looked at me and nodded, which encouraged me to continue with the reason we were here and that was to question Catherine about the dead bodies.

"Mrs. Braun, I'm so sorry for your loss," I said as I turned to look at her.

"Thank you, Heather, Joy. I guess you didn't get a chance to meet my Peter, Joy; you would have liked him."

Catherine had aged since the last time I'd seen her, but with the death of her husband it was to be expected.

As she finished pouring the tea, we all settled around the large table in the living room. Picking up the delicate china mug, I closed my eyes as I enjoyed the scent of English breakfast tea wafting over me. I took a tiny sip since I knew it would be very hot—boiling water usually was—and savored the sensation of my lips and tongue sliding along the smooth, polished rim the of the tea cup.

Lovely.

I pulled my notebook out of my large leather purse and placed it on the table

Old Bones

"Joy's nephew is Detective Ryan Falcon of the Vancouver Police Department and we're helping him," I began. "You've heard about the body they found at the empty lot the other day?" Catherine nodded. "Well, we're helping him by talking to all the neighbors in the area about it. The crime is an old one, it goes back about fifty years, but was only recently discovered. So we're trying to see what people who lived here then remember," I said.

"Oh, I see," said Catherine, nodding to herself. "It's too bad Peter is dead. Maybe he knew something. He was living here at that time. Not me. No, not me." She got up and started to clear the tea dishes.

I watched Catherine, then shifted my gaze to Joy, who shrugged. Catherine's reaction was very strange. I knew Peter and she had had their fifty-year anniversary a good five to ten years ago, and as far as I knew they moved into this house on Fifty-Third when they were first married and had stayed here ever since, at least sixty years. So they would have both lived here when the murders occurred.

Catherine rolled up her black shirt and dark gray sweater sleeves and started to pour hot water into the sink to do the dishes. I noticed that she had a dishwasher, but didn't use it, at least not today.

"Thank you very much for your time, Mrs. Braun, it was wonderful to meet you," said Joy before she stood to leave the kitchen.

"Oh, I'm sorry," said Catherine, quickly drying her hands on the tea towel hanging off the oven door. "Please let me show you the way out."

Joy and I walked down the hallway slowly, studying the paintings and family pictures on the walls.

In the entryway I turned to look at the living room again and then Joy and I entered the room to take a closer look at a large, white wicker basket filled with African violets in different shades of blue.

50

"My, they are doing do well here," I said as Catherine entered the room joining us.

"It's the north light," explained Catherine. "It's bright enough this close to the window, but the sunlight won't burn them."

We could leave now that we had seen what we needed to see. At least for the first visit.

"Oh, if you really want some more information on the case. I can—" Catherine stopped abruptly as a sad expression crossed her weathered face.

"Yes," prompted Joy while she buttoned up her forest-green jacket.

"I can ask some of my friends that I see when I'm on Fraser," Catherine hesitated as she finished.

I knew Catherine had just changed what she was going to say, but I also knew this was enough for her for one day.

Then Catherine offered me a tight smile and her eyes were bright. Her face suddenly seemed years younger and she seemed happy. "Thank you for coming to see me."

"Thank you, Catherine. Would you mind if I dropped by sometime in the future and talk to you about your window herb garden?" I asked as I checked around for the cat.

"I guess that would be fine if you came again. Mizzy went upstairs to lie in the sunshine," said Catherine as she opened the door and let us out into the cold sunny day.

Joy led the way down the front stairs until we reached the sidewalk before she spoke to me about what we'd just seen and heard.

"The living room, the master bedroom, and the upstairs bedroom face the street," I said. "They would have had a direct view of anything that was happening across the street at the empty lot."

"I wonder what she really knows?" wondered Joy, following my line of thinking.

Chapter Four

Pictures from the Past

WE DECIDED TO GO back to my house in order to complete our notes and go over questions we still had to get answers to.

"Wait a minute," called Catherine from her open front door before we started to walk away. "Peter had a younger brother named Arnold; he lived here too. What about him? Have you spoken to him?" asked Catherine as she came down the front stairs, then along the sidewalk to where we were standing.

Joy and I looked at her, surprised by the unexpected new information.

"Catherine let's go back inside. You're going to catch cold in this weather without a coat on," I suggested since she was only wearing her light sweater.

"Oh, yes." As if on cue, she started to shiver. She wrapped her arms around her body in an effort to keep warm.

Catherine looked like the wind was knocked out of her. Her face looked gray and haggard and I wasn't sure if it was because of the cold or because of what she had told us.

We quickly went into the house, down the hall, and back into the kitchen, where Joy emptied the teapot, plugged in the kettle, added the hot water to the teapot with fresh tea bags, and within a few minutes poured Catherine a hot cup of tea. I had to smile; the teapot had been sitting under a bright orange flower—a knitted tea cozy.

Probably the kitschiest thing I had seen in a very long time. It was one of those things that was so ugly it was cute.

Joy and I sat down at the kitchen table next to Catherine and patiently waited for her to sip her tea and warm up. Meanwhile I went to the kitchen sink, picked up the washcloth, and started doing the few dishes that were there.

I like to putter.

"Okay. Peter and Arnold lived in this house all the time they were growing up," summarized Joy.

"You know Peter is gone," Catherine said as she paused to look around the kitchen, her eyes reflecting her confusion as if she were waiting for her late husband to appear.

"Peter is dead, but his brother Arnold is living in a seniors' home in South Vancouver," she said, nodding as she sipped her tea.

I had finished drying the dishes and stacked them on the counter next to the dish rack, then gone to join Joy and Catherine at the table.

Joy was seated across from Catherine and was leaning ever so slightly toward her.

"What do you mean?" asked Joy, looking Catherine directly in the eyes.

"Well, he had a military pension after the war, you know. He served twenty years with the army. After leaving the army he got a job with the British Columbia government in their supply warehouse and worked there for another thirty years. So he had the money rolling in from all over the place, didn't he," she said.

"Yes, but it was his pensions," said Joy in a gentle tone of voice.

"Yeah, but the cheap son of a gun lived with us for twenty years and never paid a penny in rent," responded Catherine. "He never married, but would take expensive holidays all over the world.

Old Bones

When I asked Peter to talk to him about paying his fair share, all Peter would do was tell me to mind my own business." Catherine held up her cup, indicating she wanted a top-up of her tea.

"That's not right," I said, shifting my gaze to Joy.

"You're darn right it's not right," agreed Catherine, her tone more forceful. "I was the one who paid the bills and bought the groceries on the little bit of money Peter gave me. And Arnold never once gave us anything toward the running of the house or his upkeep." Catherine's lips formed a thin straight line and her eyes flashed with anger.

"You have good reason to be angry with him," said Joy.

"I'll get the address for you. It's in my book. You should talk to him about the night—" Catherine stopped talking and clamped her lips tightly together.

I watched Catherine and knew by her facial expression that there was more that she wasn't telling us.

Catherine turned her back on us as she got up, went to one of the kitchen drawers, slid it open, and drew out an old blue address book held together by a large rubber band.

She laid the book on the table and opened it. "I need to get a new one of these," she explained. "So many people have gone now, but I just don't have the heart to do another one for just myself." She started to cry and dabbed at her eyes with the backs of her fingers to stop the tears.

I couldn't think what I would do in her place. A big old empty house filled with dust motes and memories and no one else, except a cat that always tried to get out.

Catherine rubbed away her tears with the back of her hand and took a deep breath to calm herself.

I pulled out my small blue notebook, and when Catherine had found Arnold Braun's address, she told it to us and I wrote it down.

"Do you have any pictures of Arnold?" asked Joy.

"Sure, I have some old ones. Arnold moved out when he was in his late sixties. He'd had a small stroke and found the stairs hard."

Catherine got up and led us into the living room. I got a chance to look around a little more. There was something about the couch that tickled the back of my mind. Besides it being pink with a nubby fabric woven into a design, it was very, very old.

"Here is a picture of Peter and Arnold, taken when they were in their late twenties." Catherine picked up a small picture from the mantel over the fireplace. It was in a heavy silver frame. She held up the brightly polished frame so that we could see the photograph in it.

It was of two young men dressed in dark suits with ties, posing in front of a brick wall covered with built-in planters.

I recognized the brick wall. It belonged to one of my neighbors who lived across the street and two doors down. They had brick in the front of the house and two waist high brick planters that ran the whole of the front of the house except for where the front stairs were in the center.

They looked happy and there was even an old beige Studebaker in the driveway next to the house.

"The dark one on the right with the hat is Peter and the blond one on the left with the cigarette in his mouth is Arnold. He was always a wild one with his thin moustache." Catherine's eyes softened and her lips formed a whimsical smile as the memories flashed across her eyes. She placed the picture back on the mantel and sighed.

I thought of Tom and me. Would one of us die before the other and leave the other behind with only memories? We had spoken about this and that we would die at the same time.

Old Bones

It would be too hard to be alone. I know that we weren't serious, not really.

I looked at the mirror that hung over the mantel and saw myself, Joy, and Catherine standing in the middle of a room that was at least thirty years behind the times. It was like stepping back in time.

I looked again at the deep pink sofa. It was familiar, there was a memory there, but it just wouldn't become clear in my mind.

I noticed Catherine was watching me. I smiled easily at her.

"Does the sofa bring back any memories?" she asked, waiting expectantly.

"Yes, but I'm not sure…" I didn't finish my sentence, I just let the words drift on the air.

"It was your aunt's. Your Aunt Wilda." I looked at her, confused for a moment, and realized she was talking about my Aunt Trina Wilda, or Auntie Trina. Or at least that's what we had always called her.

"We bought it from her twenty years ago. It's as good as new."

She was obviously very proud of the old piece of furniture. Now I remember sitting on it in my aunt's place in East Vancouver forty years ago, this very same sofa. I recalled the Christmases and Easters we had celebrated on this couch with the whole family around. I started to smile as I remembered those wonderful, warm days.

There was striped tufting on the wide arms of the couch and diamond tufting on the back of the couch and chairs. They were in remarkable condition for being so old. Which to me was kind of sad. Yes, they were made to wear like iron, but since our family had used them only on holidays or when we had company, it didn't look like anyone had sat in them at all. And to me that was sad.

"Do you think we could get a copy of this picture and maybe of this one, too?" asked Joy, holding up another picture in a similar frame.

Catherine looked at the second one and a funny look crossed her face.

The first was a picture of two men and the second was of two women and two men. I recognized her husband, Peter, but the others I wasn't sure I knew. Something we'd have to check out.

A frown creased her brow. "I should have thrown that one out a long time ago. But if you like I'll get copies for you at the library."

"Great, when do you think we can come to pick them up?" asked Joy as we moved toward the front door.

"Later on this week," Catherine said, her mouth pressed into a thin line.

"I have time tomorrow," I offered. "I'll take them to Staples across the bridge in Richmond in the morning, make the copies, then bring them right back to you."

"Oh," said Catherine. Her cheeks flushed red. It seemed she was looking for an excuse not to give me the pictures. Reluctantly she finally nodded. "Fine," she said, her lips pursed.

She went back into the back bedroom and soon returned with the pictures wrapped in a plastic shopping bag.

We thanked her and left. We started to walk along the sidewalk; the wind was cold and Joy and I didn't say anything to each other until we had crossed the street and were almost at my house.

"Can I see the bag?" asked Joy.

I handed her the bag, wondering if there was a problem I was missing. She unfolded it and pulled out one of the pictures.

Old Bones

She smiled at me, then showed me the photo. It was the one of the two men, but it was also the only picture in the bag.

"I wonder how much of what she told us was the truth?"

Chapter Five
Friend or Foe

AFTER THE INTERVIEW with Catherine Braun, Joy and I decided I would go to my church, South Hill Baptist Church, and talk to the secretary, Angela Kay.

Angela was a lovely person and had been one of my first Sunday school teachers when I was a girl. That's how long Angela had been associated with the church.

Even when Tom and I had to move out of town so we could afford a home for the family, she was always there. My mom and dad had been fond of her. She and Ernie, her husband—who had been the church's caretaker for a very long time—were long-time friends of my family. It seemed Ernie had always taken care of our church while Angela took care of our community library. She had been the librarian for over thirty-five years until she retired.

She had taken care of her family and especially Ernie when he became sick, first with gout, then other health concerns, until he had a fatal heart attack. With the family grown and her husband gone, she decided it was time to get involved with her church again and took on the job of church secretary.

At least that's what everyone thought she did—everyone except me, that is. I knew better. It wasn't the elders or the pastors or the deacons that ran the place, it was Angela.

Angela was a formidable woman. She stood five feet two and weighed a little over one hundred pounds. Her posture was impeccable, her back was always straight, and she wore dresses.

Old Bones

She even gardened in a dress—none of these modern pants for her.

On Sundays she always wore a hat. She had three, all different colors. They were pinned to her hair. Her hair was always worn in a snug gray bun. She wore very little makeup, a little lipstick and a dusting of rouge, and the skin of her face was paper thin, almost translucent.

I loved her. My parents had kept an eye out for her after Ernie died until they went home. Now this responsibility had fallen to me.

So it was only natural that I was the one to take her to tea while Joy went to work.

I called Angela at the church and invited her out for coffee. I offered a choice of either going to BreakTime or to come to my home.

I was surprised when she said she'd love to go to BreakTime.

Once at the church, I unlocked the office door with my master key. I was one of the trustees and the keeper of the keys. I found Angela sitting at her desk, waiting for me, with her navy-blue winter coat and black leather gloves on, ready to go.

She was wearing an attractive dark blue hat edged with black. I didn't know if it would keep her head warm. The hat looked more fashionable, for her, than functional.

"Boy, it's gotten cold again today, Angela, but not to worry. I have the heater turned up so it's nice and toasty in the car," I said. I watched her scan the office one last time to ensure everything was in its correct place before leaving.

"I better let Brian know I'm leaving," she said before quickly calling him upstairs.

"Don't be silly, why would we drive?" she said after hanging up the phone.

"Heather, it's only one and a half blocks away; we'll walk. It will be good for you," she said, eyeing my tummy that wasn't as trim as hers was, though I was a whole lot younger than she was.

I sighed knowing I was beat. We would walk. She was right, as usual. It was a sunny day—cold, but very nice—and to be fair, my usual half hour walk with Buddy had been interrupted this morning.

After stopping in the parking lot to turn off my car, we set off to BreakTime at the corner of Fiftieth and Fraser. In about three minutes, barely long enough to stretch our legs and take in a little fresh air, we were there.

I noticed the interior windows of the bakery were fogged up. I opened the door and the smell of fresh-baked bread and coffee came rolling over us. We quickly entered so we wouldn't let all the heat escape.

Once inside, the noises were amazing. Coming from the quiet of outside, the din of human voices of various pitches and accents, all trying to be heard over the music in the background, was incredible. It was like being in the middle of a cornucopia of sound.

"Over here, Heather," said Angela, indicating the row of overstuffed chairs that were lined up against the far wall.

Every two chairs had their own little round wooden table that made for an intimate seating arrangement.

"Are you gentlemen leaving?" Angela asked as she smiled at two men who were standing and putting on coats, it looked like they were getting ready to leave. Quickly she sat down in one of the free chairs and looked directly at two young men.

She grinned at them, her blue eyes twinkling. She turned her attention to the long line of people waiting to talk to one of the wait staff behind the counter in front of the cash register.

Old Bones

The two men nodded to her and smiled back at her. It seemed to me they were thanking her for encouraging them to leave. I glanced at her, hoping it looked friendly. I wish I could have the nerve and the moxie to pull something like that off.

Quite often the coffee shop was packed. Maybe I'd do the same thing one day. One person grabs an empty table or waits for one to come available and drops off their coat while the other person gets in the line. It's the table that's a rare commodity. I think it's the only twenty-four-hour coffee shop in East Vancouver. Never mind that they make the most delicious baked goods around here.

There have been times I have come here at ten thirty on a Sunday or Monday night and not only are all the seats inside taken, but the three tables and wooden chairs outside are taken, too.

The divide and conquer tactic I learned from one of the young ladies in our College and Career group when we went out for coffee one evening. She had looked at me and said, "Table or line?" I stood there looking confused until she pressed some money into my hand and told me to wait in line while she got us a table.

"A Copenhagen, please," she'd said, then with the seeming speed of light, moved to a table with two chairs and sat down.

I'd realized then what she meant. I guess my inaction was an action so I shrugged, then got in the line and got our food orders and drinks.

I asked Angela what she would like to drink and if she would like a sweet.

"Oh, yes, please. Both," she said, her clear blue eyes twinkling as she asked me to order her a green tea with jasmine and a poppy-seed muffin. Since this was one of my favorite combinations too, I ordered the exact same for myself.

Rita Schulz

Once we got settled with our tea and muffins, we started to talk about the church, the choir, and the sermon last Sunday. I waited until there was a lull in the conversation. I wasn't quite sure how to ask Angela about the murder. She was such a delicate, dear lady.

I originally thought this would be one of the easiest interviews Joy and I would do. That's why I volunteered to meet alone with Angela. I mean, I've known her for literally all of my life. Even when Tom and I moved away, we still came home to visit the family on holidays and I'd drop by to see her on weekends if Mom and Dad needed anything.

But now, as I sat here and watched her sipping her tea and taking dainty bites of her muffin, I didn't know how to ask her or what to say.

I suddenly realized there was a lull in the conversation and Angela was gazing at me over the rim of her steaming teacup before she took another sip. She was waiting for me. I felt so nervous I held my hands on my lap so she couldn't see them shake.

I felt like a schoolgirl being asked for the answers to a question we had had for homework that I hadn't done, again. It seemed everyone's eyes were looking at me and I didn't even have a clue to what the question was. Never mind the answer.

"Um… Have you heard about the old bones that were found in the empty lot across from Sunset Elementary School?" I asked.

"No," answered Angela, gazing at me, her eyes quizzical.

Okay, that hadn't worked.

"Last week the police found some old bones at the building site in the empty lot. Apparently they were human bones. They seem to have been there for about fifty years." I took a deep breath and continued.

"The police have decided they are from a woman in her early twenties and apparently, according to what the police have told us, she was murdered."

Old Bones

I realized the people nearest us had grown quiet. Actually no one was talking. I glanced around and it seemed everyone was leaning toward us as if they were waiting for my next words.

I picked up my muffin, broke off a piece, and stuffed it into my mouth. Perhaps in the middle of a crowded public place wasn't the best place to discuss an actual murder.

Angela ignored what I had said and started to discuss the new music that the choir director was going to start rehearsing this week.

I tried to appear interested since I usually would be, because I would be singing these new songs, being one of the members of our small but mighty choir. Small in number, but with the great microphones we had a sound you couldn't beat.

I knew that perhaps we should pick up this conversation at the church. Perhaps I should have invited Angela over to my house, but Joy and I wanted to complete the interview of the people who lived nearby this week and thought I could do Angela at BreakTime.

We'd made a list and a time frame so that we could complete the interviews and move on to people that were further away.

With Angela working all week, this had seemed like a good idea, at least at the time.

As we walked back to the church, we shared a laugh at the antics of a little fluffy black dog as it walked next to its owner, a large, tall man. He may be big and tall, but you could certainly tell who was in charge—and it wasn't the man.

I walked Angela up the cement stairs to the church office door and accompanied her into the church secretary's office.

"Angela, remember what we talking about at the coffee shop?"

"Yes, dear," she said, her voice as gentle as a summer breeze.

"I know you were living in the neighborhood at the time of the murder. Did you hear about a murder or someone who went missing fifty years ago?" I gazed into her clear, smiling blue eyes.

"No," she said, her eyes locked on mine. I saw the determination in her eyes.

I nodded, sighed, turned away, and left.

My heart was heavy. I felt like I had just been punched in the gut. I didn't know quite what to do.

But I would have to tell Joy because somehow I knew I had just been lied to.

Chapter Six
Visiting Neighbors

Joy sat with me in my kitchen. The morning was gray and cold but at least it wasn't raining. Without my asking, she poured me another cup of tea.

"I can't believe she lied to me," I said as I took another shortbread biscuit and nibbled at one corner.

"I was going to ask you about whether it was a good idea for you to interview her or leave it to me," said Joy as she poured another cup of French-pressed coffee.

I knew Joy really enjoyed using Tom's French press. If she hadn't gotten one for Christmas, then I would buy one for their home.

I sighed again and brought my mind back to the problem at hand.

"Okay, so you think she knew something but didn't want to tell you?" asked Joy bringing us back on topic.

I nodded. We had already discussed this and there wasn't anything more to add.

"Well, there had to be a really good reason that she didn't want to talk to you about the murder, right?" said Joy. Her brow creased in thought. "Let's see if we can figure out what the reason could be because no matter how strange the reason is, if it's the only logical solution, no matter how improbable, then it must be the truth."
"Sorry, I don't buy that," I said. "It sounds good in theory, but unless you have means, motive, and opportunity, even with a confession you can still make a mistake.

Humans are always bound to do something stranger than fiction. I know. I'm a writer, and if I wrote half of the things in my fiction books that people do for the motives they have, no one—and I mean no one—would believe it or buy any of my books."

Joy reached out and touched my arm. I took a slow, deep breath and looked at her. I was trying to avoid another meeting with Anglia, even though I knew that I would have to do it and it was most likely going to break my heart. I really felt she was much more involved in this whole thing. I could feel guilt radiate off her and there was nothing I could do about it. The worst part was she was my friend and I still loved her regardless of what she may have done. But also the truth had to come out. And if I was the one who found it, I would have to let the police know regardless of how I felt.

"We're going to have to talk to her again," Joy said with a wry smile. "But this time I'll take the lead, and we'll have a chat with her either at her home or at one of ours. Talking to her at BreakTime? Why? What were you thinking?" she asked with a little laugh.

Her laughter made me feel like a fool and hurt my feelings. I'm not a foolish child and don't like being treated like one, especially since we had both agreed on this course of action. Enough, I scolded myself. Get over yourself.

We know how to disseminate information quickly to everyone in the neighborhood: talk about it at BreakTime and a good portion of Vancouver will know by the next morning.

I'm glad Joy had time to come over this afternoon. I was feeling better now. I'd had a miserable night even when I told her what had happened between Angela and me when Joy got off work late last night.

Buddy rose from his place under the kitchen table and started to whine softly and his anxious eyes looked up at me.

Old Bones

"I think we have company coming," I told Joy as I followed Buddy down the hall to the front door.

I quickly took a peek through the spy hole in the door and saw two human shapes standing on my small porch.

I pulled the door open to discover Manda and Beverly another one of my neighbors, looking chilled to the bone on my stoop. "Come in, ladies," I ushered them inside. "Tea?"

I noticed they were dressed very warmly. Not surprising, seeing the dark leaden sky threatening rain beyond my front door. I hoped the weatherman was going to be correct and that it would rain like crazy after lunch, then stop early evening.

I needed a good walk and so did Buddy. We were both okay for a day or two, but after that we needed to get out and stretch our legs.

"Joy's here and we've had one cup. I was about to put the kettle on again. Would you like tea or coffee?"

They both looked at me as if I had lost my mind. I hung up their coats and they slipped off their boots. I normally only served tea. I didn't make coffee, that was Tom's area of expertise, but recently I had occasionally broken down and made a pot of coffee for Joy. But that had changed this morning when she came over with her own beans and commandeered the coffee grinder and French press.

Her excuse was that she had always wanted to try a French press. At her work, One Cut Above, they had a large, twenty-five-cup coffee urn that got turned on in the morning and stayed hot until the entire thing was drunk or they all went home.

At home she had one of those drug store coffee drip machines. Apparently they're okay, but according to Tom, nothing compared with grinding your beans fresh, then pouring hot water, heated to a certain temperature, over the beans. The smell infused the entire house with coffee goodness.

"A perfect cup of coffee every time, full of flavor with no bitterness," he'd say, as if he was in a commercial. Maybe I should rent him out now that he's retiring?

I believe Tom. I had given up on coffee when I worked at the Scotia Bank at the corner of Forty-Ninth and Fraser. We would do the same thing Joy's work does. Someone would plug an immense coffee urn in first thing in the morning, so for morning break it would be okay, but by late afternoon break it was far too strong for me. Then I found out no one would ever put it on to heat; it would keep filtering the water through the coffee grinds all day. It was bad enough just being kept hot, but this way it was thick as tar and smelled and tasted burnt.

I started bringing tea to work to save my stomach lining. Soon I discovered my friends and coworkers were helping themselves to the tea and I had management start to supply it when I found the manager's secretary sneaking downstairs to make him a pot of tea, his own pot but my tea bags. Cheap man. Imagine the manager of a bank taking the receptionist's tea bags; how penny-pinching was that?

Manda and Beverly joined me in the kitchen. I noticed Joy had set the kettle on to boil already. I rinsed out the old teapot and picked a light flavored concoction with a bit of green tea and mint.

"Um…the reason we're both here is because, remember when you asked us if we knew anything about the old bones last week, we said we didn't?" explained Manda getting immediately to the point of their visit without any preamble.

Joy, Beverly, and Manda gathered around my kitchen table. I walked over to the end table by the couch in the kitchen where I usually sit to work and study. I picked up my pen and notebook, flipped it to a clean page, and waited.

Old Bones

I was surprised to see Manda and Betty seeming so nervous. Complete with deep sighs and glancing at each other and avoiding looking at Joy or me.

While Joy made the tea, I set out jugs with fresh milk and honey. Joy set the tea on a cork hot pad in the middle of the table and slipped a bright blue-and-white tea cozy over it. Then we all sat around the table and watched the teapot seep in uncomfortable silence.

I had brought my notebook to the table too, but thought that with my friends acting so strange I would just let them get comfortable and tell me what they needed to when they were ready.

"Okay, ladies," I said, finally breaking the silence, "While the tea is brewing, let's talk." I'd tried to start off our discussion but after five minutes—yes, I was watching the clock—nothing. No one spoke. I'd even used my best noir detective voice, which at least solicited uneasy smiles.

"Remember when you asked about the old bones at the empty lot on the weekend at Joy's open house?" said Manda, looking at her fingers resting on top of the table in front of her mug.

"Yes," I said in what I hoped was an encouraging tone of voice. My pen was poised to write, my notebook ready.

"You go first," said Manda, her eyes flitting to Betty.

Beverly didn't say anything. She smoothed her shoulder-length black hair with one hand, then looked at Manda, and finally nodded as if she agreed she would go first. We waited; still no one said anything.

I know both Beverly and Manda had lived in the neighborhood about the same time; their families had lived here for about fifty years.

"It happened a long, long time ago" began Beverly. "George and I had just gotten married and his parents gave us a large amount of money in cash that was to go toward buying a home. The home was to be in this area, since they lived here too," she said and then she stopped and looked down at her lap.

I sensed I must be missing something because it was as if Beverly was deeply ashamed. She emitted a deep sigh and looked as if she was going to cry, her eyes brimming with tears.

"I am a wicked daughter-in-law," she suddenly blurted out. "They asked for us to move in with them when we got married. This is our culture's tradition, but I was born and raised in Canada and I wanted my own home like many of my friends had. And when I became pregnant, I was even more willful and insisted that George and I have our own home. That's why we bought the house next to the empty lot."

"It's okay," Joy said softly. "That was a long time ago; no one here is judging you. Just tell us what you know about the old bones. I think the person who was killed really needs to be laid to rest."

Beverly nodded solemnly. "I know nothing about a murder. But I do remember the family living there at the time. So does Manda."

Manda perked up when she heard her name and nodded. "I heard on the news the police are asking the people who lived around here who might know something to come forward."

I thought it was interesting the police were asking people to volunteer information and come forward. I always found that you got more volunteers if you went to a person and spoke to them directly.

"They didn't talk to you, too?" I asked Beverly.

"Yes, they want to, but when they came to my house and spoke with Pastor Brian next door, he told them I was out. I was at the park with Fire," she stopped and looked at me.

Old Bones

Fire is a great name for her Australian with all her red coloring. She really liked to lead the pack of dogs and their owners at the annual May Day neighborhood walk down Fraser.

"Great. Why don't you tell us what you remember about the people who lived in the house on the corner across from the school," said Joy.

"Sure." Beverly nodded and her brow wrinkled in concentration. "I remember them as a couple who immigrated from Germany with two children, one son and one daughter. The girl was the younger and very, very smart; the boy was smart, too. Eventually they both went to university."

"No, I don't think so," said Manda. " As I recall the girl, Nancy, went to university and her brother went to the college down the street."

"Yes, you're right, of course, Manda." Beverly shrugged "The Martins—the boy was named Luke." She paused looking to Manda for confirmation before continuing.

"Yes, his name was Luke and hers was Irene. Were the bones they found a boy or girl?"

"They found a young woman," answered Joy with a nod, shifting her eyes briefly to me as I wrote down this information.

"I'll be talking to one of the detectives this evening so I'll let him know you remember a little bit about the family," said Joy as she nodded to me.

"And they had a black lab named Lucky," said Beverly. Her voice was firm and she wore an easy smile on her face. "I remember it was a very nice dog. Friendly. He used to come over to visit our house." She made air quotes with her fingers.

Manda nudged her and they both giggled.

"Okay, what's so funny," I asked.

"Beverly really wanted a dog then, her parents always said later, so when Lucky came to visit she would feed him and play with him. After the way she treated him, he didn't want to go home and she would tell her parents he followed her home, proof he wanted to live with them. But the boy Luke always came to get the dog at the end of the day."

Beverly's expression became serious. "He was mean to the dog, too. I bet he kille—"

"Beverly, no!" snapped Manda sternly. She glared at her friend and shook her head as if warning her not to continue.

Beverly clamped her lips into a tight line. I thought about asking her what was wrong but decided Beverly wouldn't say anything more on the subject.

"I remember another very nice girl. Jane … Janet?" Manda looked at Beverly, who looked away and wouldn't meet her friend's eye.

"Look, ladies, we're trying to catch a killer and we need your help," I said, trying to bridge the friction between the two friends.

"Her name is Janet Frissell. It was Janet Bidwell when I knew her in school then she married one of the Frissell boys.. And she was a lot of things but never a nice girl," said Beverly, scorn thick in her voice.

"Do you know anything else about her? Like where she is now?" Joy asked as I busily wrote down the information.

"Yes. I have her address," answered Beverly.

Given her obvious dislike for the person, I thought it odd that she had her address.

She saw the look that passed between Joy and me and then continued.

"We were once close friends. She got married. They were very well off; it all seemed fine until last year. I called her to see if she was going to come over for Christmas.

73

"They used to come to Vancouver and visit friends at Christmastime and sometimes they even stayed with us."

She stopped and took a deep breath.

"Go on, they should know," encouraged Manda softly.

"She told me Graham, her husband, had died and that she wouldn't be coming over again. And that she would appreciate it if I didn't call her again." Beverly had a confused and hurt look in her eyes. She handed an address book to Joy. "Her address and phone number is in here. She lives in Victoria."

"Maybe we can find out why her attitude changed so much while we're checking for information on the murder." I was trying to comfort Beverly.

Joy nodded to me and nodded at Manda and Beverly.

"Thank you very much, Manda and Beverly," Joy said as she tucked her hair behind her ear. "I'll tell my nephew what you've told us. I expect he'll be in touch with you. If you think of anything else, no matter how small, please let Heather or me know, okay?"

I watched as Joy did her little gesture and wondered if it was a nervous habit. I'd have to watch for it.

"Let's have some tea," I said cheerily, trying to break the tension in the room. "I think I might even have some of those cookies that you like so much, Beverly and Manda." I stood and poured tea for everyone.

"How is your book coming?" asked Beverly as she nibbled on a cookie.

"I really hope to use some of the information from this case in it," I said.

"I'm really stuck on my plot, or even a good murder, and a motive would help," I said in mock seriousness, eliciting chuckles all around. "It really doesn't have to be anything at all to do with this case."

"Yeah, even if it was just ideas, you know, made-up stuff, maybe I could help Heather put together some ideas. Together we could weave it into a plot," suggested Joy as she warmed up to the idea.

"That's how books are written all the time," Joy said. "They take two different plots, then change some major ideas, change the characters and their responses, the locations, then you have something totally different."

"Yes, that's true," I agreed. "It's just a matter of getting a couple of good ideas and then see how the characters would react to the situations. I plan on setting the book in Vancouver. I love the mountains and the ocean around us. We have such a beautiful city I'm going to use it as a backdrop for the book."

"Do you have a title yet?" asked Manda.

I had been really surprised to discover Manda loved to read. And not just loved to read, she was a voracious reader. She had actually read and enjoyed some of my books. She was one of the few people who knew my writing name, at least the one I used for mysteries.

"I was playing around the other day and I think I'm going to call it Home for Good, but I'm not married to it."

Joy grinned at me. "Catchy beat, but can you dance to it?"

Chapter Seven
A Little Information from the Local Law

I STRETCHED, THEN got out of bed and headed for the bathroom. This morning I was annoyed; Tom had woken me up again. I don't know if his snoring was louder than normal or if my nerves were on edge. So many things ran around in my head; and when I really want it to be quiet so I can sleep, that's when the little lady in my head seems to be the noisiest.

Let's see, I thought, maybe if I make a list and cross off the items one by one, that would help. I debated the merits of that idea as I walked down the hall from the bathroom, then into the bedroom, kicked off my slippers, and slipped under the still warm down quilt.

Then the doorbell rang.

What? I didn't hear any sirens or voices so I knew that it couldn't be serious.

I covered my head with the quilt as Buddy ran barking to the front door, doing his best to let the entire neighborhood know we had company.

I looked at my bedside clock and realized it was seven thirty in the morning. It was a little too early for visitors, at least anyone that regularly dropped by, and I wasn't expecting anyone this morning.

Was it the police?

My left hand slid under the warm covers to where Tom should be, my heart thumping hard in my chest. No Tom. Where was he? Was he okay?

I immediately felt terrible for thinking those thoughts about him and his snoring a few minutes before. I know he would never purposely try to wake me as he got ready for work. He had always been such a considerate husband. I stopped myself. I hadn't thought anything bad about him.

I certainly have an over-active imagination.

I grabbed my robe from the back of the closet door as I headed for the front door.

The doorbell rang again.

Buddy joined in, barking and yelping for all he was worth.

By the time I reached the front door, I was almost in a full run. I shooed Buddy from the door and locked him in the front room. He finally stopped barking as I unlocked the door.

I took a deep breath and swung the door open.

"Hi, I hope I didn't wake you," said a very chipper Joy, holding a bag.

"What are they?" I asked. I wasn't going to get up out of bed before eight o'clock for just anything.

"They're fresh bran muffins from BreakTime. Shall I put on the kettle for tea or coffee?" Joy said brightly.

I squinted at her, totally confused as I released the breath I had been holding. Joy stepped into the house and I quickly closed the door behind her.

I heard a small noise and looked through the French doors to the front room and spotted Buddy wagging his tail rapidly. Joy was standing next to the glass doors. She opened them to let Buddy out and headed to the kitchen.

"Good boy," I said automatically as I followed Joy down the hallway.

Old Bones

"Come on, sleepyhead. I thought you had a book to write and a crime to solve, or a crime to solve and a book to write. Why are you still in bed?" asked Joy as she looked uncertainly at me and tucked her hair behind her ear.

"No it's okay, Joy. You're right, I do need to be up and get to it. It's just that I usually like to sleep in, at least a little." I watched her playing with her hair and knew it was her tell and gave her a small grin. I like to know people.

I looked at my bedroom with its unmade, still warm bed and sighed. I knew she was right, but still I wanted to go back to bed and sleep. Not lie there and chase my thoughts around like I had all night. Now I was exhausted. I knew that it was going to be a long day.

I had finally gotten to sleep about half an hour before Tom's alarm went off at six o'clock. That was my fault, but I didn't know how to cure or stop my insomnia.

"I have stuff to tell you," Joy said far too cheerily this early in the day. "And we have a meeting downtown in about an hour and I don't think your housecoat and bunny slippers will keep you warm enough today."

"I'm not wearing bunny slippers. Buddy would eat them," I said with a chuckle. "I had a nice pair of fuzzy, lamb fur slippers once and he got hold of them before I even had a chance to wear them." I arched an eyebrow at Buddy as I remembered what he had done. Buddy's tail started to wag fiercely as he recognized his name.

"Fine," I said to the dog. "I know you're hungry too. Come on, I'll feed you. You did a good job protecting the house from the evil Joy."

Joy snorted and shook her head.

I picked up Buddy's bowl, opened the cupboard door, and scooped a one-third cup portion of his dry dog food.

Buddy didn't have to be encouraged as he followed me and

watched while I measured out his food as if I might shortchange his ration. Then he sat and waited as I filled up his water bowl and set both bowls on the floor. He moved the food dish and began to eat, scarfing down the kibble, accompanied by crunching and chewing sounds.

"Heather. You haven't told me what you want to eat this morning," said Joy.

"Coffee," I said, "and one of those muffins. What do you mean about being ready in an hour? Where am I going?"

I sat down at the kitchen table and watched as Joy buzzed around my kitchen getting the mugs and plates for the coffee and muffins.

I pulled my housecoat tighter around me and shivered. I didn't know if it was from the cold, the lack of sleep, or the emotions I had felt when I thought something had happened to Tom. Probably a bit of all three.

"Oh, we have a date with a couple of hot-looking cops," said Joy as she pressed down the French press plunger and the room was filled with the smell of fresh coffee, then poured the steaming hot coffee into two mugs.

"Anyone I know? Or are you going into the matchmaking business? What about our husbands?" I said all of that in one breath as I broke off a piece of still warm muffin, a little crispy on the outside and soft in the inside, and popped it in my mouth. Just the way I like them.

I chewed slowly, thoughtfully, as I took a sip of coffee. The scalding dark, earthy liquid burned my mouth and it started to wake up my taste buds.

After the next sip and swallow, I could feel the caffeine start to course through my body. I rubbed my eyes to clear the sleep and blinked hard.

Old Bones

"Okay," I said to Joy as I started to feel myself awaken. It was the first time in a long time I had actually felt myself change from sleeping to waking.

"I'll wait for you while you shower," said Joy. "I guess Buddy hasn't been for his walk yet?"

I looked at her as if she had gone completely crazy. She knew what time I usually got up. Then I realized it was Joy that liked to stay in bed until the sun was up and the air was warm.

"Joy, what are you doing here at this time of day?" I asked. "And why the quick summons from the cops?" I hesitated. "Have they had a break in the case they want to share with us?"

"Yes, there apparently is some new information they want to share with us, but they also have today and tomorrow booked so it's this morning," Joy said. "Early is all I could get with them. And day? What are you talking about? It's so early it's still night. The sun isn't up yet so it's still night," she joked with a smile on her face and broke off a piece of her muffin and popped it into her mouth.

Chapter Eight
Coffee at the Chinese Food Diner

I LOOKED OVER the dilapidated old diner. The floors were covered with ancient, cracked, washed-out yellow tile. I wasn't sure if there was a pattern on the floor or just cracks where dirt had accumulated so deep and hard it couldn't ever be cleaned.

We sat in a small, four-person booth. The bench seats were made of cracked red vinyl that was stiff with age and covered with stale grease. The top of the table was nondescript, grimy, gray linoleum. I was almost afraid to put the sleeve of my jacket on the seat or the tabletop.

Luckily I had decided to wear jeans downtown today. I hadn't been on Pender and Dunsmuir for a long time. Though Tom worked downtown, I only came to pick him up or drop him off on very rare occasions, and he didn't work around here anyway.

He usually took the bus to and from work, which saved us from insuring another car. This was going to be another thing we were going to have to get used to as of next week. Who gets the car and when?

The waitress came up to Joy and me and took our orders. I couldn't believe it. She was exactly like one of those stereotypical waitresses depicted in every book and television show that you know don't exist in real life.

Old Bones

But there she was, a woman in her late forties, her blonde-streaked hair tied up in a ponytail, and she was wearing a mustard-yellow shirt dress that was stretched as tight as it could get over her ample bottom. But the best clichéd thing was she snapped her gum as she took our orders for coffee and called us dolls.

I almost started to giggle, but I looked at Joy, who must have known what I was thinking because she grinned at me and shook her head slightly. I could see she was trying her best to control herself and struggling not to laugh out loud. But it just made the situation worse.

Finally I had to pull open my purse to get out my notebook and try and concentrate on the last entry I had written down in there.

Then it came to me. Angela and Catherine were about the same age. While I knew Catherine didn't grow up in the house that she was in now, I did know she'd had ties to our church before she married.

I wondered if they both knew something more about this murder than they were telling me? I knew Angela had not told me the truth by the way she avoided my eyes and her body language. I really sensed that there were things she wasn't telling me. Joy and I were going to have to talk to her together to discover what she knew.

I made a quick note in my notebook to follow up with Angela and talk to Joy about when a good time would be to talk to her and to decide where to meet.

Suddenly the bell at the top of the restaurant door began to ring, drawing my attention from the notebook.

I watched Ryan and Nigel walked in from outside. Nigel was a little bigger and more generous around the middle than I remembered him, but he still had that calm, gentle-giant manner about him I had found so appealing.

The guys approached and nodded hellos as they slid into the booth with us. Ryan sat next to Joy and Nigel next to me.

I made myself relax my shoulders and look at Ryan. I wasn't ready to deal with Nigel, at least not yet.

"Ladies," said Ryan as he sat down. He had a pleasant smile, broad shoulders, and softly wavy hair, and his voice was a pleasant baritone as the waitress came over with menus, still popping her gum.

Ryan waved the menu away and so did Nigel.

"Okay, folks, what'll it be?" the waitress asked as she took out her pen to write down our orders.

I noticed the restaurant had muffins that looked fresh so I decided to be adventurous and try one of them with coffee. I very seldom have coffee but I figured it would be safer than the tea. I took note both Ryan and Nigel ordered the coffee too, so I figured the coffee must be freshly brewed. I'd heard that cops seem always know where to get the best coffee.

We quickly ordered and I noticed that she didn't write down our orders, but she did listen intently and then repeated it back to us, then stuffed her order book back in her dark yellow apron.

It was interesting; the diner was busy for such an old place.

"It's surprising how much business this place does for how little money they put into it," said Nigel. "We've been bugging Mabel here about when she's going to do some major renovations with all the money she's made on the place in the last ten years." He spooned one teaspoon of sugar, then added a dash of milk to his coffee.

Mabel, the waitress, brought me my muffin, placing it in front of me. "I made them fresh this morning," she said before she turned to walk away.

Next she came back with Joy's toast, and a few minutes later she brought out both men's full bacon and egg special. The eggs looked fresh and not swimming in grease. Which was a pleasant surprise.

Then Mabel returned with the guys' toast and asked if there was anything else we needed. We all said no, thank you. She then told Joy and me next time we should try her eggs. She explained they were delivered fresh to the restaurant every morning and she cooked them in real olive oil. Or, she said, if we were even more daring, we could try the Eggs Benny. Her homemade hollandaise was to die for. She winked at me as if I were in on a joke.

I smelled a rat. Was this all a set-up and an act for her customers? I had noticed the regulars that she greeted by name as they came in, as well as people that were checking out the menu posted outside. It was posted in the hands of a unique wooden sign in the shape of a girl in a kimono that had been there for as long as I could remember.

I knew the restaurant was a classic greasy spoon in the heart of downtown, one of the very few of its kind left from a bygone era.

Then I was convinced this was all a set-up. A cross between good food for the regular customers and a dive for the tourists, who would be blown away by the ambiance and the food and who would recommend the place to all their friends and other tourists where they were staying.

How wonderfully clever.

"Anybody want a little more coffee?" asked Mabel when she returned with more fresh, hot coffee. It was the best I had had for a very long time. And the muffin was fresh and still a little warm too, and not the kind of warm that comes from a microwave either. Move over, BreakTime; my allegiance was shifting.

"Mabel, I must say the food and coffee are very good, thank you very much." I held out my cup for a refill.

Next time we come here, I think I will try something else. If there is a next time. Joy wore her usual bright, satisfied smile I was certain would be there until next time we came here.

I watched the two cops tuck into their food. It was actually surprising how quickly they polished of their breakfasts. And since they had very good-sized portions, I wondered, with a little sniff of why not me, where they put it all.

Ryan was a young man and obviously active given his build, though Nigel appeared to have some extra pounds on his tummy, but not too much. I looked down at my coffee.

"Hey there, Miss Joy, I sure like your sweater," said Nigel as he chased down the last of his toast with some coffee.

Joy was wearing a hot pink sweater that you'd think would look hideous on someone with red hair, but on her it worked. She wore it over purple slacks and ankle-length black boots.

She was a very interesting lady, Joy was. I was going to really enjoy getting to know her better. She had bright reddish hair cut in a short bob and blue eyes that really suited her slender, five-foot-tall body.

It really surprised me she didn't wear any jewelry, at least none that I could see. And for a hairdresser in her thirties, I would have expected jewelry, makeup, and maybe piercing, but she didn't wear any accessories. I knew she usually wore a little bit of lipstick and eye makeup, but it was so subtle you really had to look to see it.

I liked that about her too. Joy had a fresh wholesomeness that you didn't find very often these days. I know everyone has good points and not so good points, so it was going to be interesting to discover hers.

"Okay, ladies, let's get the show on the road, shall we?" said Ryan, calling our meeting to order.

I almost said, "We've been here waiting for you guys." Joy and I had been waiting for them to show up, then waited for them to have their breakfast.

Now he made it sound like they had been waiting for us. He was being a bit of a jerk, but I let it pass. I needed the information for my story and time was marching. Instead I just relaxed my shoulders and grinned uneasily at him. I pulled my notebook out of my purse, ready to write down pertinent points of our discussion.

As Mabel refilled everyone's coffee cups I quickly took down some sensory details about the little restaurant around us to add to the setting of my story.

Nigel leaned forwarded and looked at Joy and then me. "The information we have is very limited at best," began Nigel, his eyes drifting between us as he talked. "Basically we know the body we found was that of a young woman in her mid-twenties, about five feet eight, Caucasian, with blonde hair. The cause of death was a blow to the back of the head with a blunt object that they're still trying to identify."

He leaned back after he had finished as if that was the end of the conversation.

Joy looked to Ryan, indicating with a nod it was his turn to add additional information.

"It seems a lot, almost all actually, of the forensic evidence we would normally obtain from a crime scene has been corrupted over the years. At least that's what the coroner's office has told us. They're still running tests, given the information we've been able to gather. It seems our best guess at this point would be that it is the body of the daughter of the family that lived there at one time."

"You mean Irene Martin?" asked Joy.

Nigel looked a little surprised at Joy's question and I watched Ryan smile knowingly at his aunt. He looked proud of her.

"Yes, we do."

"Good, then we're on similar tracks," said Joy in a concise manner.

"Heather and I have spoken to a few of the people that used to live in the neighborhood but we still have more questions than answers. But since we've just started, that's to be expected."

I didn't say anything, preferring to watch Joy as she waited for the two cops to add something more to their scanty information.

"Have you gotten hold of the family or relatives?" I finally asked.

"Yes, that was where we went first thing this morning and it doesn't look good," said Ryan, his expression grim. "The parents are dead but they had two children. One boy and a girl, who would have been about the right age for the victim, but we can't find out what happened to either of them. The sale of the house and estate is being handled by a law firm, Kline and Schmidt."

Nigel's jaw tightened as he listened to Ryan. He covered up his reaction by picking up his cup and taking another sip of what must now be cold coffee.

I glanced at Joy. She was smiling at her nephew as he finished.

"Is there anything else?" I asked with my pen poised over my notebook.

"No, I don't think so," said Nigel, clearly unhappy with his partner's openness. "At least not at this time."

I nodded at Nigel, catching his attention. I smiled thinly at him to let him know I understood his anger, then I glanced at Ryan and winked. He spread his hands on the tabletop, looked at Joy and then at me.

"Well, in that case, it was interesting meeting you here," said Joy.

"Thank you both for the information. We'll get back to you in a couple of days, or better yet, how about next Monday? I've got work and Heather's got a book she's got to get done." Joy stood and shrugged into her dark red fleece-lined jacket.

Mabel took this as a cue to come over and give us our bill.

I pulled open my purse to put my notebook away.

"Don't, Heather," said Nigel. "Ryan and I will pick up the tab today. It's the least we can do for you volunteering to help us."

"Would you like me to email you with some of our findings?" asked Joy.

I looked at her, trying to get through the message I thought this was a bad idea. I didn't have time to be doing reports and notes for the cops with everything else I had going.

"Oh, don't bother, ladies," said Nigel in a pleasant, but dismissive, tone. "If you come up with anything that might be of interest, please just give us a call, of course."

My annoyance level started to rise and I knew my face was starting to get flushed as it grew progressively warmer. Something I never could overcome, as Tom always said, was I wore my heart on my sleeve and my emotions on my face.

Not only did he not remember our blind date, he didn't remember his promise to call me. I guess it certainly didn't mean anything to him and that's fine. But Nigel didn't have to use that condescending tone with Joy and me.

"Well, thank you very much," said Joy. Odd. For the first time since I met her, I could hear a hint of Irish lilt in her voice.

I stood and zipped up my parka. I guess I wasn't the only one who was a little shocked at Nigel's attitude.

All I knew was I was taking precious time from my writing to meet with them and if they weren't going to be open with us, it would be that much harder to solve the case.

Joy motioned with her chin to the car park. I turned and lead the way. It'd wait until we got to the car to talk.

I had set up with dear Angela Kay the next day. I'd asked her to have tea with me tomorrow afternoon. I realized I hadn't mentioned to Angela that Joy was going to be there too.

I suspected she had information that we had to have. I hated to be the heavy, but we had no other choice. Frankly, it was making me a little crazy to think Angela was hiding something from me.

Tom had asked me what was wrong when we went to the church last night for choir practice. I pretended to be preoccupied—which wasn't a lie—and while at practice hadn't spoken a word to Angela, not even my normal greeting.

I didn't like the strangeness that had come between us and I knew this chasm had to be cleared up before it started to fester like an open wound.

I was looking forward to having tea in a way. At least I hoped Angela and I would be back to being close friends again after tomorrow. I missed her. Not being able to trust and confide in her really hurt my feelings and made me very sad.

I checked the time on the car's clock and saw we would have to hurry and get a move on. I had called to check that Janet Frissell still lived in Victoria since we had a date to meet with her this afternoon.

Chapter Nine
Across the Ocean to Victoria

Joy DROVE THE LITTLE Volvo station wagon of hers like nobody's business. She drove fast, but smoothly, and seldom touched the brake pedal. I held on tight, looking at the scenery and not the road. I didn't want to show her how afraid I was. I had driven this way lots of times, but not at the speeds we achieved today.

In no time we were at the ferry dock in Horseshoe Bay and in the line to get the Nanaimo ferry. It was an hour-and-a-half drive to Victoria. There were other ways as well, but Joy wanted to check out the this ferry.

It was a bright sunny day, typical of March in Vancouver—one day it's freezing and you reach for your parka, the next day hard rain greets you, and the following day is warm and sunny with a bright, clear blue sky.

You have to be prepared for anything.

I've always enjoyed the drive along the Upper Levels Highway and love the little town of Horseshoe Bay where the ferries to Vancouver Island, the Sunshine Coast, and the Gulf Islands sail. It was a large ferry dock and served a lot of people, including the coastal communities along the Sunshine Coast and the Gulf Islands, which are located between the mainland and Vancouver Island.

It was always a treat for me to travel on one of our ferries, especially on a beautiful sunny day like today.

It was too bad we were only going over for the afternoon since the ferry ride was about an hour and a half each way, and given the time of year, it would be dark during our return trip. But at least we would be able to see the ocean and the other islands that we passed on our trip to Victoria.

I could never understand why they had decided to put the capital of the province of British Columbia on Vancouver Island and not the mainland—Vancouver perhaps? I mean, it only makes sense; it would be much more convenient for everyone if you could just drive to the capital without having to take a ferry. I guess this way the government isn't bothered by all the people living in British Columbia.

The price of the ferry was getting higher all the time, but I always thought, for the sheer entertainment value of the kind of scenery we have on the coast, it was well worth it. Seeing the most spectacular views of the mountains and oceans in the country from a ferry is incredible.

We drove onboard the ferry and, once parked, quickly grabbed our purses and carryalls. I had a couple of books, my camera, and of course, my notebook tucked into my carryall.

I saved us seats in the cafeteria while Joy got in the food line. I just wanted a cup of hot water since I had brought my own tea bags, not to be cheap, but I find most places didn't carry the kind of tea I liked. Which was usually okay, but since I had some in my carryall, I thought why not?

I was covering the cost of our trip so I felt I had the right to a nice cup of tea as I watched the ocean and islands we sailed past.

I pulled my camera out of its case and started to take pictures around the dining area and the hallways, then I focused on the views outside the expansive windows.

Old Bones

I really hoped Joy would hurry up and get back so that I could start steeping my tea, then take that opportunity to go out on deck and take some dynamic shots of the islands we were passing.

It's funny, traveling by ferry was something I never got blasé about or bored with. When I was in my early twenties, I'd had a friend who lived on Vancouver Island and I went over to visit her on the odd weekend for about two years before she moved back to Vancouver.

I loved sitting watching the world drift by as the ferry took its majestic time weaving in and out of the islands, occasionally pulling into wharfs to let passengers off and to take on new cars and people.

I really enjoyed people watching, too. I had come up with a good number of ideas that I still use parts of when I make up my characters these days.

I have met some interesting people and the really fun thing is they would never recognize themselves in my books.

I like to take different characteristics of people and blend them together, the good qualities with a few not-so-good to create something new.

I also like to take reference shots for my books. I blow up the images to help me remember different specific setting details when I write.

"Here, Heather," said Joy as she put down the dark brown tray laden with steaming cups of fluid and a couple of bran muffins wrapped in plastic. "They had bran muffins and I thought you might want one since I'm not sure when we're going to get dinner."

I took my cup of hot water and plopped the tea bag from my carryall into it.

"Thanks, Joy, that's a good idea." I took my muffin and tried my hardest not to poke at it to see if it would bounce.

Ferry muffins can be like rubber balls at times.

"I already tested them. I even asked," she grinned at me as if she could read my mind. "Apparently they were baked fresh this morning. They even passed the bounce test."

The cafeteria-style dining area was dotted with tables, mostly designed to seat four people but there were also a few two-seaters. The tables and chairs were all secured to the deck, I guess to make sure they wouldn't move in case of rough weather.

I decided to go out on deck and chose the closest side to where we were sitting. I crossed the hallway walking along the drab, multicolored rug that ran the length of the ship. Nothing exciting there, but it did seem to compliment the beige-colored interior walls of the ship.

I pulled open the heavy metal and glass door to receive a blast of cold wind in my face. The smell of salt water, brine to be exact, mingled with seaweed and dead fish smelled like the ocean to me.

I took a deep lungful of fresh air as I stepped over the high doorsill onto the outside deck, moved to the railing, and started taking pictures. Wonderful.

We were passing some beautiful scenery. Each time I take this trip I marvel at the beauty of our little planet.

The deep gray-blue of the water with the yellow-green hills and the green-blue mountains worked in perfect counterpoint to each other.

I loved taking pictures of the homes nestled among the trees above their private boat docks.

As I took pictures, it seemed the seagulls were accompanying me and were congratulating me on the shots I was taking and making suggestions with their eerie echoing calls.

Old Bones

I laughed as I tried to get a few picture of them flying overhead. They were more like hovering and riding the wind. Sometimes they didn't beat their wings at all, just glided effortlessly.

I got some spectacular shots when we went through the narrows between a group of gulf islands.

I climbed the steel stairs to the top deck and explored a little. This was an area I wasn't that familiar with. Each of the ferries that sailed this route was a little bit different. Even if they were similarly designed, it was interesting to note the little differences.

The larger ships had an outside area enclosed with glass so that people could come to sit out of the wind and rain to enjoy the view behind the protective glass.

Today was still a little chilly to be out for too long, even with a windscreen.

My hands were starting to get red from the cold. Soon my fingers were numb and I was having a trouble working the focus and pressing the correct buttons on my camera. When my fingers started to tingle and my ears and nose grew numb, I knew it was time go back inside.

I climbed down the metal stairway, holding on very tightly to the handrail. While the ocean wasn't too rough, there was still enough of a swell that I had to be careful.

The ferry was just pulling up to one of the small ferry docks and I managed to find a spot out of the wind and took some great pictures of the little beautiful tree-lined bay from the first deck level.

There were even some kids playing among the rocks, and old logs carried by the waves to the high tide mark. I took some great shots of the rocky shoreline. My goodness, those kids were having so much fun looking for treasures along the shore.

Rita Schulz

I remember the fun I had when I was a little girl when the family would take the odd trip to one of the many beaches that Vancouver has to offer. Mom would pack a picnic lunch, then we would all get into the family car and drive to one of the beaches.

We would spend the day there playing in the water and exploring for our own treasures. The beaches were a great place to find seashells and unique rocks to take home as souvenirs. Mom and Dad would go through our treasures and decide what could come home and what couldn't. I tried to bring home a couple of little crabs in a bucket of water one year and Mom explained we had nothing to feed them or the right kind of water for them to live in. So I returned them to the ocean and wished them a long and happy life.

I had originally thought all I would have to do was add a little table salt to some tap water and the baby crabs would be fine. As for food, my Mom was a good cook so I felt if we fed our dog leftovers and she did great, it would make sense for my little crabs too. Amazing the stuff you think about as a kid growing up.

It was all good clean fun. Although it sure is funny how many places sand manages to get into so we always had to have a long shower when we got home, even if we had just had our Saturday bath the night before.

After taking my fill of pictures, I decided I should meet Joy again. First I checked the cafeteria and didn't see her, so I thought I would stroll around the inside of the ship to see if she was among the people sitting in the different lounge areas around the ship.

I love the tall picture windows that go all the way from the ceiling to within four feet of the floor. The glass is thick and always cool to the touch depending on the outside temperature, but the views are incredible.

Old Bones

I found Joy just outside the other side of the cafeteria after having taken a look in the bow section's large seating area. I knew it wouldn't be hard to spot her. After all, how hard could it be to spot a woman with red hair wearing a hot pink parka? I didn't know there was such color. Most of my clothes are pretty much all in subdued colors with perhaps a colorful scarf or interesting piece of jewelry to brighten it up.

"Joy, I almost missed you," I said as I pulled off my dark green parka and sat down next to her in one of the large, overstuffed brown chairs. "You took off you pink parka. I didn't realize you were wearing a dark green fleece top with your jeans. It looks great on you. I certainly couldn't wear anything like that."

"Very funny," she said with a chuckle. "Actually, I think a little bit of color would be nice on you."

I didn't say anything. I hated it when people gave me advice on what to wear or how to wear my hair.

I decided to give Joy a chance because I trusted her sense of style and color, although they weren't my style. I didn't want to be made over to another version of Joy. Still, maybe a little bit of color would be fun.

"I love your hair," she said keeping her eyes on the view of the gray-blue ocean visible through the expansive windows across the front of the ship. "The short cut and white color are both easy to manage and very modern. You like to wear jewelry, something I don't do. I think a couple of funky accessories—like chunky jewelry, and maybe a colorful scarf or two—would complement different outfits to get you started." She glanced at me, then handed me a white plastic bag.

I liked her ideas and would be willing to slowly try a few things that weren't too crazy or expensive.

I opened the bag to discover she had bought a beautiful scarf from the on-board shop. It was a basic cream color with vibrant waves of hot pink, bright orange, and dark green flowing through it. I slowly drew it out, loving the feel of the silky fabric in my fingers.

"It's got the same colors as your scarf," I said, "but mine is so thin and light."

"You're right," she nodded. "Yours is more of a dress-up scarf and mine is an over the coat or jacket one, although you could wear either with different outfits."

Joy watched me as I gently unwrapped it and let it flow down until it almost hit the floor. I quickly pulled it up at the last second.

I held it up to look at it in the light. It was almost sheer and so light that even a light breeze would make it move. It was beautiful.

And it was fun.

I looked down at my brown, long-sleeved sweater and jeans and realized that this was exactly what I needed.

I took it with me into the ladies bathroom to use the mirror. I was so excited. It was a little like Christmas or your birthday when you get a gift that you really weren't expecting and something that you've had your eye on for a very long time.

I looked in the mirror and saw a pleasant looking, middle-aged woman looking back. Nondescript, you know the type: average height, average weight, average looks.

The only thing that is really different about me is that I have very short white hair in a cut that I can do different things with, like spike it up, or sweep it off my forehead, or mess it up and let it dry naturally.

I decided I would wrap the scarf around my neck and drape it across my right shoulder. That way it could flow freely around my hips.

I giggled; wearing the scarf made me feel exotic and just a little bit naughty.

This was definitely something Joy would wear and I was sure she had a few, but this was new to me. It was mine and I loved it.

I went back to where we were sitting and did a pirouette to show Joy how I looked.

She laughed. There was pleasure in her eyes.

I sat down at the exact moment the ship's whistle sounded, so I jumped right back up again.

"Well, I guess it's time to go back to the car." I picked up my jacket, purse, and camera and led the way down to the car deck below.

"How did you picture session go?" asked Joy when we got to the bottom of the steep steel stairs.

"It was wonderful. Too bad you didn't get a chance to go outside. I could have watched our stuff."

"I know you would have," said Joy cheerily. Suddenly her face sagged and she came up short. "Oh my!"

I stopped too and followed her wide eyes to her car. There was a nasty scratch running down the driver's side.

"It looks like it's been made with a key," Joy said, crouching down to examine the scratch. She then took her finger and ran it along the scratch. "Yeah. It's been keyed. There's a little groove in the paint." She frowned. "The car will have to go to the body shop for repair. It'll cost a pocket full of money."

I walked around to passenger side of the car and waited for Joy to unlock it. There was something white under the driver's side windshield wiper.

"Joy, there's a piece of paper under your windshield wiper."

"Yeah, I see it." Her eyes arrowed and I saw the determined earnestness in her expression.

She pulled the note free very carefully, then opened it. It was a white piece of paper folded in half. I could see there were words on it.

Joy looked around us and then unlocked the driver's door. "Let's get in the car."

I slid into my seat, then turned to look at her.

"Well?" I asked, not liking the fact that she wasn't telling me what the note said. "What does it say?" My heart was racing.

"Here," she said, handing me the note.

I opened the paper, then read the words out loud, "Drop your questioning and chasing around. Let old bones rest."

"Interesting," I said, "I think someone has taken what we are doing personally."

"What?" Joy eyed me with one eyebrow arched.

"I'm not sure." I shrugged. "I just thought it's something a famous PI or detective might say about now."

Joy raised both eyebrows and grinned at me. "Very funny."

"Yes, I can see you and me as Cheech and Chong," I said with a straight face.

"You mean Fu Manchu?"

"No, most men spit," we both said at the same time and started to laugh at the very old joke.

I looked up at the sound of vehicle engines starting.

"Okay, get ready; the cars in front are starting to go," Joy said as she as she quickly turned the ignition key and nothing happened.

Joy turned the key again and stepped on the gas. She turned the key again, nothing happened. Absolutely nothing. The car has just become a giant paperweight.

I watched the cars nearest the bow of the ferry starting to move and I knew we would have to slowly drive forward in a few minutes.

"Joy, what's happening?" I asked, struggling to keep the tension from my voice.

"I'm, not sure," she said, her lips a grim line, "but I don't think we're going to be going anywhere soon. I don't want to flood the engine. It's almost impossible with these new automatics, but at this rate that's what I'm going to be doing if I keep trying."

I watched helplessly as Joy calmly tried to start the car another few times.

Nothing.

"Here comes one of the ferry workers," I said.

A young man wearing a blue jump suit with a bright orange vest and ferry logo emblazoned on the right breast pocket came toward us. He was carrying a bright red flashlight. Joy rolled down her window.

"What seems to be the problem?" asked the man.

"It won't start," answered Joy. "It was in perfect running condition when we went upstairs, and we have lots of gas, so I don't know what's wrong."

He nodded. "Just sit here. Do not leave the car. When everyone is unloaded, we'll get a tow truck in here and get you off the ferry."

He continued to move down the rows and motioned for other cars to drive around us.

I watched people in the other cars and trucks stare as they passed us. I realized I was sinking lower and lower in my seat from embarrassment.

"Heather. Would you sit up, please," said Joy. "You do realize this has nothing to do with the car not working properly. The car was working fine when we boarded.

It will be interesting to find out what's wrong with it when we get to a gas station on the other side."

I looked at Joy as what she was saying started to sink in. The car was fine when we parked. Now it wasn't. Was someone trying to stop us from finding out who the murderer is? That was a silly thought. This isn't a spy movie, is it?

I started when I heard the loud roar of an engine. I watched as the back end of a tow truck rushed toward us. The closer it got, the louder it got. I didn't know if I should jump out of the car and run to the stairwell to avoid being hit or just sit here. My heart pounded in my ears and a knot of fear formed in my belly.

My hand went over to the car door handle. I was just ready to pull the handle and jump out and roll on the deck to get out of the way.

"Wait," ordered Joy sternly.

I sucked in a deep breath and held it. Joy was right, of course; I was just being paranoid.

The truck stopped. The driver's door opened and out jumped a longhaired, middle-aged hippy.

He had a dirty bandana around his forehead and a wide grin on his scruffy face as he strode up to the driver's side of the car.

"What's the problem?" he asked in a deep, grating voice.

"The car won't start or even turn over," answered Joy, explaining the routine again.

"Boy, you ladies really didn't have to try so hard to meet me," he said, his brown eyes twinkling. "Do you want me to take you to a reliable mechanic?"

Joy nodded.

Did we really have a choice?

I noticed one of the ferry workers as he came up to us. He spoke to the tow truck driver. "Is everything all right, John?"

"Yeah, no problem, Pete. I've got it," he said to the ferry worker.

I guess they knew each other. I felt better as my heart rate eased and the tension began to drain from my body. So this meant the tow truck driver was safe, right?

"Put it into neutral for me," he said with a wink as he started to whistle.

He signaled to us with a wave of his hand. "Okay, ladies, out you get. You'll be riding with me."

We got out of the car and went to the back of the tow truck to watch him.

He went around to the back of the truck and got the winch to lower the ramp so he could slip it under the front of the wheels of the car. He locked the car in place and raised the winch.

I thought, since the tow truck man had the car on the back of the truck, that he would go slowly. Silly me.

I was reminded of one of my favorite albums, Bat out of Hell. Because that's what he should have been playing on his CD player as he roared down the car deck of the ferry and up the ramp to the dock.

I looked at Joy and we both started to laugh at the same time.

What were we getting ourselves into?

Chapter Ten
Visiting Victoria

THE SMELL OF GAS and grease was so thick in the cab of the truck you could almost cut it with a knife.

I was afraid if anyone came within a few feet of us with a lighter or a cigarette, we would all be blown sky-high.

That was until I saw the cigarette stuck behind his left ear. I sat on pins and needles, waiting for him to pull it out and light it and send us on a trip we wouldn't ever come back from.

We arrived at Paul's Mechanics a short while later. At least I think it was a short while later; it's hard to tell how fast time is going when your eyes are closed and you're praying really hard not to be blown to bits.

I finally felt a boney elbow jab me in the ribs and heard the screech of tires as we were lurched forward and then tossed about in the cab of the tow truck. My neck twinged. Great. Whiplash. I'll add this my adventure.

"Heather, please open your eyes," said Joy. "You look really funny with your eyes closed and your face all scrunched up like that."

I opened my eyes slowly and looked straight ahead. We were in a dark garage. There was equipment hanging from the walls from brackets in an organized fashion. All well thought out. I was reminded of something I heard growing up: Everything in its place and a place for everything.

Old Bones

My right side had been pressed against the door for the duration of the trip, so when I opened up I almost fell out onto the greasy, grimy floor.

I guess I had to expect that in an automotive garage. It was bound to be a little greasy.

"Okay. When do you think Mr. Paul will be able to talk to us?" asked Joy to the tow truck driver as she nudged me to get out of the passenger door.

"All right, you don't have to be so pushy, Joy," I protested.

I tried to wiggle around on the bench seat so at least my feet were pointing toward the ground and I had a possibility of making it to the floor without landing on my bum.

I heard the other door slam as I slid down to the ground. I looked around and couldn't see him; I guess the driver has left the building.

"I need to get out to make arrangements, Heather," Joy said impatiently. "You don't want to be stuck here overnight, do you? I don't mind road trips, but not when there's no place to stay. Where are we, anyway?"

"Okay, just give me a minute. I know this is a small town but there are hotels in almost every town on the island," I said as I slid down from the truck seat and managed to land on my feet without losing my balance. "I'm sure we'll be fine."

"Are you playing a rerun of the Hitchcock film ... what was it called?" said Joy, her brow wrinkled. "It was set in a creepy motel owned by some guy named Norman." Joy started to hum a spooky tune.

"Stop already," I protested. "If I was thinking of that film, you wouldn't help. Now I'll have nightmares all night because of you. You're not helping, Joy."

"Look, ladies, don't panic just yet. If you're in a big hurry, and I'm sure you are, I can take a quick look to see if I can figure out what's wrong with the car. Okay?" said our hippy tow truck driver.

"Thank you very much, but I think we'd like to wait for Paul," I said, nodding at Joy. Strangely she avoided me.

"So your full name is Mr. John Paul?" Joy asked the driver sweetly.

I looked between them. What was happening? Now they were flirting with each other? Ewww. I actually shuddered as I watched them laugh at their own little jokes.

I almost said something to Joy, but then she looked at me and gave me a tight little smile and her expression became serious.

"Okay, then. What do you think?"

The driver popped the hood and then pulled over a directional light on wheels, pointing it at the engine of Joy's car and turning it on. The bright white light made me wince as he started poking around.

"Can you turn on the car on for me?"

"It won't—" Joy started to say.

"Sorry," he said, interrupting her. "I meant to say, try to turn it on now, please." He reached inside the engine compartment and appeared to make a couple of adjustments. At least he grunted and beads of sweat appeared on his dirty forehead, so he must have been doing something. I know nothing about cars other than you turn the key to start them and the steering wheel to steer.

Surprisingly the car engine roared to life at the same time as the lights, heater, and radio went on too.

"How did you do that?" Joy asked.

"No problem," the driver said with a shrug.

"I noticed the MAXI Fuse for the fuel pump was pulled out just enough that it wouldn't connect properly. They didn't even pocket it. Go figure."

Old Bones

He snorted as he swung the light away, reached up, and pulled down the hood of the car with a bang.

"Okay, what do we do now?" I asked Joy and the driver.

"I guess you pay me for the tow," said the driver, "then you can leave and go to wherever you ladies were headed." He paused and crossed his arms, his eyes hardening. "But I will say I don't know who did this, maybe it shook loose by itself, which I doubt, so I'd be careful and keep an eye on the car and yourselves." He took a clean rag and wiped off any finger smudges he may have left on the car hood.

I nodded to him and handed him my visa card after taking a quick look at the bill. I was pleasantly surprised, he'd charged a modest amount for the tow. He seemed a lot smarter and nicer than I first suspected. I think my wild child was responding to his charms a little more than I would like to admit.

Just don't tell anyone, I reminded myself.

"Thanks, we'll keep that in mind," said Joy, starting to get into the car.

"Before you go," he said, "here." He handed me his business card, then swung open the passenger side door for me. After closing it with a dull thump, he walked around to the other side and gave an identical card to Joy.

I put on my seatbelt. I felt my eyelids start to droop and my shoulders sag. I was so tired it felt like I had been up all night.

I couldn't believe it was still afternoon. It felt like it should be late at night.

We drove out of the garage to find the sun breaking through the clouds.

It was getting warmer so I slipped off my gloves and put them into my jacket pocket.

Off we went to find Janet Frissell. I hoped she would have some answers for us, or at least ideas. I could use a good idea right about now.

"Heather?"

"Yes, Joy?"

"I suggest when we stop I call Ryan. I was going to tell him we were going to the island today, but I thought I would wait until we knew more before I called him."

"Good idea. I'm sure he'd like to hear from his favorite auntie," I said with a grin.

She chuckled. "I'll call him first, then I'll call Edgar to let him know we're going to spend the night in Victoria. Does that work for you?"

I nodded. "Yeah. Good plan. Ask him to phone Tom and let him know about our change of plans."

"Sure. Did you pack some overnight stuff?" she asked, eyeing my carryall.

"I did," I said, covering my mouth to stifle a yawn. "Are you going to call him on your cell phone?" She nodded, her eyes fixed on the traffic ahead on the road. I thought it was a good idea to stay over too. It was getting late. By the time we conducted the interview, I had a feeling we were pushing the clock a little hard. "Besides, I like Victoria. I haven't been here for a very long time," I added.

"Yeah, my cell is good for just about anywhere," said Joy. "I don't have satellite, but if there's a cell tower nearby, then I'm good. Any ideas of where a good spot would be to bunk down for the night?"

"There are some hotels in the city center that seemed okay last time I was here," I said.

Old Bones

"I've stayed at the Empress Hotel with Tom when the kids were young. We came over for Christmas one year and had high tea. It was expensive, but boy, was it worth it. It was so much fun.

"The kids had a room to themselves. Our room had two separate beds joined together to make one larger bed. We had to keep the door open so if the kids got scared, we could get to them in a hurry. What a great memory. I hadn't thought of that in years. Have you been to Victoria before?" I asked Joy.

My stomach started growling. I was getting hungry and I knew if I ate now I would go to sleep way too early, then be awake all night. Regardless, we should have something to eat soon. With all the running around and the problem with the car, it was nearly five o'clock. A little early for dinner but I had only had a muffin on the ferry, which wasn't enough for lunch.

"What do you think?" asked Joy as we drove into Victoria.

It had changed since I had been there last. The traffic surged around us. The noise and pedestrians were like waves and we were caught in the middle. I looked around for something familiar but didn't see anything I recognized. There were more hotels, all about seven or eight floors, with palm trees out front.

Finally, a place I recognized. I could see that they were working on the Crystal Garden, a lovely indoor garden filled with butterflies and birds. And there was the Empress Hotel, a grand old place.

"Let's go up this street a few blocks, just to get out of downtown. I know there are some modest hotels up here."

"We can get checked into a motel, have a bite to eat, something light, then a power nap for an hour or so. I am soooo tired.

"After, we could go for a really long walk, look around, get some exercise and fresh air."

"It's like you read my mind sometimes, Joy," I said with a whisper of smile playing across my lips.

"Oh, I don't think so, Heather. I saw you yawn and I know the last time we ate." Joy glanced at me, then looked back at the road ahead. "On the ferry you were running around taking pictures, so if I'm tired—and I am—and you got all that exercise and fresh air, you must even be more tired than I am. Easy. But I'm glad you're impressed. I like to impress people. Probably why I'm such a good hairdresser. I actually want to make people happy and try to listen as they tell me their ideas and what they'd like."

"Oh, there's a Holiday Inn Express," I said pointing ahead and to the right side of the busy road. "How about that? It's close to the Empress so it's a nice area. I've stayed at one of them before. They're clean and reasonably priced. What do you think?"

Rather than respond, Joy switched lanes and turned into the hotel parking lot.

I was glad that I'd had the foresight to pack some things for overnight. It turned out we both did. I always try to travel light and I've found ways of traveling with just a few items that can be mixed and matched.

But right now a good, long, hot bath or shower and a change into my light travel robe, then crawl into some fresh sheets was a wonderful idea.

We got checked into the hotel; they had a few rooms vacant so we were in luck. We could each have our own room. The desk clerk told us about the complimentary breakfast too.

Joy and I were on the same floor across the hall from each other since we asked to be close, so that worked out really well.

The tub in the bathroom was deep and the water warm. I had even had the foresight to pack a few bath oil beads with me.

I had picked out a wonderful lavender and jasmine scent. When I finished my bath and after a quick rinse under the shower, I felt wonderful. My skin was so smooth to the touch and soft. I put on my robe after my bath.

I closed the drapes, turned on the bedside lamp, then slid into the bed. I picked up my book, never leave home without one, but only managed to read a few lines before my eyelids became so heavy they were closing on their own.

I turned off the lamp and was asleep before I even got my arm back under the covers.

A phone rang at the edge of my consciousness.

It wouldn't stop.

I leaned over and patted the night table.

"Tom, you're up, can you get the phone, honey?"

I rolled over so he wouldn't disturb me and started to doze off again.

But the phone kept ringing.

"Tom," I said, forcing my eyes open, and realized where I was. I guess there was no reason to ask Tom to answer the phone since he was far, far away.

"Hello," I said, clearing my throat of the frog that was lodged in it.

"Hey, sweetie," said an awfully chipper voice that sounded like Tom.

"Hi. What time is it?" I asked cleared my throat again.

"It's about five thirty. Why?"

"Oh, no reason. Thanks for calling and waking me. How's everything there?"

"Not bad," Tom chuckled. "Buddy wants to know where you are. For some reason the food I give him isn't the same as the food you give him.

And he also told me that since you hadn't fed him tonight it didn't count and he wanted extra treats."

I heard a little bark in the background and knew Tom was playing with Buddy. I missed them both. I really felt warm knowing that Tom loves me enough to call and see how I'm doing.

"When did he turn into such a little pig?" Tom said with a chuckle. "And when did he start speaking to you and you answering him?"

I threw back the bed cover and swung my legs over the side. "Hmm? Oh. He's usually pretty good. In the summer when it's warm I just leave his food out and he kind of grazes. But I guess he's having fun trying to get extra treats out of you. And remember no, absolutely no, people food." I tried to sound stern and knew I would be ignored.

"You know it doesn't hurt him to have a little treat," Tom said. "My folks used to feed our dogs scraps from the dinner table and they were all just fine. All this stuff nowadays about free range, organic, low sodium, gluten free—what a scam. I read what's on the ingredient list of Buddy's dog food. Organic human-grade food? If it's good for humans, it sounds like leftovers to me. How much does that stuff cost, anyway?"

"Nice try in deflecting, Tom," I laughed. "I mean it about no human food as well as not too many treats. And do not give him any ice cream. I watch you, when you're not looking, ya know. You leave a little bit of ice cream in the bottom of your bowl until you get it nice and melted, then you let Buddy lick the bowl." I turned the lamp on and looked around for my clothes, which I had laid out on the club chair.

"I do not," he said but didn't sound too convincing since he was laughing as he was talking to me.

"What's so funny?"

111

"It's as if you never left home. Do you have the place bugged?" I could hear the laughter behind his words. "Where is the hidden camera?"

"Very funny." We were both chuckling now.

"I'll be home tomorrow," I said, changing the subject. "I don't know what time yet. Do you want me to call you at work and let you know?"

"Yeah. You can do that or you can just leave a message on my cell. That way I'll make sure I check it."

"I'm sure I'll be home by dinner. We hope to talk to Mrs. Frissell in the morning if we can, then we'll catch the next ferry after that."

"Sounds good. Miss you, honey."

"I miss you too. Give Buddy a pat and hug for me, will you?"

"Have a nice night. And when it's time for bed, sweet dreams. Bye, darling."

"Good night, Tom."

***

After a good night's sleep, Joy and I met the next morning at about nine o'clock for breakfast to discuss the "Old Bones" case as we had code-named it.

We both had a hearty breakfast. There was an assortment of cereals, fresh waffles, fruit, and pastries, and bowls of hardboiled eggs and yogurt. Of course the coffee and tea were in plentiful supply and while good, not great, the food did fill out bellies.

I was a good girl, something I'm working on, and had bran cereal, two hardboiled eggs, and two yogurts. For some reason I have a little problem with dairy products. I like them, but they don't like me. Or they like me too much. I'm especially fond of ice cream.

Something I consider the perfect food.

After we had enough breakfast to hold us, Joy said we had to leave quickly since the little doughnuts and pastries were tempting her and calling her name. We left.

With the map in my hand and Joy driving, we discussed the questions we should cover with Janet Frissell.

We had no trouble finding the Ocean Shore Residence where Janet lives. It was located just outside of Victoria in the suburb of Collingwood, a very nice neighborhood.

The streets were lined with a variety of trees that show color at different times in the year and a number of evergreen trees that stay green all year round.

The boulevard was wide and well kept.

As we entered the Ocean Shore Residence property, I noticed all the planters with all-season plants and the well-tended grass areas with a nice wide walkway that meandered all around the property. The walkway was designed to encourage residents to go outside to enjoy the gardens.

The residence was a low, one-story building and the entrance had hanging baskets filled with winter pansies and ivy. It was nice to see the bright colors even in the winter.

The air was cool but filled with bird song and I looked and saw a number of bird feeders in front of the dining room windows that were very busy with our feathered friends.

We arrived and went up to the well-marked receptionist area and asked for Mrs. Janet Frissell.

The receptionist, a young blonde woman, looked at us; her large brown eyes grew larger as she listened to our request.

"Um, are you family?" she asked in a quiet voice.

Old Bones

"Not exactly; we came from Vancouver to ask her some questions about the history of our community," said Joy. "She used to live in our neighborhood a long time ago." Joy's eyes glanced at me and a smile played across her lips. She seemed pleased with her answer.

"Okay. I'm going to have to call the administrator so she can talk to you. Please have a seat and I'll get her." She nodded to a row of chairs against the wall next to her desk.

There were a couple of coral-colored leatherette chairs next to the wall adjacent to the desk where we sat down to wait.

As we waited I had a chance to look around the reception area. It was large and bright, with tall natural plants and a few conversation areas arranged to give the illusion of privacy. Across the hall from where we were sitting was a large, six-foot by five-foot aquarium against the wall. It was wonderful and I found myself enjoying the tranquil motion of the colorful fish as they swam and chased each other.

"Joy, look at that aquarium, isn't it great?" I nodded toward the fish tank. "We used to have a small one. I understand with the large ones, if you have the right balance between fish and plants, there's very little maintenance. We used to feed them weekly fish pellets. I'm sure you can get them for even longer periods now. They release the food slowly into the water."

"Really?" said Joy. "I like tropical fish too, but they seem like a lot of work and very little enjoyment, so I've never had a fish tank. Maybe I can start little with a Siamese Fighting Fish?"

"Oh, that would be cool," I said. "There was a hair salon in Surrey where some of the stylists had them at their station. People loved it."

"Heather, that's a great idea," said Joy with a smile in her voice. "I'm going to look into that when we get home. That's just the thing I need for my station.

"I'll do some research on the internet when I get home to find the best size of tank and combination of fish."

"You'll probably find that the fighting fish are antisocial and they recommend only one per tank as far as I remember."

"Yes, you're right," Joy nodded, her brow wrinkling. "Now that I recall, only one to a tank. They come in such beautiful colors." She looked thoughtful, then added, "Now you've really got me thinking."

Soon a woman—who looked to be in her early fifties, with short dark hair streaked with gray, wearing a blue pantsuit—appeared from an adjoining hallway walking toward us. I assumed she must be the administrator.

On the other side of the administration desk was an elevator. The doors slid open and we watched as it opened and grim-faced Ryan and Nigel appeared.

My eyes flitted between the two cops and the approaching administrator. "I think she's coming with some bad news," Joy whispered to me from the corner of her mouth. She nodded and smiled to the detectives as they stood silently watching us.

"Ladies, I'm Norma Walker. I'm the administrator of Ocean Shore Residence. You were asking for Mrs. Janet Frissell?"

"Yes, we were," I said, my eyes flitting to Joy, then back to Norma Walker. I wondered if we should be talking to her or the detectives.

"Are you members of her family?" Norma asked politely.

"No, we're not," said Joy. "But we do need to talk to her. Just for a few moments if we could."

Norma shook her head and her eyes sagged at the corners. "I'm afraid that won't be possible. Mrs. Frissell passed away this morning."

"Oh," said Joy as she looked at me, then back at the administrator. "We're very sorry to hear that. Thank you."

Without saying another word, Norma turned to walk away.

"Would it be at all possible if we could see where she lived?" Joy called to the retreating administrator.

Norma turned back to face us, her eyes perplexed. She nodded and accompanied us to the elevator past Ryan and Nigel. I saw Joy wink mischievously at the men and nod to them.

They nodded back at us. I hoped we had their approval for what we were doing.

"I haven't seen you before," said Norma as we entered the elevator and pushed the button. "How are you related to Mrs. Frissell?"

"Oh, we're quite distant relatives," said Joy.

I hoped she was thinking about how the whole human race was interrelated and this wasn't an outright lie on her part.

"We grew up in the same neighborhood," I added, trying to add some connection and a reason to our request. "My parents and she were very close. And unfortunately we won't be able to attend the funeral. It would mean so much to us if we could pay our respects to her," I added.

"Yes. She was a lovely lady," said Norma quite vaguely as she nodded to us.

It seemed as if her mind was on other things, probably going through the list of things that would need to be done and the people she would have to contact this morning to make arrangements for the release of the body, and of course the funeral.

This was a good reminder for Tom and me to review our wills and our burial arrangements too.

When my last remaining late aunt died—God bless her soul—her funeral was a piece of cake. Probably not quite the right emotion to use for a funeral, but Aunt Erna had prepared everything in advance of her death. It was all paid for.

Her gravesite was selected and paid for and so was her entire funeral, everything, even the coffin, liner, and the flowers.

It was amazing when Aunt Erna asked me to go through to make sure everything was still covered and the companies still existed and had all her records. Of course I confirmed she did. She had done absolutely everything perfectly.

Much to my surprise, the companies all still existed and even stranger when they told me that they had updated their records from that long ago. I thought, "Oh, oh." The records are gone, but I had a copy in my hands so I was ready to send them a copy, but no need, they had everything right there.

I was going to ask Tom if we should do the same as Aunt Erna. I would like to have it done right for our kids too. Then Rodney and Marie won't have to worry about anything when our time comes.

We entered the elevator with Norma. The mail girl followed us into the elevator car. She had her little push trolley full of envelopes in different dividers. I watched as Joy studied the cart carefully and then turned to face Norma.

"Which room is Mrs. Frissell in again?" Joy asked as we arrived at the third floor and the doors opened.

"She's in room number 312. Just on the right at the end of the hall," said Norma as she went out of the elevator first and let the way.

I nodded, then let her and Joy walk ahead of me.

The halls were wide and painted a light green. The floor was a mid-tone gray with a large pattern of brown and darker gray in a brick design. The ceiling was high and there was lots of florescent light.

All in all, the residency seemed airy and well taken care of.

It was almost uncomfortably warm. The heat must be turned up pretty high.

Old Bones

I know a lot of my older friends and members of the congregation at South Hill Baptist like it on the warm side too.

I noticed Ryan and Nigel had stayed downstairs and hadn't come with us. Actually they hadn't spoken to us at all.

"Here we are. I'll leave you alone," said Norma after leading us into a private room. "If you need me, I'll be downstairs."

"Thank you," said Joy as Norma closed the room door behind her.

"You look around here," Joy said to me after she took a quick look at the dead Mrs. Frissell. "I'm going to see if I can head off the mail cart." Joy opened the door to look for the mail clerk, who was at the other end of the hall.

I started to look around. I heard the echo of Joy's and Norma's footsteps in the hallway. Joy was taking her time so as to keep some distance between herself and Norma. We didn't want to attract suspicion about our motives.

I looked out of the room and I could see the mail girl down the hall and nodded to Joy. She was sure sneaky.

Then I turned and went back into the room. There was Mrs. Frissell, lying on her bed.

I closed my eyes and said a quick prayer for her.

I had thought she was no longer in the room, assuming they had moved her body; but apparently when Norma said she had just passed away, that's exactly what she meant.

I guessed that this was going to be a very short interview.

Chapter Eleven
Dead Women Do Talk

I WANDERED OVER to the bed to gaze at the late Mrs. Frissell to see if I remembered her. It had been a very long time since I had last seen her. But yes, I still remembered her, or at least she looked like someone from the neighborhood a very long time ago.

I noticed her eyelids seemed to bulge slightly, although it was hard to say if her eyeballs themselves were bulging since, thankfully, her eyes were closed. I also noted her lips were blue. Something nagged at the back of my mind about blue lips. I couldn't quite put my finger on it.

I thought I'd better take this opportunity to quickly go through her nightstand to see if there was anything Joy and I should know about her death for the investigation.

I pulled open the drawer to discover a few letters from groups trying to solicit money, a few pictures, and a few yellowed Christmas cards.

I pulled out the pictures first and wondered why they weren't displayed on her nightstand. One was of a smiling man and woman. I guessed this would be her and her husband. They looked familiar. And then I looked at the Christmas cards. I smiled as I saw the names on the cards, two of the most common being Angela Kay and Catherine Braun. There was even one from two of the other neighbors, Beverly and George Chong.

We hadn't had a chance yet to talk to the Chongs since they were out of town on a holiday in Hawaii.

I quickly slipped the cards into my purse. I looked around and opened the tiny closet. Finding nothing significant, I then went into the bathroom, but there was nothing else of a personal nature. It was very sad. I left the room and headed down the hallway to the elevator.

Perfect timing. Joy met me at the elevator door. I noticed she had a small grin on her face. I nodded to her to let her know I had found something too.

"Do you think we should stop and talk to the boys?" I asked Joy once were alone in the elevator.

"Of course," she said. "We need to keep in touch, as they requested. But mostly to find out what if anything is new on this case." The elevator doors opened.

We stepped out to discover Ryan and Nigel standing in the lobby talking to Norma. She seemed all smiles and I wondered what they were talking about. Surely not the death of Mrs. Frissell.

I wondered if they had to call the coroner or if the doctor had already been there to release the body and had left.

Every province was different in what their requirements were.

I could hardly wait to talk in private with Joy, but we had to keep a low profile and talk to the police first.

"Aunt Joy and Heather," said Ryan looking down at his five-feet-four-inch aunt from his six-feet-four height. "Funny finding you here," Ryan smiled but it didn't reach his eyes.

I felt his joke fell very flat.

"You hadn't said anything about coming to Victoria, Aunt Joy."

She smiled sweetly at him and nodded. "You're right. The last time I talked to you, Ryan, I didn't know we were coming. How about you? You didn't mention it to me, either. Change of plans too?"

"Yeah, we did know about this old lady, but when her name came up, I talked to the boss and he said we should talk to her as soon as possible," said Nigel.

That didn't make any sense to me at all. What did he mean "when her name came up"? I started to draw a deep breath, but before I could say anything, Joy jumped in.

"Yes, her name came up and we thought we'd pop in to see her too," she said with a nod to me.

"Joy, what about your car?" I asked, wondering if we should tell them about what happened to the car on the ferry.

A look of indecision crossed Joy's features but then she nodded.

"Is there a cafeteria or somewhere we can talk privately?" Joy asked Norma, who didn't seem very happy we were breaking up her little gab session with the boys.

"Certainly," she said coolly. "There is a lunchroom right around the corner. Since it's between meal times for our residents, you should be fine if you'd like to go there. Actually, coffee should be served soon so you could probably grab a cup."

We thanked her and then we all went to the cafeteria.

I wondered if they'd seen the body, already been upstairs, or were going to do that after we left?

We walked into the lunchroom, luckily it was between meals, and took a table by the windows. There was a lot of natural light and even in winter a lot of green.

"A cup of tea would be great," I said to Joy as she joined Ryan and Nigel at the service counter to get a coffee.

We sat across from each other after I got a cup of tepid tea. At least it was wet. The others got cups of steaming coffee. I was glad to have something to drink and while it wasn't hot, it was strong.

I watched the others as they took their first mouthfuls and, from the sour looks on their faces, it seemed the coffee wasn't great either.

"Okay, what made you decide to come the Ocean Shore Residence?" asked Nigel bluntly.

I waited for Joy to speak first. I could give them all kinds of answers—I am a fiction writer after all—but none of them would have been the truth. I pulled out my notebook to jot down some of my ideas. Maybe not for this project, but good ideas for another.

I quickly made my notes, waiting for them to start, and it was a quiet place to collect my thoughts. I looked up and realized that they were all watching me.

"Sorry, traveling notebook. Just writing ideas down for possible stories at some other time…" I finished the sentence, then waited.

"Right, Aunt Joy," began Ryan, "why are you here? I thought you were going to tell us everything you find?"

"Yes," said Joy without missing a beat. "Except I also remember we were going to share, pool ideas and information as we each got them.

"We don't have any information yet, we're just coming over to see if Mrs. Frissell knew anything. The other people we have been speaking to remember her as living in the area during the time of the murder. And you?" Joy's eyes narrowed as she scrutinized her nephew.

"Same for us," said Nigel, turning his coffee cup in his hands. "All we know is Mrs. Frissell lived in the old neighborhood. We came to see if she knew the missing girl."

"Right, then. Is there anything else? If not, then we'd like to get the next ferry home. How about you?" asked Joy.

"We're going to stay a while and take a look upstairs, then talk to Norma Walker to see if we can come up with something new. We'll talk to you at home?" Ryan said, eyeing his aunt.

"Sure, Ryan," Joy said with a whisper of a grin on her lips. "How much longer are you going to be able to work the case, Ryan?"

I thought this was a strange question until I remembered Ryan and Nigel said they had only a very short time to work this case since the murder happened so long ago.

"We have a little more time to work on it," said Nigel as he stood. "It's been extended so it all depends on what we find out. So really, ladies, I really mean it when I say we need your help and the community's help, too."

Simple as that, we were dismissed.

I quickly gathered my notebook and pen, dropping them into my purse, and stood too.

I looked at Nigel and wondered if he remembered me. I knew I was most likely being silly, but I did wonder.

They walked us out to the front door and I found myself walking beside Nigel. I was still amazed by the sheer bulk and strength of the man and the warmth he exuded, even when he was being a bit of a bugger.

"Heather," he said very softly.

I shifted my gaze to him.

"I still remember that night," he said in a soft whisper and smiled slyly at me.

My heart hammered hard and my throat went dry. I knew then I could not let this part of my past rest. I would have to have a long talk with Nigel, after which I'd put my childhood fantasy behind me.

I could see it in his sky blue eyes: he knew it, too. I opened my purse to pull out a business card and gave him one.

Old Bones

I saw Joy and Ryan had stopped and turned to stare at us. I quickly handed Ryan a card, too.

"I didn't have any on me the other day, but now you both have my card." I smiled weakly at both Nigel and Ryan. Though my heart was beating hard, my voice stayed steady and I hoped I appeared as cool as ice cream on a hot day on the outside.

I joined Joy as we walked to the car in the parking lot.

"Don't you think that you should have told them about the car?" I asked Joy when we got in and started to drive away from the Ocean Shore Residence.

"No, it's too early yet. Did you get a good look at the woman?"

"You mean Mrs. Frissell?"

Joy was staring straight ahead, her eyes intent on the road. Usually I find this kind of attention by a driver reassuring, but I was starting to know Joy a little bit and I could bet you the last thing she was thinking about was the road. She nodded and the car accelerated.

"Yes, I did," I said, breaking the silence. "I found some interesting Christmas cards too. What do you mean did I get a good look at the woman? I saw her body, if that's what you mean. I guess they're waiting for the police before they take her to the funeral home. Why?"

"Did you notice the color of her lips?"

"If you mean her lips were a strange tint of blue, then yes. Also I think her teeth were fitting her strangely. It seemed her mouth wasn't closed naturally."

"Yes. I think she may have been asphyxiated," said Joy grimly.

Joy flicked the right turn signal on and we sailed around a corner. Never mind stopping at the stoplight.

"Ah, Joy, are we in a hurry?" My voice betrayed my nervousness.

"Yes. I want to catch the next ferry before the killer gets away from us," said Joy.

"If I'm right, we just missed him at the Ocean Shore Residence. If we had gotten there on the first morning ferry, we may have prevented her murder. If she was indeed murdered."

"Joy!" I said. "And you didn't think this was important enough to tell your nephew and Nigel?"

"It's all just a guess and may be nothing at this point. That administrator, Norma Walker, didn't seem unduly upset at Jane's death, and it didn't seem as if she was hiding anything. Although she really isn't the sharpest pencil in the box, is she?" Joy added with a derisive snort.

"Yes," I said, "I see what you mean. You walked right past her and got the mail from the trolley. I bet you had a little chat with the mail girl, then met me at the elevator door, didn't you? And Norma Walker saw you going down the wrong way in the hallway. Why didn't she stop you and correct you?"

"Very good questions, Heather. Maybe she has a lot on her mind? Right now, though, we have to get to the ferry as quickly as we can."

Chapter Twelve
A Beautiful View

J OY PARKED IN LANE 34 at the Swartz Bay ferry terminal. We were heading for Vancouver. With a bit of luck, we'd make the three o'clock ferry. It was now five after two, so we had a little time to look around.

It was a beautiful afternoon. The gray clouds from the morning had disappeared; now the sun was shining. The air was fresh, although the wind was a bit cool, and the seagulls soaring high overhead were calling to one another.

Everyone in the vehicles around us seemed to be relaxed, chatting and smiling. I joined the crowd at one of the terminal coffee bars. This one promised Salt Spring Coffee. I much prefer tea, but I didn't mind a good cup of coffee once in a while. You know, the kind that actually tastes as good as it smells. I also stood in line for a cup of ice cream. I'd had a tip that the ice cream at the terminal was some of the best around.

As a friend once said, and I agree with her: ice cream isn't a vice— it should be listed as one of the food groups. It contains everything your body and soul need, fat and sugar. If you want to get really fancy—and occasionally I do, although it is very occasionally—I like my vanilla ice cream with some creamy hot fudge and some roasted, salted peanuts sprinkled over top.

To me that is the perfect food: hot and cold, sweet and salty. Who could ask for anything more?

Well, my doctor could. He asked me to eat and drink everything in moderation.

He wasn't impressed with my idea of an ice cream diet. Once I went on an ice cream diet. Every day I would eat a bowl full of ice cream and make sure I took a good vitamin supplement; it wasn't healthy as far as he was concerned. I wondered if he ever tried it?

As I came back to the car with my coffee and ice cream, I promised myself this ice cream was a special treat and I would give myself an extra-long walk with Buddy every day for the next week. Also, this was my sweet for the week. I found that one treat on the weekend worked well for me. I savored it and I could tell myself during the week to wait for it.

I sighed, closed my eyes, then slipped a spoonful of the cool, creamy, sweet ice cream into my mouth and wondered why vegetables didn't taste this good. Yes, I know; if they're fresh and crisp they tasted very good, but come on, there is no comparison.

I opened my eyes to discover Joy watching me. She had closed the book that she was reading and held it in her lap.

"What?" I said. "I asked you if you wanted anything. I would have brought you back a coffee, or a muffin or..." I held up my cup of melting ice cream.

I took another small spoonful. I was not disappointed. My friend was correct: it was cold, creamy, smooth, and had flecks of vanilla bean in it. It was the best ice cream I'd had in a long time.

"I was just watching you enjoy it. You have a very expressive face, you know," Joy said, grinning at me.

"Okay," I said with a chuckle. "Once I've finished ice cream, we can go over our notes."

Joy started the car.

I must have been daydreaming a lot longer than I thought. I know the ferry lines were long and I enjoyed poking around in the ferry shops, but I didn't think it was three o'clock already.

Old Bones

I pulled out my cell phone and realized we were starting to load about ten minutes early. Of course, they would have to have time to load the boat. It was a good thing I came back to the car when I did.

I nodded as I took the last spoonful of ice cream into my mouth.

We drove up a broad ramp and onto a metal gangway. Our car made loud thunk as it drove across the connecting ramp between the dock and the ferry.

Once we were onboard we parked, got our stuff from the back seat, and headed up the steep steel stairs to the upper passenger decks.

There was quite a lot of seating onboard this ferry. It was one of the large boats. We didn't want to sit in the main cafeteria. We wanted to find a quiet little table so we could talk in private and compare notes.

We each got a beverage; a bottle of water seemed like the best option for me this afternoon after the ice cream.

I pulled open my black leather purse and took out my notebook and cell phone. I checked the time. Sure enough, it was just a little after three. I could hear and feel the vibration of the large ship's engines through the deck as we started to pull out of the dock. The ship's horn sounded a few short bursts to signal everyone we were pulling away.

I started to open my purse again to get my camera. The midafternoon light wasn't as good as the morning or late afternoon, but I could still use a few reverence shots.

"Go ahead. You know you want to," said Joy with a sly grin as she opened the latest book she was reading.

I grinned at her. I wasn't sure what I was going to do with all my photos. But I was sure they'd be useful.

I crossed the deck to an outside door and tried to swing it open, but the heavy door wrestled with me. It was as if it were determined not to open. But I was valiant and fought back to eventually win. I stepped onto the outside deck straight into what I was sure was a gale force wind.

The other people who were already on the outside deck taking pictures of themselves and their friends had their hair whipped around their faces by gusts of wind. They kept trying to keep it out of their eyes so that people at home would be able to recognize them in the pictures.

I almost took a picture of them taking pictures. It sure looked funny. Then I got serious and started to lay out some shots that would work. Trying to get an interesting composition and enough contrast was difficult, but I think I got a couple of shots I could work with.

The ship was one of the new Spirit-class vessels. The Spirit of Vancouver Island is a beautiful ship.

It was fun in the brisk air on deck, watching people. They were really struggling to keep their footing and some were almost bent double trying to get across the deck. Some of the people were women and very tiny; I thought they should have been tethered to the ship's rail, just in case.

I quickly snapped a few shots and headed down the stairs to the lower outside deck.

I looked down at the bottom of the stairs and didn't see the foot that suddenly kicked my ankle. Yes, it was hard.

My heart pounded hard and I yelled as I pitched forward. Without thinking, my hand gripped the solid cold metal railing in a death in grip. I could feel my hand slip on the railing as my feet shot out from under me at the top of the stairs. I became airborne, my one hand desperately gripped on the railing.

Old Bones

My body twisted around and I landed on my side on the steel stair, my right knee striking the metal step hard. Pain shot up my leg. I knew I had torqued my shoulder because it ached terribly, but I hadn't heard anything pop or snap so I was praying nothing was torn or broken. I had landed upside down. I was looking up at the top of the stairs at my feet. My left knee and leg were stretched out on the next couple of stairs.

I heard people screaming and voices all around me but I couldn't focus, my hearing and eyesight were all muddled.

"Oh, my. Hold on there, I'll be right with you," said a deep male voice close to me on the stairs.

"Come on, I'll steady her shoulders while you grab her legs and slowly turn her so she's sitting on one stair," said another higher male voice.

"Okay, honey. Once they have you straightened up, you can let go of the handrail. I'll tell you when," said a soft female voice in my ear and I felt someone hold my left hand and gently squeeze it.

I finally was able to let go of the handrail and the men carefully swung me around so that I was sitting on one stair.

I took a deep breath and quickly did a physical check as best I could. I started with my toes and wiggled them. My hearing and sight were come back so I looked at my knees. Yup they had taken a bit of a bashing and my right should screamed when I moved it. I could feel bruises already coming up on my back, but surprisingly nothing seemed broken.

I righted myself and swung my feet and legs down the stairwell so I was sitting upright.

I had been very lucky. My imagination focused on the hard, unyielding corners of the steel stairs and what a really hard landing could do to your head. Not a pretty picture.

I shuddered at the thought of what might have happened.

More people were gathering around me, asking if I was okay or needed help. I think a few even got some of the crew members since I had questions asked and then, when they determined that there weren't any serious injures, I felt arms reaching to help me stand and I saw they were wearing the crew uniform.

As the sign says, the boat may pitch, please hold on to the railings. Well, it doesn't really say that, but that's what it means. I've been on enough boats that a sudden swell can always come up to pitch you across the deck. So hang on tight.

I had wretched my shoulder and skinned my right knee when my momentum swung me around, but I was really annoyed. Even though I looked up searching for the person who purposely tripped me, he or she must be gone because all I saw was a sea of concerned faces.

I was shaking badly and took a deep breath to help steady myself. I would have to wait for my heartbeat to calm, then take some time and try to retrieve the few impressions that I had about the person.

I had to find Joy and tell her what happened so she would be on the alert.

I held on to the other side of the railing with my left hand and slowly made my way up to the top of the stairs. I stood to one side at the top of the landing and blinked my eyes hard, trying to get them to clear, trying to get my bearings.

I located the hallway and area we were sitting in and made sure I didn't limp as I walked to where Joy was sitting and joined her at a little table outside the onboard shop. As I sat down, I stole a quick peek at the goodies in the window: all kinds of unique jewelry, tee shirts, and handbags that particularly caught my attention.

But, since I was on a major de-cluttering campaign at home, I decided I didn't really need any of these items since I had two or three already; these could stay in the store for someone else to buy.

"Water?" I asked when I sat down on the little round stool permanently attached to the floor. Joy sat reading across the table from me.

I felt like a big girl sitting at a Miss Muffet table waiting for the spider and thankfully not having to eat any curds and whey.

Joy looked up at me, but I smiled weakly at her.

"You're bleeding," she said in a calm voice, looking down at my feet.

I looked down at my white-and-gray running shoes and, sure enough, there were drops of blood coming from under the cuff of my jeans.

"I'll be right back," I said, "and yes, I'm fine. Although I guess someone was trying to kill me." I rose to my feet, turned, and quickly limped off in the direction of the ladies room.

Luckily it was close, and since it was half an hour into the trip, it wasn't as full as it usually is at the beginning and the end of a trip.

I made sure to stop and step over the high doorframe before entering the washroom.

I wasn't sure if I should try to clean up the blood in the stall or by the sink. There's something a little strange about standing in the middle of a cold, large room surrounded by strangers, pulling down your pants and standing there in your underwear as people walked in and out.

So I got a big handful of paper towel and got it good and wet, and a few dry ones too so I could dry myself off.

I went into a toilet stall and closed the door behind me. I pulled down my pants, sat on the toilet, and started to cry.

I knew it was just a silly reaction to the fall, a sudden adrenalin rush, or my frustration about not seeing the person who tripped me. And relief that I hadn't been hurt worse than I was.

This attack had taken our investigation to a whole new level. Someone was willing to hurt or even kill us to stop us. That much was clear. I was afraid.

I decided we must have a meeting with Ryan and Nigel to share with them our information and to get theirs. Especially about the car being keyed, the threatening note, and now this attack. We were obviously making someone very nervous and that meant that we were getting close.

We had two ladies to talk to as well and we had to do it quickly.

Right now we didn't know the name of the deceased, but I had a strong feeling the police did.

Chapter Thirteen

A meeting of minds.

I LIMPED OUT of the ladies washroom and knew I had to take something for the pain and the swelling in my knee and shoulder.

"Heather, sit down," Joy said, her voice edged with concern, handing me a water bottle. "Here, I have something that will help." She handed me two Tylenol tablets.

I accepted the pills and the water and quickly downed them both and then sat down across from her.

"What happened?" Her concern knitted Joy's eyebrows and wrinkled her forehead.

I shook my head.

We had to talk, but I didn't want to be overheard. Someone had deliberately tripped me going down the stairs, which decreased the likelihood of the keying of Joy's car not being part of this case to nil.

"We should meet with the boys at my house," I said. "Give them a call and maybe we can get together tonight. How about we have coffee together after dinner?"

I had a Bundt cake in the freezer at home. I planned to take it out and warm it up for our coffee, if everyone was available.

"It will have to be a quick meeting," said Joy, trying to for a smile as she looked at me with intense concern. "I have to open the shop tomorrow morning and need my beauty sleep, Heather."

"Bundt cake?"

"That's not fair," she said in mock horror. "Marble?"

Rita Schulz

I knew the cake was one of her favorites. I had seen Bundt pans on her kitchen walls and had asked her about them. Apparently she collects Bundt pans and recipes too.

"I'll call Ryan and Nigel to set the meeting up when we get on the other side," she assured me. "I'll give you a call right away afterward."

I nodded and was going to pull out my notebook to go over some of the points for the meeting, but thought better of it. Just in case someone got the idea of stealing it. I couldn't afford losing my notes. Not just were my notes on the case in the notebook, a good portion of my synopsis for my mystery was in it too.

***

Joy, Nigel, Ryan, and I were gathered around my kitchen table in awkward silence. We seemed to be waiting to see who was going to talk first. It was really interesting, like watching a game of Chicken only in the comfort of your own home.

How civilized, I thought with amusement.

I looked over at Joy and watched her sit there, her jaw tight and her eyes like a hard emerald. I knew that she wasn't going to go first. As she had told me before Ryan and Nigel had gotten there, they asked us for help and said they would share information.

I finally took the leap and broke the silence. "The reason I asked you all to come to this meeting is I think it's time to really be honest with one another and pool our information together. If we're going to help you, then we have to be on the same side." I paused to let my words sink in and saw eyes flitting back and forth. I was getting through.

"And the more information we have, the less likely we will duplicate our efforts like going to Vancouver Island and tripping over our own feet. So we all need to be forthcoming with each other.

"Don't you all agree?" I saw the uncertain expressions of Ryan and Nigel.

I picked up my pen as I a pulled my notebook close to me. I had opened it to a nice fresh clean page.

I waited.

No one said anything. Joy, Nigel, and Ryan even avoided looking at one another.

I waited for another five minutes and then saw Joy look at the kitchen apple clock attached to the wall next to the cupboards.

Her actions weren't surprising. It was after eight o'clock and she still had to take Kirby out for his walk.

"Okay," I said. "Let's start with something simple. Do you have the name of the victim?"

Ryan looked at Nigel, who gave him a small nod. The younger man smiled at Joy, then at me.

"You're right, ladies. We do need to cooperate with each other. We did ask for your help and said that we would share information. But you have to understand that it can't go any further than between us. Right?" Ryan appeared very serious, his eyes darkened.

I didn't say anything; instead I took a sip of hot jasmine green tea and nodded. I understood. We had covered this ground a long time ago and either they trusted us or we were all just spinning our wheels.

They would have to stop wasting my time or I would have to make stuff up rather than taking a really good premise and just changing a few facts and rearranging things for my fictional book.

I could almost feel my editor looking at me. I could imagine her emails to me and her disappointment at me not making my deadline. I have always met my deadlines and I wasn't going to fail now.

I needed this story.

Yes, I could make stuff up; usually that was a really fun thing for me, but times have changed. Tom was home. Everything felt different and I was off my stride.

Ryan took a deep breath, put down his coffee cup, and pulled out a small three- by six-inch notebook. It had a hard black faux leather cover and a snap closure. He opened it. I noticed there were two rubber bands holding some of the pages together, kind of like a double bookmarker.

"Okay, this is what we've got so far," he began. "Bear in mind this is just basic tombstone information. Nigel is right: we don't know whose body it is yet, but we've narrowed it down. The family that lived in that house at the time were the Martins, James and Beverly. They had two children: the older a daughter named Irene June Martin, and the younger a son, Luke Ervin Martin. So we think this is Irene June Martin who we found buried at the old lot. We won't have confirmation until next week, and yes, we are pushing the lab guys as hard as we can on this. They're checking the DNA and dental records, but you have to understand this is an old case."

I was writing notes furiously. I would have to check the names, get their DOBs, and then start my hunt from there. If they were living in this area, then there should be school records for the children. And I could probably get a line on what kind of work Mr. Martin did. I bet it was either landscaping or working at one of the sawmills on the Fraser River just down the street from where we were. That's what a lot of European immigrants did when they first arrived in Vancouver in those days. Those were usually the only jobs they could get with their limited language skills.

Then there were church records. Now I had the names and the police confirmed they suspected the Martins and I could get the information we needed.

Old Bones

The church records would be the easiest place to start. I would need to talk to my friend Angela Kay, the church secretary, to gain access to the records.

I would ask her; and if she lied to me again, I'd have to go over her head and speak with the elders. This was a police investigation; we had to have the information. Even if I wound up losing a very dear friend that I loved very much, I would have to do it.

"We have things to share as well," Joy said as I nodded to her and handed a quick summary of things we had found and things that had happened to us. Joy shared the information but nothing about the car being keyed or me being tripped down the stairs.

I knew that she had to have a reason and kept quiet.

***

The morning was cold, with heavy clouds overhead. It looked like it would start to rain any moment. I climbed up the gray cement stairs not knowing what I was going to say, just knowing that I had to say something to Angela. I had wanted Joy to take this interview, but as things worked out, she had to work early; and since we had to get the information as soon as possible, I decided to conduct the interview myself.

At the top of the stairs was a heavy oak and glass door. I rang the bell for the office and waited for someone, most likely Angela, to let me in.

I had called ahead of time and made an appointment with her and hoped that the chill I detected in her voice wouldn't be an indicator of how the interview was going to go.

I watched Angela closely as she came to the door. She was a short, spry woman in her early eighties who loved God, the church and congregation, and gardening,

She had her short white hair done in a pixie cut that, with a touch of eye shadow and lipstick, looked good on her.

She held her head high and was looking at the hall wall, then she glanced into the associate pastor's office as she came past the door to that office on the left. I knew she had seen me in the mirror designed to reflect whoever was at the outside door. Anyone in the office or walking past it could easily see who was there.

Her eyes went to the door handle as she gripped it, then turned it, before pulling it open. So far she had looked everywhere except at me.

The office phone rang as she pushed the outside door open; she quickly turned away from me and hurried to the office to answer it, leaving me to catch it before it closed. I was a little annoyed. She hadn't greeted me or even made eye contact—not quite the greeting I had hoped for. It almost seemed as if she was angry with me.

I followed her to the office where I heard her talking in a soft voice to someone on the telephone.

"I told you it would be fine," she said in low tones. "Don't worry, there's no reason for them to know. Yes, of course I remember the promise I made, although…" Her words became a whisper; finally I couldn't hear what she was saying..

I had only heard a bit of her conversation before she lowered her voice and I couldn't hear anything more.

I wondered whom she was talking to and what it was about. It seemed too much of a coincidence it being a random caller with me being at the office this morning.

I decided to file this tidbit of information away for future reference. I pulled out my notebook and made a quick note. It might be nothing or it might be something, hard to tell right now. But with her attitude, everything she did was now making me suspicious.

Old Bones

"Angela, hi," I said, trying to sound cheery. I knew this was going to be an awkward conversation. She was seated at the desk in her office chair with the receiver held to her ear.

Her sullen eyes shifted to gaze at me. "Bye; yes, I'll call you later," she said before she hung up the phone.

My stomach was in knots. I hadn't had an opportunity to talk to her since our coffee the other day and now I would have to confront her about what she said and also why I had to know.

I wasn't sure about the right way to approach the subject so I thought seeing her face-to-face would provide the inspiration I needed. I hoped.

So far, nothing but an uncomfortable silence filled the church office. She looked at me and I looked back at her.

We were both waiting for the other to say something.

The clock in the corner of the room on the four-drawer metal filing cabinet ticked away the minutes.

I smiled weakly at her and she smiled back at me. I felt my throat starting to close. For a moment I thought maybe I shouldn't be asking questions Angela didn't want to answer. She didn't need any more grief in her life. I was getting ready to tell her to forget it when she finally broke the silence between us.

"Heather, we need to talk," she said. "I know what you're thinking right now and I have a good idea about what you're going to ask me, but really—" she paused.

I gazed into her bright blue eyes. She was the only adult friend from when I was a kid left in the old neighborhood, and the only old family friend I had left. She had been my Sunday school teacher and my kids club guide and my teen and adult mentor.

I didn't understand how or why she lied to me and why she was holding back critical information.

But I still loved her and didn't want her to be hurt, even if I was the one that was hurting her.

"Let's make this as painless as possible," I said. "We're working with the police. Joy and I are helping them solve a murder committed in the neighborhood about fifty years ago."

I watched her facial expressions as I talked. I was going to approach this delicate subject as simply as possible. I didn't want her to feel as if she was betraying a confidence. At least not right away. I just wanted basic information that was a matter of public record.

I was trying to lull her into a false sense of security.

"The police finally received confirmation of the names of the people that used to live at the old empty lot," I explained. "They think they might be connected to the murder. I would like to know if James and Beverly Martin were members of this church?"

"Yes," she said simply. Her voice was curt, her eyes hard.

"Could you let me know which dates they came here?"

My heart beat heavily and I was breathing shallowly; this Angela was someone I had never seen before.

I waited for her to access her computer, but she didn't. She just sat there, her lips forming a tight little smile.

I decided to press on. "When did they become members and when did they stop coming here? I'd also like whatever information you have about their children. I believe the girl's name was Irene and her younger brother was Luke."

I watched as Angela turned on her computer. I was surprised to see how quickly she typed the request for information into the machine and searched the church records.

Boy, for an elderly lady, her fingers really flew across that keyboard. She'd been keeping her typing skills updated on the computer.

Old Bones

I sure knew that if you didn't keep up, the technology just flew by you.

"Okay," she said finally, "here is the information you're looking for. The Martins were German immigrants who came to Canada as part of the Canadian-German Baptist Sponsorship Program. Actually they were immigrants before the war, and when they arrived in Vancouver they started attending this church."

There was a certain note of pride when Angela spoke about the Sponsorship Program so I thought I'd get a little more information on the program as background. "Do you know much about the Sponsorship Program?"

"Sure," said Angela with a tight, small smile on her face. "It all started at one of the small Baptist churches in Winnipeg, Manitoba, in the nineteen-twenties."

"That's not what I meant." I was getting frustrated. I needed to know about the Martins and the old bones, not a history lesson on church history.

"Actually it is. You wanted to know about the Martin family. In order to know more about them, you need to know a little of the church's history and the Canadian Baptist Conference."

Of course I knew she was right. I had to get the back-story to understand the entire story.

I took in a deep breath, relaxed my shoulders, and nodded. I glanced down at my notebook, then back into her bright blue eyes and couldn't help but grin. "You're right. I do need to know the whole story if I'm going to understand how it all fits together. If I'm going to write about it, I need to understand it. I'm not going to write the church's story specifically, but I need to write a story with similar elements in it."

Angela nodded. "It will be a good story, I'm sure."

Angela had always been one of my biggest fans and she had always supported me.

"How about coming over to my house for tea after work and we can talk?" I suggested. "Tom will be home by then. I'm sure he would love to hear about the start of the church and the immigration from Germany in the early nineteen-twenties. You know how much he loves history."

Angela chuckled easily. Her face had relaxed; her usual calm, peaceful smile was back.

"You've always been stubborn and focused. I guess you won't let this go, will you?" she asked and looked at me. Her eyes looked tired.

"I can't, Angela. The police are looking into the deaths and have asked for Joy and me to help them. Besides, I want to use the basic story for a novel I need to get done in a hurry. So I really need your help. How about it? Come over and tell Tom and me." I was really hoping that she would be willing to help me.

"That sounds like a good idea. I don't have any plans right now, so that would be perfect. It's almost three o'clock now and that's my quitting time. Let's go," she said cheerily.

The minute she said this, I felt better. I didn't think she would tell me everything I wanted to know, especially after the phone call I overheard. She seemed to be protecting someone, but at least our getting together to talk was a start in the right direction.

Angela accompanied me to my car. I had driven to the church. Though it was only a block away, Angela might have wanted to go somewhere other than my place for coffee and I really needed to talk to her. Removing any barriers to our getting together was all part of my plan.

I pulled my cell phone from my purse and dialed home.

Old Bones

I spoke to Tom and let him know I was bringing Angela home with me and invited him to join us. I knew if I didn't call ahead, he would make himself scarce to give us our privacy. Today I wanted him there especially to ask the usual insightful questions he was so skilled at.

***

"How good to see you, Angela," said Tom as he helped her off with her coat and hat, putting them into the small entryway closet.

I eyed Tom in his comfortable tan Dockers and light green golf shirt as he welcomed Angela. He always has such a nice way with people, a real gentleman. It was one of the things that attracted me to him when we first met. Even when he had to be firm on the job as a Customs Officer, and now a Senior Canada Compliance Verification Officer he was polite. He wasn't a pushover, but he was calm, assertive, and not aggressive with people.

"Shall we go into the kitchen?" I asked as I took off and hung up my coat and gave Buddy a quick pat on his head.

Together we followed Tom into our large kitchen-dining room combination. Our house's configuration is strange—the only one I have ever seen like it. At one time we thought of putting the kitchen against the outside wall next to the sliding glass doors, so we'd have it run halfway down the joining wall, and then knock out the wall between the kitchen and the living room. We even priced it out but it would have been far too expensive since that wall was a supporting wall.

I would still like to do it, but ours is a small, old house and I know when it's sold it will be knocked down so a larger house can be built on the lot.

For Tom and me, the house as it stood worked well enough so we had decided not to bother.

"Angela, would you like tea or coffee?" I asked.

"I know you like your tea and Tom likes his coffee and I like either, so I'll let you decide," she said with a gentle curl of her lips and softness in her tone.

"Fine, I'll do what I do when we both get up at the same time."

I turned away and smiled to myself. Tom is a night owl and I like to get up early in the morning. Now that I'm retired from my bank job, I've found that I like to stay up late too, especially if I've had an opportunity to nap during the afternoon. So I get the best of both worlds: up to see the sunrise and the sunset, with a nap in the middle.

It would be interesting when Tom retired from Customs in the next while as to what our schedule would be, or if we'd just go with the flow.

I've no doubt Buddy and I will find this change confusing at first.

I pulled out the kettle and the teapot to brew a nice blend of loose green tea with jasmine, then reached up and pulled down the bag of coffee beans. The fresh beans I just bought Tom, from Salt Spring Coffee, was something new I tried on him the other day. He said he enjoyed it, so I thought I'd make his coffee using them again.

I boiled the water, then poured some into the teapot as I ground up some fresh beans in a coarse chop, then dumped them into Tom's French press. I then filled the four-cup press with boiling water. Green tea doesn't take very long to brew—just a few minutes—after which I take out the diffuser.

While I readied the tea and coffee, Tom and Angela chatted about the church and the different programs that were being prepared for the summer and fall.

Old Bones

Tom got up and put the mugs, milk, and sugar on the table while I pulled out the round cork mats and put them on the table along with the teapot and the French press.

I then went to my office to retrieve my notebook and joined them around the table with our steaming mugs of coffee and tea.

Angela looked at me, then at my notebook. She picked up her teacup and gently blew across it. Tom sat there with his coffee and I sat there waiting with my book open and pen in hand.

I was wondering why she was stalling. Or maybe it was my impatience. My shoulder and knee were throbbing from the fall on the ferry, but I didn't want to take anything in case it made me dopey. I really just wanted this day to end, but I knew I would be having another group of guests from the neighborhood for coffee after dinner tonight. And their information was critical to our investigation.

"Angela, why don't you tell us about German immigration in the 1920s," suggested Tom, smiling encouragingly.

I nodded but remained silent in case our disagreement embarrassed her and made her feel ill at ease. But that wasn't the end of it between us either, that I could promise her. And she knew it. It wouldn't be the first or probably the last time she commented on my tenacious nature.

I tore my mind from that thought and focused on the dynamics in my kitchen right now. The wooden apple clock on the wall ticked loudly as if marking time until doomsday. Finally Angela started to speak.

"It all started in a little church in Winnipeg, Manitoba." She paused as if for dramatic effect. "You know how sometimes God can use the smallest actions and ideas?"

Tom and I nodded as one, encouraging her to continue.

"Well, there is, or was, a small congregation of Baptists in Winnipeg in a little church called Red River Baptist Church. When they heard off the plague epidemic in Europe, especially in Germany and Poland, they decided to do something about it.

"I don't mean just pray about it, which is all well and good; they decided to put their money where their faith was," she paused to take another sip of her tea.

"Pastor Bergermister was the senior pastor at the time, and when member after member of the congregation asked what they could do to get their family members from Europe to Canada, he went to the Canadian immigration authorities and, after much discussion, came up with a plan.

"It meant the church would have to sign as sponsor for these people and be financially responsible for them. If one person defaulted, it could be the end of their church. A church they had cleared the land for and had built with their own hands.

"They were very careful about who they selected to head the project. It had to be a family member of a member of the congregation as well as a Baptist. That way, each person who immigrated would have a family to stay with and people they would already know in Canada to help them get settled and find a job." Angela paused and took another sip of tea.

I was writing my notes quickly in point form. I felt Tom get up, go to the cupboard, get plates, and come back with cookies and some slices of raspberry pound cake.

Tom served Angela first and she nodded as she took a plate and cookie, then continued.

"It was a success. Once the people immigrated, they stayed for two years in Winnipeg to work on farms or landscaping until they found other full-time work for themselves.

Old Bones

A lot of them put down roots in Winnipeg, but a lot came to Vancouver, too.

"The Martins, Remples, Brauns, Frissells and others were part of the immigration flow and they came to Vancouver in the early 1920s.

"You have to understand: once the other Baptist churches heard what that little Winnipeg church was doing, they all pitched in and did the same. There were tens of thousands of immigrants from Europe who came to Canada that way.

"In Vancouver, here in this community, they went to work landscaping, logging, or carpentry. They had family and a community when they came here. They weren't alone. And the Martins were part of the group who moved to Vancouver."

I glanced at Tom. He had arched an eyebrow. I knew he was as surprised about all this as I was. This was something I had heard about the Winnipeg churches but never knew it had happened right here in our own community.

"Karl Rempel came first and got a job with one of our congregation and then Brigitte came about a year later. We sponsored them both and may others."

Angela took a deep breath, then sighed before taking a sip of her tea. I could see that she was struggling with something.

"Theirs was not a happy marriage. At first I thought Brigitte was one of the luckiest women alive. Karl was so kind and funny. I was just a young girl with little life experience and you never know what's really happening behind closed doors, do you?"

"Do you know what happened?" asked Tom. "Was it their daughter in the empty lot? Was it her body that they found?"

"I don't know," she sighed, shaking her head. "All I know is that one day they're here and the next they're not.

They had owned the house then it was torn down, the empty lot has been empty for a long time. It was a big house, you remember?"

I nodded. "I remember as a young girl going by there when I walked with my father in the evenings after dinner. We'd walk our little dog."

I looked over at Tom to see him give me an encouraging nod.

"You knew her, didn't you?" I said, my heart beginning to beat faster. "You know who the body is?" My voice got higher and higher as my excitement grew. I pushed my glasses up my nose and gripped my pen harder, ready to write her next words.

Angela started to shake her head and sighed.

"No, I don't." Her brow wrinkled. "I don't think. I got married just before that time and we moved to Toronto where Otto's parents lived. We were gone from the neighborhood for fifteen years. We came home and heard some rumors but nothing specific. I only heard about it through friends and it was all third hand."

I watched her play with the handle of her mug, then start to tap her fingers on the rim.

"What about your brother and the other friends Irene Martin may have had?"

Angela shrugged her shoulders. She pursed her lips. I knew a stubborn look when I saw one. I sensed there weren't any more questions she would answer for me today.

"Angela, would you like some more Bundt cake?" asked Tom.

"After we have our cake, Tom will run you home," I offered. "It looks like it's going to be very cold this evening and I have to get dinner ready." I quickly drained my tea, then ate a small slice of cake so not to spoil my dinner.

Old Bones

It seemed the story was mostly true up to the immigration part, but she knew something more about the murder, of that I was fairly certain.

Normally I would run her home myself but I had to make a quick dinner since Ryan and Nigel were coming over to exchange information.

Hopefully we'd know more in a few more hours.

***

Joy was the first to arrive after dinner and couldn't sit still so I knew something was up. She started pacing up and down the long kitchen as I did the dishes and tidied up.

I glanced at the kitchen clock and realized I wouldn't have time to make any more sweets. The Bundt cake and cookies were almost gone; I was going to send Tom out to the bakery when the doorbell chimed and Buddy raced barking to the door.

"Joy, tell me what's going on," I said as I caught up with her in our hallway. We walked into the living room and the doorbell rang again. I looked up and saw Tom coming down the hall toward the front door, with Angela behind him.

Joy was deep in thought, her brow was furrowed, and her blue eyes were narrowed in concentration.

"I just heard from a source of mine, unofficial of course, that it wasn't just a female human body. That is was a—"

Tom opened the front door and both police officers were standing on the front stoop bundled up in their heavy parkas.

"Come on in, gentlemen." Tom held out his hand in greeting. "I don't know if your remember, my name is Tom, I'm Heather's husband and I met you at Joy's house party.

150

Please come in and let me take you coats."

I heard the tone of deep male voices come from the entryway; it sounded like they were introducing themselves again.

"Heather, I'm going to run Angela home. I'll be right back. Is there anything we need?"

"Yes, please," I said as I leaned close to Tom and put in an order for sweets from the bakery.

"Thanks for coming by, Angela, it was really interesting," I said as I gave her a quick hug. It wasn't over yet, but it was done for tonight and I wanted us to both feel good about our discussion about the case so far.

"Let's go into the kitchen and have a cup of tea," I said. "Or coffee if you prefer," I added when I saw Ryan pulling a yuck face at the mention of tea. I got him this time.

I offered the two cops a tight smile, then led the way down the hall into the kitchen. The kitchen is the social center of our home and a good place for meetings.

Tom was back in ten minutes and took over the duties of brewing the tea and coffee and setting out the sweets, the china clinking as he pulled mugs from the cupboard.

"So you're a writer too, are you, Tom?" said Nigel. "Have you written anything I may have read?" Nigel looked at Tom as he rocked back on the back two legs of his chair, waiting for a response.

"Actually I had a new book come out last month. It's a mystery entitled The Dark Window. I write under my own name, Tom Ross, and you can pick it up online."

Nigel nodded as he grinned at Tom. "That sounds good; I'll check it out. I've just discovered a fabulous new mystery author—well, new to me; she's been writing a while. Susan Applewood. Have you read any of her stuff?"

Old Bones

I almost started to laugh and caught myself just in time. Susan Applewood was my mystery nom de plume. Tom had read me a lot, especially since we were each other's first readers.

Tom wore a smile on his lips as he leaned over to pour the hot water into the French press. He took a deep breath, straightened, and turned to face the detective.

"Yes, I believe I have enjoyed her books over the years."

"Okay, everybody, I think we need to clear the air and actually work together," said Joy, her eyes flitting between the two police officers. "I have the feeling we're treading on each other's toes. Remember, you asked for our help with this case."

I watched the facial expressions as the two police officers looked at each other, exchanged a nod, then looked stone-faced back at us.

I sighed in frustration. They were still playing games. I was certain they would have discussed exactly what they were going to say to us. And what information they were going to release, and what they were going to withhold from us.

"Look. Enough with the games already," I said, trying to stay calm. I was getting frustrated, especially with the incident onboard the ferry. "We need you to tell us everything. If you hold back, and we hold back, do you think this case will ever be solved? It won't."

Okay. Enough said. I clamped my mouth shut. I decided not to say anything else. Just observe and note everything.

Ryan and Nigel glanced at each other again.

So much for my resolve.

"Stop it. Stop the acting and the game playing," I sputtered as I watched them. "You've already decided exactly what information you're going to tell us. You might fool other people, or witnesses, but you can't fool me."

Nigel had the good sense to appear embarrassed. His cheeks were bright as Santa's red suit. Ryan smiled and arched an eyebrow at his aunt, who looked very pleased with herself.

What else was going on here? Had I missed something entirely?

"Gentlemen, it seems that you're frustrating my good wife here," said Tom as he moved the French press and poured coffee into the cups on the table. "And you really don't want to do that."

I wondered how hot that water really was and what it would do to a person if it was thrown at them. Okay, that's gross. I quickly dismissed the image in my head.

Maybe I could retrieve the image later if I was going to work on a short horror story. It's all grist for the old story mill, as I always say.

"Look, it's simple," I said. "I don't know if Joy agrees with me or not, but I have a book to finish and I'm on a very tight deadline. The plan was to use the bones of this story, change the names, the location, and some of the details, and write a fictional mystery novel." I smirked.

"But of course you know all of that already. Only I sense I'm not getting anything but a runaround rather than the information to actually help you with this case and help my story.

"I'm sure Joy has better things she needs to do, too. She's just moved into a new house after all," I added, finishing my tirade.

Boy, when I'm determined to keep my mouth shut, I certainly don't do a good job of it. I sighed and my eyes flitted to Joy. She was smiling at me but I could see a determined glint in her eyes.

"Fine," said Nigel, scanning all our faces. His eyes were dark and serious. "Tom, you haven't been involved with the ladies and this case, so I'll repeat that what I'm going to discuss now has to stay in the room."

Old Bones

We all nodded as his eyes fell on each of us, confirming we would do as he asked.

"There was more than one body in that shallow grave. There was another one as well, a baby's," Nigel said, a grim edge to his voice.

I was scribbling madly in my notebook. Taking down not just his words, but a brief description of our responses as well.

Tom nodded and pursed his lips while Joy steepled her fingers and pressed her fingers against her bottom lip, her eyes unfocused as she digested this new information.

I was shocked. I just figured they had the identity of the body, so together we would have a starting point to find out which of the family it was.

"That's why we were waiting until we had the forensics in hand first. And we needed to find out if the bones were related to each other or not. Our initial thought was the two sets of bones were a mother and her child. We just found out they're not."

Nigel let that information hang in the air as he got up to get the coffeepot and poured himself another cup of coffee while the rest of us digested this startling information.

"Are they closely related?" asked Joy.

"Not really, at least not immediate family."

"Do we have any more information concerning the family living here at the time that would help us, and when they left the area?" asked Ryan.

"Yeah, we do," said Joy. "But first you need to know that someone has been following us, and whoever it was damaged my car, sent us a warning note and then tried to hurt Heather by pushing her down a steep flight of stairs on the ferry."

Until now I'd been hiding my injury. I slowly rose from the chair and limped to the counter.

Since my injury, I found if I sat for too long, my knee would start to stiffen up. I poured more hot water into the teapot and added tea leaves. My back was turned to Tom and the others.

I really wished Joy hadn't said anything. The jury was still out if these events were related to the case. I sighed. Who was I fooling? Certainly not myself.

They were obviously warnings that I was purposefully ignoring. I was concerned about what Tom would say. I hadn't had time to talk to him before this.

Joy went on to describe in detail what happened to me and to her car and showed them the note. When I sat down, Tom reached out and took hold of my hand. I knew we would have to talk later but right now the look of concern in his eyes was enough for me.

"Okay, so we know that they weren't mother and child or any immediate family" said Joy, recapping the new information. "Not the same immediate family. But the one body was female in her early to midtwenties and the other, buried under her, was a baby."

I nodded and looked over to Joy.

"Tomorrow morning, Heather and I are going to go back to the community and have another visit with some of the nice people we've met and then start to visit others. Maybe that will loosen a few memories," Joy said determinedly.

"Actually, tomorrow is Friday night; how about then?" I suggested.

I was losing time and I knew this case had to move forward. I didn't want to be bossy but I wasn't going to make my deadline unless I was.

"Why don't we have them over for a get-to-know-the-new-neighbors party?

155

"Maybe we will get more information with a little wine and cheese rather than intimidation," I said, throwing out the idea I had been thinking about on the ferry until my short trip down the stairs.

"Great idea," said Joy.

I nodded. "Tonight is our choir practice so I'll invite a few of the ladies to a party and call the others tomorrow."

Everyone nodded and I got up.

"Another thing, before we go," said Nigel. "We've been given until Monday to solve this case. So we have three days before we have to move on to other more current cases."

"All right, that will work well; we can party tomorrow—Friday—then on Saturday we can catch up to people that didn't come. What do you think?" I asked.

Joy grinned and Nigel and Ryan nodded.

Chapter Fourteen
Visiting Old Friends

It was Friday night and our little house was full. I was always amazed how quickly the word gets out that the neighborhood was having a party and everyone was welcome.

Luckily we have two floors and although the house isn't that big by today's standards, it works well for parties. We had people playing board games in the kitchen on the big table, and there was a conversation pit developing in the front room. In the guest bedroom we had a couple of the kids playing a game on my laptop. I shuddered at the thought of it being used for this purpose, but this was all for a good cause. I needed more clues.

Downstairs in the family room, we had the large television playing a movie. We have a great selection of DVDs since Tom and I both loved our movies. Right now there was a kids' movie playing. We had agreed with the parents we would have stuff for all age groups so they could take turns.

One of our friends had actually created a list, after talking to Tom, and posted a schedule of show times for the selected titles.

This was a bring-your-own-bottle type of party. We were supplying the snacks and later we would have hot food served buffet style, and of course we had tea and coffee, and juice for the kids; but we wouldn't be serving anything stronger.

Don't get me wrong, I like a cocktail or a glass of wine and Tom enjoys an occasional beer, but we didn't want people to get drunk and have to be carried away.

Old Bones

Tom had turned on the stereo in the living room, running extra speakers into the kitchen too. The soft music was a nice background noise over the hum of conversation.

"Yahtzee!" I heard Joy call as a sudden whoop of noise went up at the end of the long kitchen table. I laughed. I hoped she was keeping her mind on why we were throwing this indoor block party.

"Heather," said a familiar male voice softly from behind me, "we need to talk; and the sooner we do, the better." I didn't have to turn around, knowing already it was Nigel.

I looked for Tom and discovered him playing another board game with a group of people right in front of me. I smiled as I leaned toward him to tell him I was going to talk to Nigel for a few minutes in the office.

My face grew warm and I dreaded the idea everyone here knew my secret and how uncomfortable I was. I realized if I wanted to get past the ancient history with Nigel and move forward, we would have to talk. It might be painful but it was better to know what happened or didn't happen than carry it around all my life.

At the time I'd really liked Nigel and he'd said he liked me too. So why hadn't he called me? He said he was through with his previous girlfriend and wanted to be with me. Though we had only had that one blind date, there seemed to be a connection.

My self-confidence had been completely shattered and I had spent the next thirty years getting over it.

I needed to focus, to get my book in on time by meeting or beating my deadline. I was going to have to put this thing with Nigel behind me once and for all. I needed to kill it and put it to rest.

"Let's go into my office," I said, leading the way down the hallway.

I opened the door since it was closed and had a Do not enter sign on it.

The sign was a souvenir from the days we had our teenage children living with us.

I led Nigel as we entered the office with its warm, cream-colored walls and big window facing the north garden. I always kept this window open regardless of the weather. Only at night did I pull the light blue curtains closed; it gave the room a cozy feel.

Nigel pulled the door almost closed but not quite, leaving it a crack ajar.

Okay, my thoughts were racing and focusing on the mundane. I tried to calm myself as Nigel and I sat down in two chairs opposite each other. I sat in the executive chair I used when writing while he sat in the reclining wingback chair I use to curl up in and read.

I smoothed my sweater with shaky hands, a nervous habit I've had since I was a girl, and stared at Nigel.

He still reminded me of the boy I had known all those many years ago. His hair had silver in it now and his face had lines from worry and laughter, but to me it was still the same as I remember.

His mouth was full and his nose straight, a bit more prominent than is considered handsome these days. But his eyes, they hadn't changed. They were warm, brown, and kind. They were gentle eyes. With all the things he would have seen and had to deal with as a police officer, I wondered how his gentle eyes could have remained the same in the intervening years.

"Let me start first," began Nigel. "I know I said I would call you and didn't. I did check with Paula and she told me she had spoken to you and given you my message."

"She did," I said, crossing my arms over my chest. "Why did you take the coward's way out and not talk to me yourself?" I looked him straight in his eyes. I had wanted to ask that question for a very long time, over thirty years.

Old Bones

I never understood how someone could tell another person that they really cared about them, that there was something special between them, and not let them know in person. Especially when he had gone back to someone that he said he didn't love and didn't want to be with.

I know it's difficult, but a person should at least let the other person know. My rule is be honest—don't just leave people guessing what went wrong between the two of you. Or you will leave them blaming themselves.

I knew Nigel had married Sara, the girl had had returned to after our blind date; they had two children and Sara died about ten years ago.

"I'm so sorry," he said. "I was a coward. I should never have gone back to her. I should have called you the next day like I said I would and wanted too. But I felt like a heel leaving her. We'd been together for a very long time, over five years."

I waited for him to continue. I looked down at my hands at my wedding rings. Marrying Tom was a decision I had never regretted.

"I assume things turned out well for you?" he asked.

"Things turned out great." I looked up and said confidently, "If we had been together, I wouldn't have met and married Tom. Now I know this was the right path and the right decision for me.

"I don't know what would have happened if you and I had started dating. I don't know what kind of person I would have become." I paused to let my words sink in. "But it was very special meeting you for that one special date all those years ago. When the dust settled, that date shattered me and after a time I had to pull myself up and move on which gave me more confidence in myself. And it gave me the belief that love can and does happen," I smiled.

Nigel nodded and he too smiled.

My stomach burned and bile rose to the back of my throat. Now came the real question. The question I had to have answered to finally put our past to rest. My heart pounded hard as I formulated the question.

"Nigel, was there anything I could have said or done differently?" I asked. "Anything that would have made a difference, to help you like me more?" I asked my voice thick with emotion.

"No," he said shaking his head. "That was the worst of it. I was turning my back on you, someone I had fallen in love with. Yes, with you, it was love at first sight. I wanted so badly to stay with someone I owed my love to and didn't. It was a very confusing time for me," he whispered, his eyes avoiding mine. "I betrayed myself. I didn't stand up for myself; I took the coward's way out and just let it be." His gaze dropped to the floor and he blinked his eyes hard.

My mind went back to that day. The day he didn't call. I felt a sense of relief come over me. There was nothing I could have done differently. Good. It wasn't my fault. My whole body felt as if the air had been let out of it. I became limp, weak. It was finally over.

The day my heart was broken, I had survived it. Life had gone on.

"Friends?" he asked shyly, his eyes coming up to meet mine.

I nodded. "With the understanding that if you have something to say or tell me, you will tell me yourself. Not via email or through someone else. It's not fair to leave a person hanging and wondering what happened. Can you do that now?" My heart beat harder and my mouth was dry.

Nigel shrugged. "Yeah. I've grown up and had to deal with lots of emotional and very unpleasant situations too. Friends?" he asked again.

I stood, wrapped my arms around him, and hugged him. "Friends," I said with a deep sense of relief.

"Now we have to get going on that murder case. And I have to get back to the party to see if we can shake any information from these good folks."

Nigel's brow furrowed, his expression one of confusion.

"Oh, yes," I said realizing I'd forgotten to tell him the real reason for the party. "The reason I'm having this impromptu little house block party is that Joy and I are going to mingle and try glean any kind of information we can shake loose from these people. We felt if we put them in a different setting outside their own homes, someone might say something that we can work with. Then we're going on a one-on-one tomorrow with the ones who provide information to follow up on. What do you think?" I said with a sly grin.

I watched the corners of his eyes crinkle up as he shook his head. "Dangerous, but effective. I think it's a good thing that we never did get together. We would have made a dangerous team." He chuckled.

"I concur with that remark," said Tom as he pushed open the door and came into the room. "I'm glad you didn't get together with her either." He walked up to me and put his hand lightly on my shoulder.

I turned and put an arm around his waist. He leaned down and gave me a light kiss on the cheek. "Yes, after all, who would you have had to nag at you all these years?" I gave Tom a quick squeeze.

I can't say I was surprised to see Tom, but I'm glad he was here to hear what was said. I had told him about my one night date that I still questioned but now the question was answered for good.

The three of us walked down the hallway into the kitchen. I was so relieved that discussion was over. And it turned out to be nothing at all. My heart had been broken all those years ago and it really didn't matter anymore. I couldn't regret what hadn't happened, but I'd learned to appreciate what had.

While I'd be gone, some of the players at the table had changed and they were ready to start another game. Angela and Catherine were setting up for Monopoly and I wanted to join them.

I didn't really like playing Monopoly. My brother in-law and Tom used to play what I called Killer Monopoly. They played the game as take no prisoners, win at all costs. I guess I'm too much of a wimp, it just doesn't sound like fun when your main purpose in a game is someone else's destruction.

Don't get me wrong. I am competitive, very competitive, but I don't like to be so stressed over a game. By the way, I usually win.

Then there is the fallout from people who don't lose gracefully to look forward to after the game. It sometimes gets ugly.

"Hi," I said cheerily. "Rather than play Monopoly, can we play Sequence instead? We just got it a little while ago and I haven't had a chance to play it." I walked to the end of the table carrying the large box with the special game board and cards in it for Sequence.

It was a good game because, while you played, it also allowed you to talk a little while players were taking their turns. Unless of course you were playing Speed Sequence and slapping your cards down as fast as possible, which was an entirely different game than I was used to.

I needed a game that would encourage people to talk. I got funny looks all around and a little grumbling, but finally they agreed to play my choice of game. That was after I promised we would only play one game and then play Monopoly if they wanted to. Who would have thought Angela and Catherine were so into playing games? But I could see it in their eyes: they were out to win no matter what we played.

I had a feeling this was going to be a long session. Oh well, the things I do for my Queen and country.

Old Bones

Okay, so I'm being a little over-the-top. What I wouldn't do to write a good book was a lot closer to the truth.

While they were setting up, I decided to check on how the others were doing in the living room. The children were probably all downstairs watching an old Disney movie, so everything should be under control.

I poured myself a tall club soda with a slice of orange. I was really thirsty and decided I should crack a couple of windows open. With all the people crammed into our small house, it was getting warm.

"Hello, everyone," I said as I walked into the living room, "Can I get anyone a refresher, coffee, tea, juice, club soda?"

Joy was there. She had a lovely assortment of people around her, and Manda and Dillon on one side. Manda honored us by wearing a beautiful deep purple sari and Dillon was in western dress clothing.

Beverly and George on Joy's other side were both sporting their retirement togs of dress jeans and Beverly had on a deep red silk top while he was sporting an Hawaiian shirt with small flecks of red in the pattern. Directly across from Joy were two comfortable wing chairs. Pastor Brian Jeffery sat in one while another was empty. Nigel appeared and I watched him slip into it.

"No, thanks," a few voices called back to me.

"All good here."

"Just got some."

"Great party, Heather, you should do this more often," Manda said, showing her plate filled with goodies, which people laughed at, including me.

Everyone, it seemed, would be fine for a while.

I returned to the ladies who were ready to play Sequence. I was surprised at to how fast and how much fun the game was but I could only stay for one quick game.

I spotted Joy and she gave me a nod and a knowing wink.

Good, now to put our plan into action. Joy and I both had two good ears. I was going to throw out the topic of the old bones, then we would all listen to the people around us who hopefully would talk to each other about it.

So here goes nothing, I thought as I took a deep breath and walked up to Nigel, looking dashing in his black jeans and dark gray sweater. I hoped he'd play along.

"So has anyone heard anything about the old bones that were found down the street a while ago? Any ideas or theories?" I asked.

"I'm going to get a fresh drink and some of those wonderful seafood tarts," said Pastor Jeffery as he got up. "Anyone want anything?"

I let our pastor pass me. It suddenly dawned on me I hadn't thought to talk to him about the murder. After all, he hadn't been here during the time frame of the crime. But everyone talks to their pastor, don't they? Maybe not as a priest or confessor, but I find they are usually a depository of people's tragedies and happiness. A confidant.

Sometimes I am silly. Now how were we going to get the information out of him? I mentally shrugged. The direct approach sometimes worked. I'd put his name on our list of people to question.

Nigel was embroiled in a conversation with Tom. I glanced at Joy, who was trying to listen to both Beverly and Dillon, who were trying their ideas about the old bones on her and each other.

The volume in the living room had certainly gone up since I entered. I smiled and turned to leave. I love stirring up the pot.

"Pastor Jeffery, can I help you get something to eat?" I asked after following him into the kitchen.

Old Bones

Pastor Brian Jeffery was a nice looking, single man in his midforties. I estimated he was about five feet ten and was on the husky side—actually he was a little larger than husky, but that made him a favorite of all the women in the congregation as a guest for lunch or dinner. And he had a lot of invitations, and the men liked him to come over too since then they would be able to get a great meal. Especially if it was on a Sunday after church—then they would be able to watch football since Pastor Jeffery was a fan too.

I smiled at the pastor and started to refill the serving plates of hot snacks on the kitchen counter I'd set up as a buffet bar.

"So, Pastor Jeffery, which of these are your favorites? Or I can get you some hot, fresh ones?"

"Well, the bacon-wrapped scallops are wonderful, and so are the shrimp balls with the mango sauce," he said.

I opened the oven door and took out some extras that were being warmed and filled the serving plates. I noticed Pastor Jeffery was pouting slightly as he surveyed the other offerings on my makeshift buffet bar.

"Is there something you're not seeing?"

"Actually, if you happen to have another piece of that wonderful lemon cheesecake that Angela made, I would really appreciate it," he said. "But if it's all gone, I understand. It is wonderful, after all."

He was so cute with his dark hair combed back from his forehead and his bright blue eyes. He really was a good-looking man. I wondered why no woman had snapped him up yet.

I'd love to introduce him to Marie, our daughter, but she hadn't been home to visit in the last couple of years since she lost, James, her husband.

I pushed the gloomy thought out of my mind. I knew I hadn't been interested in being a pastor's wife when I was thinking about getting married. The thought of living in a fish bowl with everyone watching everything you did and everything you said wasn't my cup of tea. It must be a hard job being a pastor's wife. I admire the women that can do it.

I looked at the plate where the cheesecake had been and saw it was empty. I smiled weakly at the good pastor, then went to the fridge and pulled out another cheesecake ready to go.

"I think there might be a few slices looking for a home right here," I said as I placed it on the counter. I reached for a serving knife that I slid under a piece.

I would wait until he was fed and relaxed before I asked him more questions. Once I was in his good graces, I'd invite him into my office for a talk. Might as well find out what he knows, if anything, right now and cross him off my list.

I waited a few minutes—ten, to be exact—until I heard Pastor Jeffery talk to one of the kids who came upstairs to see what goodies the adults had. I had made sure that downstairs was stocked with the appropriate kids' snacks, even some stuff that was good for the little darlings.

I knew I had to act quickly; the pastor is a favorite with people and they like to talk to him since he's such a good listener and a very nice person.

I grabbed a bag full of apple chips and scooted the teenager downstairs.

"Pastor Jeffery, do you have a few minutes?"

He looked at his now empty plate, then looked at me and nodded. I could almost hear the sigh he didn't utter, but I knew what was on his mind.

Old Bones

There was more of his favorite food, but he really was comfortably full. Yes, the temptation was great. I knew exactly the war that was going on in his mind. I could empathize.

He followed me as I led him to my office and swung open the door. I left it open for propriety's sake, not so much for me, but for him.

Unfortunately some people like to gossip about something juicy so they can be the center of attention. They seem unable to consider what effect their supposed juicy gossip will have on someone else. I wasn't about to allow any such opportunity to embarrass Pastor Jeffery, not on my watch.

"Please take a seat," I said, indicating the recliner as I pulled out my writing chair behind my desk and turned the tall black leather chair to face the pastor.

I shivered slightly, it seemed cool in my office after the warmth of the rest of the house with all the guests.

"Are you cold?"

"No, I'm fine, thank you, Heather."

The room felt a little chilly because of the large window and coming in from the rest of the warm house. I took an old blue sweater that always hangs on the back of my chair and put in across my shoulders. I knew the room would warm up quickly since the door was partly open.

As I adjusted my sweater, I watched Pastor Jeffery and tried to form a plan in mind of how I was going to approach him about the topic of murder and what questions I should ask him.

He surveyed the office, his eyes filled with curiosity. He had been over to our house a few times for dinners and barbeques, but this room is usually off limits to visitors. It was my little hideaway.

Now that Tom was home for good and writing as well, I knew we would have to give him someplace in the house he could call his own too. There was a spare bedroom downstairs next to the family room, but it was usually very chilly even in summer and darn-right freezing in the winter.

I pulled my mind back to more immediate things rather than finding Tom a writing room.

"Pastor Jeffery, I don't know if you realize this or not, but Joy and I are working with the police, Ryan and Nigel, trying to discover the truth about the old bones that were found down the block at the empty lot a week ago. We're asking a lot of the long-term residents of the neighborhood what they remember about the family that lived there, or anything else they may know about the murders." I watched Pastor Jeffery for any indication he might know something as I spoke.

He nodded his head as I was speaking, although I wasn't sure if he was agreeing with me or hearing a favorite song since his eyes seemed to be focused at the wall of books across from where he was sitting.

"Really?" he said softly. "I thought you needed to speak to me about a personal matter, Heather. How is Tom? We haven't seen him very much at church lately. Are you sure this other mater can't wait until next week and we can meet at the church?"

"No, Pastor Jeffery, everything is fine between Tom and me, but thank you for asking." I said. "I would like to ask you some questions about the murder case."

His eyes widened and he gave me an embarrassed smile.

"I was wondering when you were going to get to me, Heather. And by the way, I thought I asked you to call me Brian when we weren't at church. Why so formal tonight?"

Old Bones

"I guess I'm not really comfortable in calling you by your first name. The way I was brought up you would never do that to your pastor,"

"Times do change Heather," he said with a smile.

"I'll try to remember. Anyway, I'm not sure how to really handle this situation," I confessed to him.

He gazed at me, nodded, then folded his hands in front of his ample stomach. "I understand you're a mystery writer, Heather. That must be fascinating. And Tom writes as well? It's nice to have a hobby, isn't it? Have you written anything I might have read?"

"It is a fascinating job, Brian. And, yes I am published—both Tom and I are—me under a pseudonym name Tom under his own name." I stressed the word job. It certainly is interesting how many people think writing is a hobby and don't take my writing job seriously.

When I worked for the bank I never got asked that question, but since I've been writing, people think it's just a hobby. Maybe it's my fault to a large degree. By trying to be available and accommodating people, they think that writing isn't serious or important to me. I try to be available and shift my writing time around, because I can. Which is one of the reasons I took writing up as my second career. I can write anywhere at any time for as long as I want.

Pastor Jeffery or Brian, I corrected myself, looked interested in what I was saying. He also knew I tried to help out at the church whenever I could, trying to be flexible with my schedule. Maybe I would have to re-think that a little, especially lately.

"Anyway, getting back to why I asked you to this meeting," I said, trying to interject a little humor into the situation and getting him to smile.

I was getting a very strange vibe from Pastor Jeffery and I wasn't sure why.

I really wanted to play that game with the ladies so I could talk to them too, maybe I could sit in with them later. I could just put him on hold until we could meet at the church later as he suggested.

"Pastor Jeffery, do you know anything about the bones found at the old empty lot?"

Pastor Jeffery's face was suddenly split in a wide grin. He shook his head. "No. What do you know about it? I've been really interested in those bones and checked our church records. I discovered information about the family, which of course you're welcome to, but it really isn't much. Mostly the records are about the births of the two children and their registration in the cradle role, and when they were baptized and became members of the congregation."

I sighed. I had hoped someone would have confided in him a story about the history of the neighborhood that would be relevant to our investigation. He looked at me earnestly as he spoke and he appeared to genuinely want to know about the mystery surrounding the bones.

"Thank you, Pastor Jeffery. If I could come by your office before church on Sunday to pick up the records, I would really appreciate it."

"I have a file on my desk right now so, if you want it, I can place it in the trustees' cubby hole," Brian suggested. "Do you still have a key for the office door?"

I shook my head. "But Tom does. I can borrow his key for the church office and pick up the documents in the morning."

"Perfect." Brian grinned. "I'll drop into my office on the way home; it's not out of my way."

This was a standard joke since the parsonage was right next to the church. We often joked the pastor didn't have much of a commute to get to work.

His brow wrinkled slightly. Something else was obviously on his mind. "Heather, I see you have a couple of Susan Applewood books I haven't read yet. I saw them in the front room. Do you think I could borrow them?"

A sense of relief came over me. I didn't need any more shocks than this case had already given me. And Pastor Jeffery looked so hopeful I couldn't say no to him. "Sure, I think we have another copy downstairs; somehow we ended up with a couple of extra copies. Tom and I need to make a list of all our books, especially the hardcopy first editions we've collected over the years."

That was all true. We did have extra copies of the books I had written so I have no problem in lending them to him.

"Let's go back into the living room and see how everyone is doing. I'll make sure you get those books before you leave," I assured him before I accompanied him out of the office.

He grinned as he left and was very animated as he told me which of the Susan Applewood books he hadn't read yet. I wondered what he was like at Christmas. He certainly was a man who wore his heart on his sleeve.

He would certainly be a perfect love match for Marie, our daughter. She lives in Toronto and had lost her husband in a car accident two years ago. I think she and Brian would get along fabulously and her kids would love him, too.

But being a matchmaker wasn't my job so I was going to keep my nose out of my daughter's love life. Totally.

I popped my head into the kitchen to see how everything was going and saw Angela and Catherine had started to play another game of Sequence.

"I'll be back in a few minutes," I said. "Keep me in mind for the next one."

The kitchen counter still had enough food and drinks stocked to keep people happy so I didn't have to refill anything. I quickly went into the middle bedroom that I'd kept open for guests who wanted a quiet place to talk. I had put a card table with four chairs in here so guests could talk privately or even play a game if they wanted to. Two of the older men were seated at the table playing cribbage. They barely acknowledged me as I entered.

I cracked open a bedroom window. The evening wasn't as cold as it might have been. Even crocuses were blooming and some yellow forsythia was starting to bud in our yard.

With the windows open a crack in the kitchen and the middle bedroom, we'd start to get a little airflow throughout the house. I was going to go into the living room next and open a window in there a touch, too, then we'd get some nice air circulation. I'd wait for the older folks to complain before closing any of the windows.

It's always a delicate balance. You can't please everyone.

I ducked into the living room to discover lots of conversation and laughter had broken out. I quickly cracked a window, then retreated right away, not wanting to disturb the synergy in the room.

I grabbed a bag of popcorn and headed downstairs to the family room. We used to have the TV in the third, unused bedroom upstairs but had converted it to my office.

At one time Tom and I shared a large room in the basement as our writing spaces but as I wrote more I found I needed the silence and my own space with a door that I could close. Tom had stopped writing for about ten years so we put his books on bookshelves in the family room. Now that he was writing again, we would need a space to call his own.

He's deciding where he would like his office. Once he decides, the other bedroom will become a guest room.

Old Bones

We never have more than one group of guests at the house at one time anyway, even with both the kids and their families living out of town.

Downstairs in the family room, a movie was on. Even some of the adults had gravitated to the family room and the big television. The husbands were doing a great job watching the kids. Some of the kids were on the floor playing with some of the action figures we always had on hand, while others were playing board games our own children once enjoyed.

In one corner of the room on our well-worn sofa sat one of the girls, reading to two of the younger kids sitting on either side of her. She was doing a great job, from their attention to every word she read. The older girl looked up and caught me watching them. She smiled at me. I nodded and smiled back. All the while she kept reading and didn't miss a beat.

It was great seeing her taking an interest in sharing books with the younger children. Maybe one day she would be a teacher or a college professor. At any rate it seemed like the youngest ones would grow up enjoying stories and that might encourage them to read. Which is a good thing for everyone.

The adult men, both old and young, had been warned they had to be careful with the movies that they chose while there were little children at this indoor block party. I was pleased to see they'd chosen age appropriate films that were on the schedule.

Some of the kids, young and old, were spread out around the room in front of the large television set paying rapt attention.

There were little bodies on the couch, in the chairs, lying on the floor. I saw Beverly and George's grandchildren, twin boys, leaning against one another on one of the couches watching the television.

Usually they barely stopped fighting long enough to eat, and for teenage boys who eat whole refrigerator's worth of food in one sitting, this was saying quite a bit.

I found Tom on one of the overstuffed chairs. I hadn't seen him leave the living room, and he was not in the recliner that was normally his throne. He had given up his seat for one of the elderly gentlemen who lived down the street. Mr. Rempel, I think.

Yes, Martin Rempel; he was someone I had forgotten about. He was a short man with piercing blue eyes. He had a bit of a stoop and an extreme comb-over. He still lived about three blocks down the street and one block north on Fifty-Second in a little two bedroom bungalow. I think his was the only house of its kind left in the neighborhood.

Martin Rempel was a good friend of Catherine's. He was definitely one person we should speak with about the bones and the murders.

Tom was having a conversation with Mr. Rempel. He spotted me looking at him and nodded. I couldn't quite make out what they were saying over the sound of the movie.

I wasn't sure if I should interrupt them or not. I didn't want to disturb them if Tom was getting new information about the murders. I waited to see if Tom would give me a sign, but he kept his eyes on the TV and nodded while Mr. Rempel continued to talk.

I finally decided to see what the plans were for the next couple of movies. If I didn't check every so often, our impromptu movie palace would slowly become a shoot-'em-up and explosion film fest. Not intentionally, but it was fun to hear the sound system at its fullest.

Mr. Rempel was always someone who didn't care much for kids so he was probably thankful they kept to themselves. Not that he was mean or anything like that, but he did have his moments.

Old Bones

One moment his mind was clear as a bell and could remember events that happened a long time ago and the next he was totally vague and sometimes yelled at people who weren't there. I wasn't sure how his short term memory was but I knew that people from the church and old friends helped him a lot.

These episodes only happened every once in a while now, but seemed to be getting worse, I really don't think he will remember anything at all soon. But it was sweet of Tom to give him the gift of time and listen to him.

I was pretty sure they were rehashing World War II, not that Tom ever served in the army. War was one thing that my generation missed, thank God. You could, of course, enlist and serve as part of Canada's peacekeeping force, but Tom had seen enough of the ugly nature of humankind, working for Canada Border Services as an inspector and then as an auditor. He even had the fancy title of Senior Compliance Verification Officer when he retired. He enjoyed the work, but was looking forward to doing his writing full time.

I put the snacks on the card table in bowls and was glad to see there were still a variety of beverages. I looked around the room; everyone seemed content. I turned to leave, hoping I could get in a game of Sequence with the ladies.

Chapter Fifteen
Company Coming

"Oh, Heather," Tom said loudly so I could hear him over the television, "did I forget to mention the kids are coming to visit?"

I stopped dead in my tracks. "What do you mean that they are coming to visit?" I asked.

Tom and I had invited our two kids, Rodney and Marie, and their families for Easter; they both said that they couldn't make it. That was one of the reasons I agreed to the deadline for my book. I knew the house would be quiet and I would be able to write undisturbed by the patter of tiny feet. Once I had a story, that is.

"They called today, first Rodney in the morning and then Marie in the afternoon, and said they had a change of plans and that they were coming after all," he explained.

Of course this meant major cleaning and organizing, but nothing that we couldn't handle. My mind started to sort out sleeping arrangements.

"Is it Rodney or Marie who is coming?" I asked, interrupting my mind amid organizing the work we would have to do to accommodate more people in our house.

Tom had started talking again to Mr. Rempel so I walked to stand beside them. I really didn't want to yell over the television and the noise of the playing children around us.

"I'm sorry, Tom. I didn't hear you correctly. You said the kids were coming and then I asked which ones. And I thought that you said all of them."

Old Bones

That would mean that our oldest, Rodney, and his wife Jennifer and their sixteen-year-old son Chris would be here. As well as Marie, our youngest, and her daughters Tracy and Morocco.

I watched him nod like one of the bobble-headed dogs you see on the front dash of cars.

"Yep, both," he said with a wry smile. "It seems they had a change of plans and Rodney can get away, and Marie is really homesick and misses us and Vancouver, so they're all coming."

"Okay," I said uncertainly. "You do know we usually coordinate one family at a time, right?"

"I know," he said with a nod. "Who do you want me to say no to? Rodney, who hasn't been able to visit because of his job for the last two years, or Marie, who's homesick and wants to see her whole family?"

This was a completely unfair question by Tom but I understood completely why he couldn't say no to our children.

I nodded, sighed, then smiled at him. "I know, somehow we'll manage. We always do. After all, there will only be eight of us with two bathrooms. I know, we can pretend that we're camping. Marie and the two girls can stay in the spare bedroom and Rodney, Jennifer, and Chris can camp out in the family room. Or maybe this would be a good opportunity to clean up the spare room." I shrugged. "We were going to do that anyway. Just not right now." I turned to walk away, planning and muttering to myself.

I stopped and turned to face Tom again. "Oh, when are they coming?"

Tom smiled at me again. Not the this-is-funny smile, more like the this-is-going-to-hurt smile. I walked back to him and leaned down so he didn't have to shout.

"They're all arriving next Saturday," he said. "They'll be staying for two weeks, an extended Easter break. I know your book is due in the middle of that time so I'll help out with the cooking and entertaining so you can work. How's it going, by the way?"

My heart clenched, missed a beat, and my face went numb as my stomach felt like it was in free fall. Were these the signs of a heart attack? I slowly nodded.

"Fine. It's going to be fine," I mumbled as I slowly went to climb up the stairs.

I needed a story now more than ever, and I needed one fast.

I had to talk to Joy after the party. I needed her help to piece some stuff together for a story. I needed a character in a setting with a problem. It didn't need to be the main problem, just a problem. Hopefully it would be close to what we had in our neighborhood; if not, I guess I'd have to make stuff up. After all, this is what I do.

"What's happened?" asked Joy as I softly shut the basement door behind me.

"Nothing," I said as I walked in a daze past her into the kitchen. "Just our entire family is coming to stay with us for a long Easter vacation. Not just one of the families, but both, at the same time. Yup, all the kids and grandkids too. No Problem. And I've got a book due in four weeks, at the end of April since I was talking to my publisher today about the next book and asked for a deadline extension on this one," I added.

I opened the fridge door and gazed unseeing at the shelves. I don't know what I was looking for, but I couldn't find it so I closed the door.

I then looked at the buffet on the counter. Still looked fine. Then I remembered. Yes, the game. That's what I needed right now. I was going to play a game, then try to figure all this out.

Old Bones

After everyone went home I would work on an outline for my book.

"Heather. Really. What's wrong?" Joy had followed me into the kitchen and was watching me. Her forehead was wrinkled in concern.

"Oh, nothing; it will all be fine. We'll just juggle a few things. I can make some casseroles and write while they're heating up. We could have chili and soup with fresh buns, lasagna, tuna casserole, chicken burritos, and lots of salad and fresh vegetables. That would work; see, I already had enough for five dinners for eight people. That's the ticket. Tom said he would help too, so while I write he can heat up food. That should work." I was muttering out loud to myself and tried to stop but couldn't.

"Let's go into your office and talk about this," suggested Joy as she tried to lead me down the hallway.

But I didn't want to go to my office. I was tired and my brain was turning to mush. I wanted something cold to drink and then I wanted to play a mindless game with my friends.

Joy came back for me.

She smiled as she took my hand. I could see her eyes looking into mine with concern. She tucked her collar-length red hair behind her ear in her familiar, nervous reflex action.

I really didn't want to deal with this tonight. I had a house full of guests and I was ignoring a bunch of them. Bad Heather, I scolded myself. You need to be a good hostess right now.

"You look like you're totally stressed out," Joy said. "I don't think you should be with your company right now. Do you? Let me know what the problem is and maybe we can work something out." Joy appeared very calm and rational.

I nodded. She was right. I took a deep breath. Nothing is an emergency. Nothing is an emergency.

Somehow those words made me feel better.

I went into my office with Joy and picked up a pad of paper from the bottom shelf of the bookcase next to my desk and grabbed a pen from the desk.

"Please, let's sit. Okay, let's prioritize," I began as Joy sat in the other chair and watched me carefully as I started to write. "First I have to write a book that I've barely started. I know I can do it if I pull a few all-nighters. I've done it before, at least the first draft."

Joy nodded, though I was certain she had no idea what I was talking about since she isn't a writer. "Yeah, I could do that in a couple of weeks if I had someone to take care of everything else. Then if I had Tom read through it, I could brush it up during the second week as I finish the first draft. I'll do a quick edit-read myself. That would give me the weekend to make the changes I'll need. It will be rough, but it would be fine to turn it in to the editor. Then together the editor and I will polish the manuscript in the final edit." I nodded to myself as I played out the plan in my head.

I wrote down who, what, why, and when. Then I sketched out quick character traits, plot points, motive, and a rough story's time line that I knew would change as I wrote the book. I was feeling much better now.

I stopped writing and looked at Joy. "The kids are coming into town next Saturday for two weeks. Both families, which means Tom and I'll have an additional six people to feed and entertain for that time. To make room, we need to completely clean out the spare bedroom downstairs and freshen up the spare bedroom up here. And get the family room set up to be used as both an entertainment room and a sleeping space."

I stopped talking when I saw Joy smiling at me.

"You're doing okay," she said with a chuckle.

181

I nodded and continued.

"It's not that the work wasn't going to be done, it was. We were going to make one of the rooms downstairs into an office for Tom and the other would stay as a guest bedroom. But I didn't expect it to be such a great rush for time, not now, not so soon."

"Speaking of kids," said Joy, " are there four kids?"

"No, three," I explained. "There are two girls—one fourteen, the other twelve—and one boy, sixteen."

"Fine," Joy said as her lips pursed and her eyes narrowed. "Out of this whole thing, which is the biggest problem? The book or the family coming?"

I sighed. I knew what Joy was getting at. It was the book I was really stressed about. I now had an even shorter deadline than before.

"The book," I said, trying to sound firm in my conviction but failing. "It's my priority and I don't have a story yet." My bottom lip started to quiver as my eyes filled with tears. I couldn't believe I was going to cry. At this rate I might as well start singing, "Nobody likes me, everybody hates me, I'm going to the garden to eat worms."

Maybe I should throw myself a proper pity party. I took a deep breath and clenched my jaw tight. This was a stupid way for a grown woman to act. The only way I'm going to get this fixed is to get on with it. Not to sit here and blubber. I do not do blubber.

"I can work on a story with you," Joy offered. "I managed to get more information tonight and I think t it might just be what we need." Joy's voice was hopeful.

I let out a deep breath I hadn't realized I'd been holding.

"Perfect," I said and meant it. "Once I have a chapter outline, I will sit down and follow it until it takes off on its own. For me, the outline is the key.

"Then if I get lost, I always refer to the outline, amend it if necessary, then continue. I know it sounds like a strange process, but it works for me."

Joy reached over to take my hand in hers and gave it a squeeze and nodded. "Okay, and Edgar and I will help Tom de-clutter the big downstairs bedroom and freshen up the other bedroom. We'll make the family room into a multi-use space. I think this is going to be fun." She smiled. "I love doing this kind of thing." Her blue eyes sparkled with anticipation.

"But you have your own unpacking to do," I said, my voice rough as I took a deep, jagged breath.

"It can wait; we have enough out so we can make do. You're the one that's going to have a houseful of people."

I emitted a long sigh and grinned at her. She was one strange woman. Most people would tell you they'd help but wouldn't; I felt that I could trust her and I was glad she was on my side.

I smoothed my hands down my thighs. "I'm going to go and play a game with the ladies to see what I can shake loose, then I'm going to talk to Tom." Joy nodded. "If you'd check with Nigel and let me know if he has any more information, it would be great." I looked around but was unable to see Joy's nephew amongst the little knots of party guests in the kitchen or in the living room beyond. "What about Ryan? Where is he?"

It dawned on me I hadn't seen Ryan since the party started.

"Look, never mind about Ryan right now," she said. "Let's get something down for your book. How about the first couple of chapters? We can always amend them or change them later. I'm off next week. I took a week of holidays. I have a lot of unpacking to do. And it's nearly spring so I need to take a look at the yard. Do you have any plants that your going to be dividing?"

She shook her head. "But that stuff can all wait for a couple of weeks. We have enough already put away to keep us going very nicely for now."

"I don't think—" I started to say when I saw Joy smile at me and I stopped.

"But my job is done and you can go and play a game and relax for a bit. How about we get back and compare notes in an hour?" asked Joy as she looked at her watch.

"I don't know. I mean about the story. Sure, you can have some hostas. I have some really great daylilies too. They actually have two colors on the same flower. One petal is a medium yellow and the other is a dark orange."

I realized that Joy had done it again and totally distracted me as my hand went to the bookshelf containing some of my plant books and magazines. That was twice in a few minutes.

"Okay. Are you feeling better?" She chuckled as she looked at me. "We will do that plant thing, but first is the mystery. I hope what we find out tonight and this weekend will give us our answers. Or at least a good portion of them."

I could feel the excitement build in my gut. It's the feeling I get when I land on a good story idea and set it down, on paper or in the computer. I love this feeling, it's why I write.

"I'll give you what I have in a while but really think that we need to all get together. What time is it? Tell you what, I'm going to see if I can catch the guys, maybe we can go over what we have right now."

"Heather, I know that you want to do it now, but it's late and I think we should just get an early start; and besides, you still have company," Joy said.

No more delays. I had to move this along. I had my notebook out and my pen at the ready.

I remembered the conversation Tom was having with old Mr. Martin Rempel, and Pastor Jefferies gave me information too.

"Tom may have some information," I said. "I'll invite him to join us. I have an old white board downstairs I've used in the past to outline books.

"We'll use it to record all the clues we've gathered so far. How about we meet at eight o'clock tomorrow morning for a breakfast-and-idea meeting?"

"Sure. I'll go over to BreakTime and get some fresh muffins," said Joy. "How big is the white board?"

"Come on," I said, "I'll show you. It's either in the storage room or the big downstairs bedroom. Before I go to sleep, I'll work on the characters I'll be using in the story and start the story outline. I'll make up their names and get their personalities straight in my mind. We better see if Ryan and Nigel are available." I rose from my desk chair and opened my office door.

Perfect timing: there were Ryan and Nigel, walking down the hall toward the kitchen.

"Oh, guys," said Joy, getting the two detectives' attention. "We were just talking and we think it would be a good idea to meet tomorrow morning to talk about the clues we got this evening to plan our next move. Are you available at eight o'clock?"

"Joy's bringing fresh muffins," I added.

"Funny," said Ryan with a smile, "we were just going to suggest the same thing to you. Not the muffin thing, but the meeting thing." He chuckled lightly as he and Nigel got their coats, said their goodbyes and left.

"Yeah, and we have a white board we can set up downstairs to start compiling our clues and other information," I said.

Old Bones

"Thank you for the lovely party, Heather," said Angela with a smile as she approached me. "It's too bad you didn't get a chance to play a board game with us."

"But it's still early," I said. Glancing at my watch, I realized it was after nine o'clock already.

It was indeed dark outside and would be very cold already. This year had been so much colder than normal. It should be spring soon, but only the bravest buds were out.

I saw that the migration from the party had started and Pastor Jeffery was volunteering to walk Catherine and Angela home. Angela declined him walking her and then Catherine since they lived in different directions. She told him she was fine since it was only two blocks to her house and the street was well lit.

"Angela, are you sure you want to walk alone? " I asked in surprise. It was very dark outside, but the one thing Angela had always been stanch on was her walking to and from the church in all kinds of weather.

Tom disappeared into our bedroom to gather coats and hats to hand to our departing guests. I wondered what would happen if we mixed them up? I guess they would have to sort everything out at church on Sunday. It would be funny, though.

"Edgar and I will give you a hand cleaning up," said Joy, who stood behind me.

The front door opened and our guests started to leave, shaking Tom's hand and thanking him for the wonderful party. A few nodded and smiled at me.

Suddenly we heard a dog barking. Nothing unusual in this neighborhood, but then it went from a regular bark to a high-pitched whine, then a yelp.

Rita Schulz

Someone was in trouble and it sounded as if it was coming from next door. Kirby. It had to be Kirby. He was hurt, I just knew it.

Chapter Sixteen
Uninvited Guests

I QUICKLY PICKED up Buddy and gently dropped him into my office, closed the door, and ran out our front door past startled party guests to Joy's house next door. Joy and Edgar were racing ahead of me. I had plucked up my cell phone from the hall side table on the way in case we needed to call the police.

I saw everyone gathered in the backyard and headed toward the side gate. I made sure the gate was closed in case Kirby decided to go on an adventure and run around the neighborhood again.

"Is he okay?" I asked as I came to where Joy and Tom were standing.

"Yes, Heather. At least it looks like it. We'll know more once the ropes are off him."

I steeled myself as I looked to where their attention was. Kirby was tied up tight like a little calf at branding time and I saw Edgar was cutting away at the rope that was holding him.

There wasn't any blood that I could see, so someone had taken care and to tie him up without hurting him, thank goodness.

I scanned the yard and then turned my attention to the back of the house. I noticed the back door with its half window was open a little bit.

"Joy, have you noticed the window to your back door is ajar?" I asked.

I didn't want to upset her but I suspected the reason someone tied up Kirby was to break into their house.

"What?" asked Joy as her gaze flitted from Kirby to the back door.

"Edgar," she said, distress evident in her voice. "Our back door window appears broken and the door is open. I'm going to check out what's going on." Joy sucked in a deep breath and marched up the back stairs.

"No, Joy, wait," said Edgar as he went to cut and unwind the rope securing Kirby's legs.

But Joy didn't stop . She charged up the stairs. I quickly followed her, with Tom next to me.

"Joy, wait. Let me go first," said Tom as he pushed first past me, then past Joy.

Joy wore a stern expression on her face. One I certainly wouldn't want to be on the receiving end of, that's for sure.

At the top of the back stairs was a good sized deck that had room for a barbeque, a table and chairs, and even a recliner with a little table beside it. The deck was partially covered so that they could still barbeque if the weather wasn't good.

The deck was painted a light gray with a white railing. The deck led to the back door that opened into the kitchen. Because of the partial roof, the back door was in shadow and was a perfect place for someone determined to break in.

There was broken, jagged glass spread on the deck near the door, washing away any doubt. But why was the broken glass on the outside of the door and not the inside?

I went to the railing and looked down at the lower level to discover what looked like an open window into the basement.

"Edgar, take a look at the window by the climbing rose underneath the deck. What do you see?" I said.

"It's open," he said, sounding bewildered.

"Someone forced the window to the downstairs bathroom open and climbed in. They must have been really small to get in through there," he added.

"But why break the window to the kitchen door?" asked Joy.

"Didn't you tell me the other day that it was sticking really badly and was hard to turn?" I said. "Maybe they needed someone stronger to get their arm in to undo the lock."

"Look," said Tom as he studied the door. "I think that we need to call the police right now."

"Tom's right. Let's go back out," I suggested. "And don't touch anything."

"Do you think Nigel and Ryan are still in front of the house?" Joy asked. "I saw them talking to a few of the neighbors."

"I'll check if they're there," I said. "If they've gone, I'll call the emergency number. I'm willing to bet this break-in is related to the murders." I quickly went back down the back stairs to our house.

As I came around the corner, I saw a few people from our party still milling around in the front of our house.

"Is everything all right?" asked Mr. Rempel. "We heard a dreadful noise coming from Joy's house, but thought it better to stay out of the way."

"That was a good idea," I assured him with a grin.

I saw other of my party guests coming toward me and it brought to mind one of those old zombie movies. I thought I better make an announcement before things got out of hand and someone disturbed any evidence.

"Everything is fine. There had been a break-in but everything's fine." I said raising my hands to stop the incoming hoard. "Joy's dog was tied up and didn't like it, but he's fine too.

"Are the two police officers, Ryan and Nigel, still here?" I asked as I started walking through the murmuring crowd.

I spotted them standing by Ryan's car. With both men being so tall it was easy to see them. They certainly looked like cops right now.

I smiled at the memory of when I was younger. I used to say you could tell if a person was a police officer just by their walk. I was usually right, too.

The evening was cold, though it was the end of March, and I hadn't had the chance to grab my jacket. I was wearing a long-sleeved light sweater with a scoop neckline.

I could really feel the cold wind as it whispered among the bare trees and shook the branches back and forth, their shadows making patterns on the grass and sidewalk.

I would have to get into the house quickly to grab my jacket before I turned into a popsicle.

"Ryan! Nigel!' I yelled, hoping they would hear me and meet me at my house so I could quickly get my jacket, then talk to them about the break-in.

Nigel turned toward me and then he said something I couldn't hear to Ryan, who nodded, then they both started to walk toward me.

I decided to quickly trot to meet them, partially to shorten the distance between us and partially to stay warm. I hadn't done any running since Kirby escaped a little while ago and before that I knew it had to have been years.

"Ryan, Nigel," I called as the gap between us shrank. "Joy and Edgar need you. Their house has been broken into. A window in the basement has been broken and the kitchen door window has been smashed from the inside. They didn't hurt Kirby. Joy, Edgar, and Tom are waiting for you. I'll be right there once I grab a jacket." I said as quickly as possible.

Old Bones

I was pleased with my short, concise report.

Ryan and Nigel nodded in unison and started to head toward Joy and Edgar's house while I trotted to my house to grab a warm jacket.

When I entered our house, I realized that in our hurry we had left the door unlocked and there were still a few people downstairs watching the television that didn't know about the excitement next door.

I decided to let them all be since they were doing well. I did remember to let Buddy out of my office. He was so happy to see me he did a little dance and ran to the back door, wanting to be let out.

I wondered if he had heard his friend next door yelping and wanted to check him out to make sure if he was all right, and to get caught up on the doggy news line. He had always been a very social dog, one almost bordering on being nosy.

I started to laugh at the thought of a nosy dog, like he was one in a comic strip or a short story. There had been books told from a cat's perspective and I wondered if there were ones told from a dog's? I would have to check that out. If there were books like this, they would be interesting to read; and if there weren't any, then maybe I would write one.

Children's books told from a puppy's point of view might be fun to write. I know there had been lots written with dogs as characters; our kids really enjoyed a book called The Pokey Little Puppy when they were young, which we read to them at bedtime—I'm sure at least a hundred times. It was a favorite when they were young.

I let Buddy outside. I knew he wouldn't be ready to come in for a while. He started to bark at the people next door until he heard Tom's voice telling him not to bark.

I grabbed my keys, locking the exterior doors of our house as I went.

I needed to discover what the police were doing and what they were finding out.

I opened the front door and heard Ryan yell for the crowd of people to get back and clear the area.

As I rounded the front of our house, I looked at Joy's place to see Ryan with his gun drawn by the front door. He leaned over and used a key to open the door, then stood to one side, his gun at the ready.

"Police! Identify yourselves!" he yelled loud enough for the entire block to hear.

I watched in rapt attention, trying to absorb and catalogue this incredible scene. I was trying to remember everything I was seeing and sensing. The smell of the damp earth, the cold air against my face, the taste of the wet, soggy evergreen trees across the street, the dark gloomy night, and the shadows created by the streetlights. The murmur of the people talking became quiet, replaced by the sound of the wind in the trees and bushes as Ryan prepared to enter Joy's house.

"Police! This is your final warning. Identify yourselves!" he shouted even louder.

He waited for a few seconds, reached for the door and flung it open, then disappeared inside.

I heard the echo of a slamming door coming from the backyard, which I assumed meant Nigel was entering simultaneously via the back door. I heard the door smash against the kitchen cabinets with the force of his entry and I suspected he would also have his gun drawn.

Then I heard the echo of their deep voices calling "Clear!" as they went from one room to another, starting with the top floor and working their way to the basement.

Old Bones

I had been expecting to hear the sound of gunshots or something, but nothing. Then the murmur of the voices of the people still on the sidewalk grew louder as they started talking while they watched this drama play out. I hurried around to the backyard and went to stand with Tom and Joy.

"Okay, what did I miss?" I said, my breathing coming in gasps.

"I gave Ryan my key and he went in the front door. At the same time, Nigel went into the back," said Edgar, stating the obvious.

I noticed he was shivering and wasn't wearing a jacket. I guess living next door, he decided to come over in a shirt, dress sweater, and jeans.

"Edgar, you're freezing," I said. "Are they going to dust for prints or anything?"

Joy glanced down at Edgar's clothing and shook her head as she looked at me and grinned. I nodded. It really was a boy thing to do, go out without a jacket, but it did make sense, too. We live close to each other and I'm pretty sure he wasn't planning on having his house broken into tonight.

Then I remembered I had gone out without a jacket but I had an excuse—I needed to catch Kirby as quickly as possible.

"Yeah, Nigel said something like that. He said they may have enough to warrant getting the fingerprint guys over. But they'll know more once they've gone through the house."

"Heather, Tom, where are you?" someone from next door called.

I saw Mandy standing out by our back door calling to us. I saw Buddy diving between her legs as he ran into the warm house.

"We're over here," I called back. "We'll be right there. Please help yourself to whatever you need."

I hugged my jacket close around me, trying to keep as warm as I could.

"Tom, do you want to go home to see how everyone is doing and put a pot of coffee on?" I asked.

Tom shook his head. "No, I want to stay and see what happens here. It sounds like they're almost finished. This is really great material for the books we write, don't you think?"

"Yes, it's all good material. Grist for the mill, as they say. I'll just stay a little longer, then I'm heading back," I added, trying not to sound petulant.

Now that Tom was retiring, he was planning on writing more. I had really hoped that he would pick a different interest than writing. I hoped that it wouldn't become a contest between us.

But if Tom were to be fair, I had already published a few books before he came up with the idea of writing after he retired. He was good, too. But our styles are totally different. I like the cozy approach with some suspense and he likes it where stuff blows up with a lot of action.

I nodded; he was right. We both should use this experience as a source for our books. After all, we didn't have much real crime in our neighborhood to use for story fodder.

Suddenly Ryan and Nigel appeared, coming out of the house. They looked in our direction where we stood at the back of the house next to the garage. They had asked us to move as far from the house as we could before they had gone in. I was really nervous and at the same time really excited.

They had holstered their weapons. Ryan followed Nigel slowly down the back stairs. I guess their adrenalin must have really been high as they went through the house, not knowing if there was an active shooter inside.

Nigel waved us to come join them next to the bottom of the back stairs.

Old Bones

When we'd joined them, Nigel explained what they'd discovered. "Well, it looks like they made quite a mess. And, no, we didn't find them."

"Are you going to call in the fingerprint people?" I asked.

Ryan shook his head. "When you moved in a little while ago, did you wash down the windows and the sills downstairs in the little bathroom? If you did, then we might have a good chance of getting a clear print; if not, then it may just be a jumble of a bunch of prints. We'd have to fingerprint everyone since you moved in and those who moved out before you. It would take a long time. And I suspect whoever broke in was wearing gloves." He added, "From the methods used, it appears to be a professional job."

I nodded and looked at Joy and thought back to the last time I had really cleaned my own downstairs bathroom windows and sills. I couldn't remember when. This task would have to be added to my to-do list.

I stuffed my cold hands into my jacket pockets, trying to keep them warm. The soft fuzzy fleece lining of the pocket prevented the cold air from reaching my fingers.

I looked expectantly at Joy. Had she cleaned everything when she moved in?

Joy gave Ryan an amused smile. "What a thing to ask your aunt. You know what a tight ship I run around here and my division of labor. I clean and Edgar messes things up. He's my forever child and the reason we decided not to have any of our own." She wrapped her arm around Edgar's and pulled him close to her.

"That's the first thing I did even before we moved in," she said. "Before the furniture arrived I was here at the crack of dawn and I cleaned from top to bottom every surface so that when they came with the furniture, the house would be spotless.

I also cleaned the downstairs bathroom." She smiled. "When will we be able to get back into the house? I'm getting too cold standing out here."

That's when I noticed Joy was wearing a pretty, light knit navy top with lime green piping. Edgar and she had just come over to our house not expecting to be outside for long.

"Okay, we'll go in with you and tell you what is okay to touch," said Ryan. "But I think our best bet will be the downstairs bathroom. I don't think anyone was down there when you had your housewarming, were they, Aunt Joy?"

Joy shook her head.

"No, the downstairs was off limits. That's where we were storing a lot of the boxes we hadn't unpacked yet," explained Edgar.

Joy and Edgar shivered as the warm air of the inside of the house wrapped around them when they led the way inside.

"Is it okay if I sweep up the broken glass?" asked Joy. "I don't want Kirby to get into it." Joy had remembered to close the little gate on the deck in front of the stairs.

"No, Aunt Joy. This is a crime scene now and you should stay out until the lab processes it. I would suggest that you get Kirby from the backyard and all of you go back to Heather and Tom's and wait until you hear from the police. Then you may want to get some cardboard and cut a piece to cover the broken window, Uncle Edgar," suggested Ryan.

The kitchen didn't look so bad and neither did the living room or dining room, but when we got to the bedrooms, it was different. Especially the spare bedroom. Joy and Edgar had moved boxes up from the basement and put them in here as they sorted things out after the housewarming party.

Old Bones

I guess they hadn't decided what to do with this room yet so they had stored full boxes and empty ones as well. The empty boxes had been broken down, then piled in a neat stack in one corner of the room.

It seems someone else had dumped the full boxes all over the floor; at least those at the top of the stacks. It looked to me like a halfhearted attempt to search for something. Did they find what they were looking for?

"Joy, where do you keep your special things?" I asked as we looked around upstairs.

"Some I have upstairs in the spare bedroom and the very fragile stuff I have in a room downstairs. I can't believe how much room there is in this house," she said.

We next went downstairs to the basement and saw short stacks of still full boxes. I could see that at this rate Joy would have everything unpacked and organized really soon.

"Joy, where do you keep your books?" I asked.

When we were on the ferry, she'd told me she loved to read and she had been reading a book then. It was one of my favorites, one of a series by the author Nora Roberts set in Ireland. We had discussed that if a book was good, it was like you were actually in a place you had never traveled to before.

But there were no bookcases or books. I remembered seeing a few books on one of the nightstands in their bedroom, but nothing that would fit someone who said they liked to read.

"In case you're wondering, Heather," said Joy, "we have a bunch of stuff in storage too. We're planning on making the downstairs into a library, lined with bookcases. And Edgar will finally get the pool table he's always wanted. And we're going to tear out the middle bedroom to put in a huge walk-in closet and a spa en suite."

I nodded. That explains why the house still seemed empty, though the boxes I'd seen were mostly unpacked.

"Do you want a hand with taking care of the window? Just remember don't touch anything else," a Nigel.

I watched Edgar grab an X-ACTO knife and cut up a box. He then taped a large piece of cardboard to cover the broken window in the back door.

"Anyone want a coffee or tea?" ask Joy without enthusiasm.

"No, thanks," I answered. Nigel and Tom we looking around the room.

"It looks like whoever broke in was looking for something specific," said Nigel, his eyes burning with curiosity and his brow wrinkled, he surveyed the room. "It's evident they didn't touch your stereo or your art." He walked slowly around the living room and then walked into the kitchen.

"What I think is really funny is they didn't even take my jewelry that was in my top drawer," said Joy. "And my jewelry box is where I left it in the linen closet."

She seemed pleased her jewelry had escaped the eyes of the robbers.

"Joy, did you open your jewelry box to check?" Tom asked.

I looked at him and nodded. We had a theft several years ago and I remembered what happened to us. I had been so happy when I saw my jewelry box had been untouched.

Joy disappeared down the hall to her bedroom. I heard the thump as she move something in the closet.

"Oh, Tom, you're right!" she yelled, the despair evident in her voice. "It's gone. It's all gone." She hurried into the kitchen carrying a pretty rosewood jewelry box in her hands.

Old Bones

I noticed she was taking great care to carry it in a towel and only held it by the bottom. Smart. Maybe the police would be able to dust it for prints. I decided to remember this point and make a note of it in my notebook about this murder case. It had to be connected to the murders in some way.

Chapter Seventeen
Morning has Broken

THE NEXT MORNING dawned clear and bright. A very welcome change from the cold rain and dreary, overcast skies of the past few days.

Some springs are like that in Vancouver. March and April can be wet and cold and even the first half of May. Then toward the end of May, just when most people have given up on planting any kind of garden, the wind comes up to whip away the clouds and the sun gets to work and quickly warms the soil.

If you're smart, you can get some great deals on bedding plants; but if you plant them too soon, they won't grow—they'll just lie there in a miserable lump if you're lucky. If you're not very lucky, you'll get a cold frost or a sprinkle of snow that will kill your new, tender little plants.

But if you put in a greenhouse, even if it's not heated, they'll be protected until the time is right for planting. Failing that, then a cold frame will do great in starting seeds if it's tall enough to protect your little plants.

Or you can be like me and buy them and keep a very, very close watch on the weather channel in case you need to quickly cover them and hope there isn't a freak storm while you're at work. It really helps that I'm working from home now.

Although I really would like to explore the concept of growing fruit and vegetables all winter long. The one problem in Vancouver is our cloud cover.

Old Bones

It may not be raining or even that cold, but we do have clouds and plants get droopy when they don't see the sun for months on end.

Maybe I'll do some research this summer and save up a few dollars to put in a greenhouse—a small one, but where? The yard is small and I really don't want to do a whole bunch of work all winter. I think I would prefer lying by a beach in Mexico or Hawaii rather than worrying about putting the lights on and off for a bunch of plants. I know about timers but, still, it is a lot of work.

I shook my head and squished my eyes closed, trying to focus my thoughts. I glanced at my alarm clock. Did it really say six in the morning? On my alarm clock? Who had done that?

How daft was that? No one in their right mind wanted to get up so early! Going on holidays, maybe; an early flight, perhaps. Much as I tried, I couldn't think of another reason.

Then it came to me. I had set it myself. What was I thinking? Right. I had a book to write, a mystery to solve, and the kids and their families were coming to stay soon. I needed to get up at the crack of dawn and get moving or I'd be in real trouble. I heard someone groan in the quiet of our bedroom and realized it was me. Tom was still softly snoring next to me.

First thing. Get into my office and start the novel chapter outline. Okay, I could cut it into thirds and focus on the main plot for the first third.

My body ached all over, especially my leg and shoulder. I felt that my left arm also was in a lot of pain and realized that when I hit the stairs on the ferry, I had cushioned my fall by landing with my arm outstretched and my head had landed on it.

I quickly turned off the horrible noise that was supposed to be music coming from the radio alarm clock. Then again, nothing could sound good at this time of the morning.

Regardless, this music was definitely not something I wanted to listen to. Besides, I didn't want it to wake Tom.

After the music was off, I rolled over. I'd closed my eyes just for a minute and promptly fell back to sleep.

I suddenly sat upright in bed, my eyes wide open, my heartbeat pounding in my ears.

Food. Book. Now.

I realized what I had done. I turned off my alarm clock. How could I? Lots of people were counting on me. Tom, our kids, even the poor ghost of the dead girl and the baby. How would they ever rest in peace if I didn't catch the killer?

Okay, it may not make any sense to me in the light of day, and talk about being overly dramatic, but at six o' five in the morning, it made perfect sense to me.

I looked over at Tom and almost shook him to wake him up, but decided to let him sleep. It was my crazy idea to get up this early, not his.

I had to get my notes together, and if that failed, at least I could start pulling the two bedrooms downstairs apart.

I'd sort the stuff into three piles as I cleared the bedrooms. What we could still use, what needed to be donated to charity, and what we'd throw away.

I pulled on a pair of jeans and a sweatshirt, then went to the kitchen to put the kettle on. With a cup of hot tea in hand, I went into my office. It didn't take me long to go over my pitifully few notes. I checked my emails.

I heard a doorbell ring.

There was an email from Joy.

And what an email.

Old Bones

There were exclamation marks all over the page. I shook my head; I knew what this meant. This meant I would have to see her and go over this jumble. It wasn't in bullet points and certainly wasn't a narrative. It appeared to be a bunch of unrelated points and observations. I blinked my eyes hard—maybe it was just me? My mind couldn't focus yet. Too early. I needed more tea

I ran my tongue around the inside of my mouth. Gross. I would have to go through at least some of my morning rituals.

On the way I stole a quick look around the second bedroom and made a quick mental picture of the accumulated stuff to convert into an inventory. Then I ran downstairs to check out the rooms down there. I needed to make a plan to house the family and when they were gone for Tom's very own office.

I heard a doorbell ringing again and a dog barking.

I shifted my attention to the second basement guest bedroom. Good, it wasn't nearly as bad as I thought. For some reason I had the impression the bedrooms were wall-to-wall boxes but they weren't. The boxes were stacked in the middle of the room. Once I completed my quick look-around I realized the possibilities.

"Heather, are you there?" Tom yelled down the stairwell. "You've got company."

I realized the sound I had been ignoring was the front doorbell. I remembered that the ringing had stopped.

Yes, that would have been the front doorbell and Buddy barking. I also realized I should really have gone to answer the front door, but who would be visiting us this early in the morning?

It was still dark. At least it had been when I had gotten out of bed. Now, as I looked out one of the basement windows, I realized the sky was brightening and it was indeed morning. I didn't like it, but when I looked at my wristwatch, I realized it was eight o'clock already.

"Hi, honey," I said to Tom as I approached the door at the top of the stairs. He was holding it open for me.

"Hi, yourself," he said, his features lit by a wide grin. He wrapped his warm arms around me and gave me a quick hug and a soft kiss on the lips as I stood in the open doorway.

I smiled to myself as he released me. Even after all this time he made me smile, especially when he said and did things like kissing me. It made me feel good and very happy.

"Who is our guest at this time of the morning?" I asked.

"You mean guests, don't you?"

Tom nodded toward the kitchen. I heard the low murmur of voices. Walking to the kitchen, I discovered the three musketeers—Joy, Nigel, and Ryan—seated at the kitchen table drinking my coffee. They were, no doubt, waiting for me.

"You might want to freshen up while I put more coffee on," said Tom with a wink.

I went to our little bathroom with its green and white tiled walls and looked at myself in the mirror over the white porcelain sink. Oh, now I see why Tom suggested I freshen up.

My hair was standing up in odd patches and I had soot and dirt smudged along my forehead and chin. In my old work clothes, I looked like a homeless dumpster diver on a bad day. I had even chipped a nail, which is really hard to do since I always keep them trimmed short.

I didn't have time for my customary morning shower—or did I? I remembered in high school I had actually gotten changed and ate a hot, home-cooked breakfast in less than ten minutes. I also remembered Mom wasn't impressed at the way I inhaled my food, but when I explained my friends and their mother were waiting for me outside, she understood.

Old Bones

I ran out and got into my friends' car with a minute to spare. I also remember it was a bet, something I never do, especially on a Sunday, but it was one of those empty bets. You know the type, one of those I bet you can't, I bet I can. Yes, at times, the scintillating, deep conversations we had as teenagers were really something.

I decided to take a chance. I quickly stripped and turned on the shower. I took my toothbrush, squeezed on some toothpaste, then ran it over my teeth. It felt wonderful. I really hated morning breath, especially my own.

"I'll be there in a few minutes, talk amongst yourselves," I called out as I got into a nice warm shower. Soon steam filled the room and I could feel the tension ease from between my shoulders.

I washed all my bits and pieces and soon was squeaky clean. It felt so good. I didn't like the idea of jumping into clothes that I had been wearing yesterday, but they had been fresh when I put them on first thing the previous morning.

I quickly pulled on my day-old clothes and wiped at the fog with the flat of my hand to clear out a spot on the mirror so I could see to brush my hair. It took no time at all to brush out my short, white hair. Then I leaned forward and used my fingers to fluff it. I was done in record time, too.

I opened the bathroom door just as the kettle in the kitchen started to whistle, and I looked down the hall to see Joy getting the beverages ready.

I walked into the kitchen with my notebook under my arm.

"I'll leave you guys alone once I've made more coffee," said Tom as he got the mugs, milk, and sugar out and put them on the center of the table.

I looked at Joy and waited. I was of two minds.

This wasn't Tom's case and the police never actually invited him, but they did ask for everyone's help. So I thought he should stay, but I wasn't sure what Joy thought.

"Nigel, what do you think?" asked Joy as she poured the tea Tom had put out with the first round of coffee.

"I think Tom is welcome to stay," interjected Ryan before his partner could respond. "We need all the help that we can get."

Nigel nodded his agreement.

"Okay, what do we know?" asked Tom as he took a seat at the kitchen table. He blew on his coffee to cool it and his eyes scanned the assembled players at the table, waiting for someone to speak.

I pulled my gray sweater close around me, feeling a little cold after the hot shower. My hair was still wet and the house was still cool from the overnight temperature. I did what my parents always did and turned down the furnace at night. I picked up my mug of tea and wrapped my fingers around the handle, immediately feeling the heat radiate through my fingers, hands, and up my arms. It warmed me.

We all went over what we knew to this point, which was precious little. We had the names of the people who lived in the old house. They were the Martin family from Germany, who lived at the house during the time of the murders. But the parents were long dead and the two children, Irene and Luke, had gone to places unknown. No one we'd spoken with who had lived in the neighborhood at the time knew where they went. We had completely lost track of them.

"What about the cousin?" asked Tom as he stood up and went to get the fresh pot of coffee.

"What cousin?" I asked, starting to draw doodles in the margins of my notebook.

As I looked up from my handiwork, I saw Ryan and Nigel were staring at Tom and nodding at his offer for more coffee.

Old Bones

"Well, answer her, Tom," said Joy.

My beloved husband shrugged his broad shoulders. "According to Mr. Rempel, the last year he remembered the Martins living here, they had a cousin living with them. He had the impression June, the cousin, was from Germany. He wasn't sure about it, but what he was sure of was that the two girls were blonde, beautiful, and looked like twins.

"Then he started getting mad, calling the Martins Communists or something like that." Tom looked at me with a satisfied grin, very proud that he had some new information to share with us.

Mr. Rempel wasn't quite lucid most of the time, so extracting anything from the old man was truly impressive. Yes, there were a few times he was almost with us, but most of the time he really wasn't there. It was sad to see. He was physically fine, and his family loved him, and so far they were able to keep him at home with them rather than in a care facility.

"Oh, honey," I said gently. "I don't think Mr. Rempel would really know any real information. Yes, he was around the neighborhood back then, but his mind is not as sharp as it once was."

Tom appeared a little confused. "But he sounded so calm and it was like he knew what we were talking about. There were a few of us downstairs talking about the case and that the police wanted information. He piped up and told us about the Martins and even knew they had the large double corner lot. He sounded so lucid and sure of his facts." Tom stopped talking and looked around at all of us.

I nodded, waiting for someone else to say something.

When no one said anything, Tom continued. "He even told us the cousin went to UBC and was involved with the UBC newspaper. That's when he started talking about Communists and got upset."

"I think that's a good clue to follow and check in to. UBC should have old copies of the school newspaper. Anybody want to check it out?" I asked.

Joy reminded Ryan and Nigel about the scratch on the car and me being pushed down the stairs on the ferry. Then I remembered the old Christmas cards and letter I found when we went to Victoria, got them out, and put them in the middle of the table.

We each looked at them but there was really nothing that was interesting and none of the names were different. A couple of the cards were from the neighborhood and a couple from the States and one from Germany.

I hoped someone recognized a name from some of the neighbors they had spoken to, but they all shook their heads.

"Aunt Joy and you too, Heather," said Ryan rising from the table.

"Thank you for all your help, but we're going to recommend the case be closed," said Nigel as he too rose from the table, and together the two detectives headed toward the front door. "We've tried our best, but there's nothing here and no clues to follow."

"What about Joy and Edgar's break-in?" I asked. "And the attack on the car and me on the ferry? There has to be something behind all these incidents, doesn't there?"

Nigel shrugged. "Sorry, it's all unrelated as far as I can see. Joy said there was nothing taken except her jewelry. It looks like just a bunch of punks robbing a house that people have just moved into."

"It happens," added Ryan as he walked ahead of me. "We'll notify robbery of our findings. I'm sure they'll look into it. We need to get going."

We were all silent as we walked to the front door. There really wasn't anything to say to each other.

Old Bones

The case was over, it was going to be closed, and now we'd never know who was killed and who the murderer was.

"Heather, can we talk in your office when you get back?" asked Joy.

I nodded to her. "In a minute."

I brought the guys their jackets and they slipped them on before I opened the front door.

Out of the corner of my eye I saw Buddy watching attentively as we said our goodbyes. He held his head lower than usual and there was even a droop to his perky tail. He followed me back to the kitchen where Joy and Tom sat at the kitchen table and looked at their coffee as if they would find the answer to the questions we'd been asking at the bottom of their mugs.

"Come on, guys. There's no reason or time to mope, we have too much to do. Joy, your not going to work today? You don't seem dressed for work." I said, tilting my head slightly at her colorful outfit.

Joy was dressed in her funky, colorful clothes. She always picked wild, bright colors. It was an interesting contrast to her classic shoulder-length red bob hairdo. I liked that she was traditional in one area but wild in another.

"Tom, we can tackle the basement right now. We have to get started making sleeping quarters for six extra people, then we have to get cleaning and buying groceries as well."

I stood by the kitchen sink, dumped the teapot, and rinsed it under warm water and then did the same for Tom's French press. I had my back turned to Tom and Joy as I rambled on. I didn't want them to see my tears. It felt so stupid to cry, but who would ever morn people that no one knew had died if I didn't?

And no one would ever be brought to justice. It just wasn't fair or right, but I knew life wasn't very often fair or right.

Something nagged at the back of my brain. It was as if I had an annoying itch. Something didn't add up. I dried my eyes with the back of my hands and then dried my hands on the blue-and-white striped tea towel hanging off the stove handle.

I turned around and sat down at the table once again.

"Tom, something you said is bothering me," I said as I picked up my pen and opened up a nice clean fresh page in my notebook. "Can you repeat what Mr. Rempel told you? Take it slowly; I want to write it down."

"He said that the Martins had a cousin, or some such, staying with them. They had two kids, a boy and a girl, themselves. The cousin was a girl. Their daughter and the cousin were blonde and blue-eyed, pretty girls in their early twenties. I had the impression he meant the relatives in Germany sent their daughter here to go to school." Tom paused in his narrative.

Joy looked at him and nodded for him to continue.

"Keep going. You said something about a newspaper and the Martins being Communists?" Joy urged.

I wondered if she was being as bothered by the information and the lack of knowledge as I was. Never mind the whole concept of justice.

She took a lock of her hair and started to wind it around her finger and then tucked it behind her ear.

None of us spoke for several minutes. We were deep in our own thoughts considering this new information.

Then I felt eyes on me and looked down. Buddy looked up at me, his brown eyes sparkling with anxiety, his tail wagging furiously. I checked the clock on the stovetop.

Sure enough, it was ten o'clock. This is about the time I usually have coffee, after which I take Buddy for his morning walk.

I do try to keep a schedule; if I don't, I won't get any writing done or get any exercise.

I'm one of those people that say "tomorrow," and tomorrow never comes; so for me, keeping a flexible schedule is a good thing.

"Joy, what are you doing today?" I asked.

I needed to get back to either writing or cleaning up the house to prepare for the kids and their kids' impending visit. I had no time to sit around and twiddle my thumbs.

"Um, ten thirty," she said, coming out of her trance after looking at her watch. "Oh, great, I have to go," she said. "I've just enough time to get there. I'm getting my nails done, a treat to myself," She looked at me. "Listen. I'm going to go shopping after that and then meeting a friend for a late lunch I could be here to give you a hand four o'clock. What if I come over and we can talk about the case and the book then? Or I can help you with preparing the downstairs for your family and then we could work on the case? I'm good either way,"

She turned to face my husband. "Tom, could you please write down as much about the information Mister Rempel provided as you remember, please?"

Joy stood. "We can go over it then. We may need to see Mr. Rempel tonight, if we can, to confirm his story." She went out of the kitchen headed for the front door.

I walked with her. "That gives me an idea," I said. "I'll try to do some research while you're at work. Something is bothering me in the back of my mind, something about the university newspaper." I glanced at her. "Do you really think there's something there?"

"We'll see," she said and smiled at me. "Even if there isn't, I do have some excellent ideas for an interesting murder mystery. Some I think you'll love."

Okay, so that was good. All I had to do now was get everything organized downstairs and get the extra bedding ready. Then Tom and I would go grocery shopping and I would have to get a haircut and a new outfit for Easter. Maybe I would hold off on the last two items for a couple of days. Oh nuts the Easter Tea. I would have to get hold of a couple of the ladies at the church and see how the ticket sales and ideas for the tea were coming. I had asked them for their ideas and help. I'm sure glad that these ladies have done the Tea so often they can do it with their eyes closed. But I felt bad, like I was just dumping everything on them.

My mind whirled around with all the things I had to get accomplished as I tried to put the bedding together in my mind. I didn't just want it to be okay, I wanted it to be especially nice for our kids and grandkids. I hardly ever got a chance to see them and this was the stuff that memories are made of, about visiting Grandma and Grandpa and camping out in their basement.

I pushed the thoughts away since the family would only be here for two weeks, and with me writing the book the first week, I would hardly have any time to visit with them. But we could still make awesome memories. I made a mental note to take some pictures and send them to all of them after so we could share these good times forever.

Tears started to well up in my eyes. What was wrong with me? Was I turning into one of those emotional weepy women, the kind I couldn't stand? Sure, I cried when I had a reason, but this was getting silly.

I should be happy I would see my children and that I had a book under contract. Both were great things that I was thankful for.

As of now, I would have two weeks to write a book. It was certainly a good thing I was a fast typist.

Old Bones

I would need all my speed, accuracy, and endurance to finish the project by the deadline. I had only done this kind of sprint writing once before and I had promised myself never to do it again. It was so stressful it had almost crippled me and it was two months before I could write anything new again.

"Honey. You're not alone," Tom said, sensing my agitation as he closed the front door behind Joy.

He wrapped his arms around my shoulders as mine went around his waist. My head found his shoulder and rested on him. I could feel his warmth, the course, nubby fabric of his shirt against my cheek, and the fresh smell of shampoo in his hair.

The tension in my shoulders relaxed as we held each other.

I looked at him feeling my eyes starting to tear up again.

"Come on, Heather, let's get going," he said as he released me and swatted me on the bottom, then quickly jogged down the stairway to the basement.

I chuckled as I ran after him, determined to give him as good as I had received.

Chapter Eighteen
Brand New Office

My mouth was dry and the skin of my face felt grimy. I was thirsty and exhausted as I looked around the spare room downstairs but was pretty happy with what we had accomplished so far.

It was late Sunday morning and the sky had decided to clear to let the sun shine through. I could see the dust motes in the air as I decided that the curtains were going to have to come down and get thrown into the washer; since I didn't have time to get new ones, these would have to do.

I was missing church today and felt unsettled about it. I always felt good after service and got a lot out of the music and the sermon, today it was missing.

I pulled the spare chair against the window and climbed up so I could reach the old-fashioned curtain rod and pull down the cream-colored curtains with the bright red, yellow, and green pattern of roses and leaves.

I smiled to myself when I recalled suggesting to Tom that the curtains were fine and would last us another ten or fifteen years.

"I don't know, dear," said Tom with a wicked grin on his smiling face, "I think the pattern on those old curtains is going to clash with the posters I'm going to put down here."

"Are you saying if we change the curtains you won't put posters up, or that you will in any case?" I asked with a straight face.

"I have ideas about what I would like to put up on the walls and in the bookcases," he said with a grin.

Old Bones

"I was think more of displaying some of the art we've collected over the years that we haven't gotten a home for upstairs. Some of the landscape and water scenes would be great down here since it is a basement."

"Yes," I agreed. "I guess I do like that idea a lot better than posters. Mind you, I know some posters are worth a lot of money and I thought you might want to relive your childhood and adolescence." I chuckled.

I finished slipping the curtains off the rod and then replaced the rod in its holder, finally climbing down from the chair.

Looking around at our handiwork of moving furniture and bookshelves, I thought the room looked really good. It had four tall, white, six-foot-high bookshelves along one side and under the opposite wall we had placed a good-sized desk for Tom's computer. And we had found a beautiful old oak rolling chair that we had stashed away to use once we had organized the space.

Next to the desk was a worn oak chair that we'd have to get a cushion for. I planned to buy matching cushions for the desk chair and the guest chair. There was space for a full-size hide-a-bed couch to fit nicely against the third wall.

It looked like a really great office where you could work in comfort and quiet, and it also was a place to curl up and read. At a yard sale we had found a couple of great lamps, one floor lamp and one for the desk.

The curtains released a swirl of dust and cobwebs as I looked at the dirty windows and sill.

It was then I recalled Ryan and Nigel were supposed to have fingerprints taken at Joy's house and I hadn't heard anything about it.

"Tom," I called but didn't hear him answer as I bundled up the curtains, trying not to disturb any more dust than I could avoid.

I went out the basement door and closed it behind me and shook those curtains for all I was worth. It was amazing the amount of dust and dirt that came out of them.

When I came back inside, I could hear Tom calling or saying something from his would be office in the basement and realized that I had called him, then gone outside.

"Sorry, I just went outside to shake the curtains out. Come here and look at how great your office has turned out," I said proudly.

We had done a really good job and I think whoever ended up in this room was going to consider themselves lucky. It was a really cozy room. All I needed was to buy a couple of pillows, the chair cushions, a couple of shams, and of course a matching comforter for the dark brown sofa bed to finish off the room.

I smiled to myself when I realized what I was doing. I had it on good authority, from Tom, that women do that. When they're referring to a house, they say, "It's perfect. Now all we have to do is redo this and that and the other thing."

I heard Tom come into the room. "This will do quite nicely. Good job, honey," he said as he surveyed my handiwork.

He looked so happy. He wore a wide grin on his face and his eyes were shining. I realized during all our married life he hadn't had a room to himself before. We called the recreation room his, but it was reality the entire family's room.

I, on the other hand, had had my own writing space for the last two years. I hadn't really thought his own space was that important to him. He hadn't said anything and seemed quite happy to work at the kitchen table when he was writing or editing and, if needed, he would go into the living room where it was quiet so he wouldn't be disturbed.

He stepped up to stand before me, then gave me a hug.

Old Bones

"It's not quite finished yet," I said. "I'm going to get new drapes and stuff and clean the windows…" My words trailed off as I felt his warmth transfer to me.

I stepped back to look at him again and saw him beaming and nodding as he scanned the walls and the bookshelves that he could put whatever he wanted on. It was his room and he wouldn't have to share with anyone except the kids every couple of years if we were lucky.

I almost said something, but I knew that's not what he saw. He was a generous man and he saw his own space, his own little place in his own home.

I knew exactly how he felt because that's how I'd felt when I got my writing office. I should have realized that and done this a lot sooner for him. At least it was done now.

"Listen," I said. "I know how you feel and the same rules apply to you as they do me; when the door is closed, I won't come in unless it's an emergency. It's your space."

Tom walked to the closet and opened the door wide to let the light in and started to pull out paintings that we had put there twenty years ago until we had time to find places for them.

"I wonder what some of these are worth now?" he said as he turned one of the paintings over. "I should check the Internet and see."

There taped to the back was an envelope with the bill of sale and a write-up of the artist.

"Oh, speaking of the internet," said Tom. "That reminds me. Mr. Rempel said one of the Martin girls went to UBC and she was involved with the communist newspaper. I did a little research and found some of the old papers from fifty years ago. They even have a picture of the students that were working on the UBC Workers'

News, that's what they called it in those days. I printed them out; come on upstairs, I'll show you."

I looked at Tom and a funny feeling I'd had earlier bubbled to the surface in my mind again. You know, when the butterflies in your stomach start flying in formation and the hair at the back of your neck starts to rise. Something very good or very evil was going to take place.

I swallowed hard and followed Tom up the stairs to the kitchen. He went to his laptop computer. Soon his computer would have its own permanent home.

Maybe we caught a break and got a solid lead from Mr. Rempel—a most unlikely source.

Chapter Nineteen
Family at Home

AFTER TOM SHOWED ME the information he'd found in the old UBC newspaper archives, I jotted down the site address, then went into my own office and closed the door behind me.

I turned my notebook to a blank page and powered up my computer.

I quickly found the website and the relevant story. There it was.

The article was about a female student at UBC in the sixties named Baker. The student newspaper was indeed called the UBC Workers' News and they had a front-page picture with an article about a founding member that had disappeared. There was a picture with a young blonde woman in her early twenties and two other people, one a man and the other a woman with long blonde hair, too.

The article went on to say the blonde woman in the middle was June Baker, who had disappeared, but the university and the Vancouver City Police were not investigating. Some staff of the newspaper thought June Baker may have been murdered.

I understood this article was probably just sensationalistic journalism, but I didn't care. This was something to go on. The other woman in the picture was Irene Martin, the daughter of the family that had lived in the empty lot off Fifty-Third and Fraser. Both girls would have been the right age to be the bones found in the empty lot.

I printed out the story and then pulled up the number of an old friend of mine. Actually she was more Tom's friend and worked with Canada Immigration Inland Branch.

The names of some of the federal departments in Canada seemed to change daily so it was really hard to tell who was doing what and who had responsibilities in what areas.

I needed to know if she would be able to check out a name and a date on the databases for me. I was going to go with what Mr. Rempel said about her coming from Germany. I could go through the government 'access to information' and get it checked that way too, but that would take a very long time and time was something in very short supply right now. I would let Ryan and Nigel know and leave it us to them if the wanted to follow up on it.

So that task was only half done, but right now I needed to concentrate on this research before I went back to lifting and cleaning and organizing.

Once the rooms and beds were set up, then I could go shopping for the few odds and ends I needed. That would be fun and my reward.

I watched the printer as the pages with the article and the picture came out. The old picture was really grainy. Maybe if I went to the school, I could get a much better copy. This would have to do for now. I quickly read the article and the continued-on pages with other articles about other women that had gone missing from UBC and the response, or lack of response, from the University and the Vancouver Police Department.

It seemed all the cases were treated as runaways and the person who was writing the article seemed to have the very strong opinion that this wasn't what had happened. What the author didn't have was proof, only suspicions.

Then I remembered I hadn't gone to pick up the information the pastor was going to leave at the church for me about the Martin family. I would have to drop by there on my way to UBC.

Old Bones

The printer finished its work and I picked up the neat pages and slipped them into an envelope.

I really wanted to get the information on the Martins and add that to my pile too. My stomach was in knots as my excitement grew.

I wondered if there was any way of finding out who the other people who served on the newspaper staff were at the time. The photo hadn't said anything about the two other people who were with June Baker, but the girl looked very familiar and so did the young man.

I felt good about this morning's work.

Based on what Tom said, Rempel was really set off by the word "communist," a word that meant something completely different from his generation to mine—at least to most of us living in Canada today.

It seems whichever side you were on, it was a time of misery and heartbreak. But after the war, Canada took in the people they were fighting against to help build a united, strong country.

All I knew was that Nazism, a political party, was evil and the world suffered because of it. But that wasn't the same as communism. That was a problem between the USA and Russia. It was the time of the so-called cold war.

I didn't know much about politics; it wasn't something I was interested in growing up. I guess it had a lot to do with my teachers and trying to memorize a list of dates and battles. Something I really wasn't interested in.

Now if my teachers had concentrated on the human interest stories and the reasons why these battles had occurred and how war affected the real people before and after, well, that would have been different to me.

It occurred to me that people who love history do so because of who the teacher was and how the information had been taught to them.

It made some people passionate about the subject and others hate it.

"Tom, I need you," I called as I left my office and headed to the kitchen.

There was a lot more information I needed to get. And various ideas that were starting to form in my mind about how to accomplish this.

The doorbell rang, causing me to change direction. Buddy joined me at the front door. I picked him up as I opened it to discover my son, Rodney, and his family on my doorstep.

"Hi, Mom," said Rodney.

"Hi, Grams," said a young man's voice.

"She likes 'Oma' better," Jennifer, my son's wife, said.

I was being hugged by three different sets of arms.

"Okay, everyone, give her some room and let's get into the house before we let all the heat out," said Rodney, my eldest child.

I saw bodies of different height and felt them push against me. I heard Buddy barking in my arms with short, staccato barks indicating his delight. They smelled of warm, wool coats and shawls, a trace of Old Spice, with a hint of Chanel Number Five.

I smiled nervously. Rodney, Jennifer, and their sixteen-year-old son, Christopher, had arrived early. They were home.

I moved aside to make room as best I could, then opened the living room door so that I could back up and stand to one side as they all came into the house.

"Mom, I'm really sorry, I know that we're a week early and I just phoned and told Dad we were coming. I probably should have called you about the change of plans, but we got a super deal so we decided just to come out early and surprise you. Surprise!" said Rodney as he gave me another hard, long hug.

I felt my eyes tear up; I had missed them so much.

"Oh, honey, it's so good to see you all and the more time we can spend with you, the better," I said as I rubbed my eyes dry with the back of my hand.

I laughed as I hugged them again. It was so good to see them all. Now that Tom was retired, I hoped to spend a lot more time with them. Either visiting them at their place or having them over here. We could even have Christopher over for a visit in the summer. He was old enough now to fly by himself if he wanted to.

I was shocked to see how much the boy had grown. Two years ago he had been about the same size as me and now he was half a head taller. I knew he was on his way to being a six-footer like his father.

"Christopher, how could you?" I teased him as I held him at arms' length to get a good look at him. "Now I'm the shortest one in the family again."

"Right, Oma," said Christopher as his smile migrated from his lips into my eyes. "Oh, by the way, can you call me Kit?"

I looked at him, confused. I understood the need for a person to have their own persona, but Kit? I knew better than to ask right now. He would be telling me everything soon enough. I'd look forward to that. I would also look at some of my name books and see if indeed it was a variation of Christopher as I had a feeling it was. No, all I had to do was to get used to it. It was his choice and his request, so I would honor it.

"Come on, son," said Rodney. "Let's get the suitcases from the sidewalk." I looked out the still open door and there were their suitcases on the sidewalk next to their car. There were a couple of bulging, overstuffed duffel bags and one hard-sided suitcase.

I realized I had lost track of Buddy. When I heard a familiar woof, I looked toward the neighbors' house and spotted my little guy at the front of Joy's house.

"Rodney, could you get Buddy for me and bring him inside? He seems to be visiting the neighbors."

"Hey, Buddy boy, come on into the house and you can help me get our bags in the right room," Kit called to Buddy. "If you're really good, maybe you can even sleep with me; but we won't tell Oma, okay?" Kit picked up his duffel bag and swung it over his shoulder. He whistled once and walked up the front stairs into the house.

Buddy's ears perked upon hearing his name and the playful whistle. He came running after my grandson and bolted up the stairs into the house. Kit had always had a good way with animals.

***

I got ready to walk down the street to the church and grabbed the church keys.

It felt funny, walking to the church office without a scheduled service, a meeting, or choir practice. I had been a member of the trustees for a very long time. I guess it was nearing about twelve years that I'd served on the board. The men did the heavy plumbing and electrical work while I took care of the security and the keys for the church.

Now that Tom was retiring—and he had done a lot of service for the church, too—we were going to take a year off and concentrate on our writing and then see where that took us.

I knew we were going to undergo a major shift in our routine, and as much as we enjoyed being together in the evenings and on weekends and holidays, this was going to be completely different.

Old Bones

I'd had the luxury of having the house to myself for the last couple of years but now I had to share.

"Tom, I'm going to run up to the church," I called to him. "Are you ready to go after that?" Before he could respond, I added, "Oh, before I forget, Rodney and Jennifer are here and they brought Chris, I mean Kit, with them too."

I was chuckling as I said that to him.

I heard him mumble something softly under his breath, then I heard his men's size tens hurrying up the basement stairs. I knew our son and his family being home would excite him.

I pulled on my warm, sage-green fleece jacket. I thought it was mild enough this week that maybe I could put the old winter parka away. But I wasn't rushing it; I knew what Vancouver weather could be like. Unpredictable.

"Tom?" I asked as I saw him open the basement door and almost collide with Rodney, Jennifer, and Kit, who were standing at the top of the stairs anxiously waiting to greet him.

"Yes, yes," he said as he collected his long overdue hugs. "I'll be ready. I'll put the water on and we can have a cup of tea before we leave.

"Come on downstairs. Guess what? I have my very own office. We just finished it this morning and I think that you will be staying there," said Tom as he led the way with Rodney, Jennifer, and Kit.

"That's a good idea," I said. "We'll blow up the air mattress and put it on the stand it came with, then Kit can have it and Rodney and Jennifer can share the hide-a-bed."

Chapter Twenty
Church Information

It was really cold. I rubbed my hands, then put them into my pockets. I hadn't even brought a pair of light gloves with me and I could feel the cold seep into my skin and bones. I was almost tempted to start to jog, but that was something I had never done and I wasn't going to start now. So I picked up my pace and walked faster.

The church looked so strange and deserted. But it was early and I knew that in another hour we would have people arriving for morning bible study.

I went around to the entrance to the office and not the large, double oak main doors that opened onto the foyer. The office door was a wide old oak door with glass windowpanes that went from about the middle of the door to the top.

It took me just a minute to open the door and turn off the alarm, then another minute to go to my little mailbox along the outside wall of the office.

There was a manila envelope with my name on it in Pastor Jeffery's handwriting. I checked to make sure there was nothing else that I needed to attend to, locked the door, reset the alarm, and left the building as the alarm sounded its farewell chime.

All was well. I could hardly wait to take a look at the information the pastor had found for me.

As I walked home, I looked at the envelope and realized that someone had opened it.

Old Bones

The flap with the glue had been sealed very unevenly and when I took my finger and ran it along the flap, it felt damp.

Maybe I was letting my imagination run away with me. I thought back to the car being keyed, me being tripped on the ferry, and the break-in at Joy's house. It didn't make any sense at all; or maybe I was seeing ghosts in the shadows.

There was something about the Christmas cards that I brought back from the island that was nagging at the back of my mind, too. I wanted to go through and check the names and find out who they were and try to discover where they were now. I was going to look in the UBC newspaper archives to see if I could find all the names and addresses of the subscribers to the Workers' News and not just the founding members.

As I hurried home, I shivered. The sun had ducked behind a large gray cloud and I could feel the cold hit me hard after leaving the warmth in the church. I walked even faster, my little legs shifting into a gliding trot so that I could get indoors and get warm sooner than later.

I got home and found everyone was downstairs in the basement. Good. That would give me a few minutes alone to see what was in the envelope before I went out shopping with Tom.

I took a closer look at the sealed flap of the manila envelope with the magnifying glass I always keep in my mug that holds my extra pens and brass letter opener. I'd been correct. It had been opened and then re-sealed. I could see where someone had tried to open it without tearing the paper, but there were a few places where the paper was ripped. Also the glue was gone in a few places so the envelope wouldn't seal properly.

I would have to call Pastor Jeffery and ask him if he had forgotten something and had to reopen the envelope.

But how do I do that without looking like a fool or sounding really paranoid?

I placed the envelope on my desk and realized that I still had my fleece jacket on. I took it off and went to the hall closet to hang it up when I heard the tip tip sound of Buddy's nails as he ran up the basement stairs.

"Heather?" called Tom. "Do you want to come down here and see what we've done?"

I really didn't want to answer him. I wanted to check the contents of the envelope. What could they have done in the few minutes I was gone?

"Okay, I'll be right there. Just give me a minute," I answered. Tom sounded so pleased I didn't have the heart to tell him I wasn't really that interested.

I went back into my office, opened the center drawer of my desk, and slipped the still sealed envelope into the narrow drawer. It was actually a false drawer I had made when I had the old oak desk refinished.

I had made an adjustment to the center drawer for a keyboard tray and under the keyboard tray was an empty space for things you didn't use very often or wanted to keep secure. It also had a key so you could lock the center drawer. I fished out the little brass key from the pencil holder where I kept it, put everything back the way it had been, then locked the drawer.

I wondered why I had done that. Was I really starting to see things around corners or hearing mysterious things that go bump in the night?

No, recent events so far had to be for a reason, but I had the sense I was really getting close to finding out what the reasons were.

Old Bones

I left my office and went into our bedroom and slipped the little key into my purse that was sitting where it always was, next to my night table.

I turned on my night table lamp and looked toward the closet. I wondered if I should move my purse into the closet behind the laundry hamper. I picked up my purse, went to the closet, and slipped it between the plastic hamper and the wall. This way it couldn't be easily seen. A burglar would really have to look to find it. I just hoped I would remember where I had put it.

I better let Tom know, too, since he was used to my purse in the old spot and I didn't want him to think it had been stolen. I had better tell him about the other things that had happened too. I hoped we would soon have a good explanation why some of these terrible things were happening. Too bad the police had just dropped the entire case.

I looked once around the room to see if I missed anything important. Satisfied, I pulled my purse out of the closet and opened it up. I took out the little key, the post cards and Christmas cards I had gotten from the island, and put my purse back in the closet.

I didn't realize until just now how much Joy's burglary had really affected me, so much so that I was hiding my purse.

There was nothing in my purse that anyone could want: cash, only a little, and my credit cards. Although it is a nuisance, credit cards can always be cancelled.

I quickly went back to the office, closed the door, opened the hidden drawer, put the cards on top of the envelope, and locked it again.

"Heather, where are you?" called Tom from the basement.

"I'm coming. I'll be right there," I said as I quickly went back to our bedroom and hid the key back in my old black-and-tan leather purse in the top shelf of the closet.

Buddy followed me from room to room and as I started to move faster, he thought that this was a new game I was playing and he tried to grab my pant leg as he barked. I stopped and looked at him and gave him a stern look. "No," in my best intimidation voice.

It didn't stop his tail from wagging, but he did calm down a little bit and follow calmly after me down the basement stairs.

I thought everyone would be gathered in Tom's office, but no one was there. I heard voices coming from the back of the house and I closed my eyes. Surely Tom hadn't taken them to the other room that we hadn't even started to fix up and organize yet. I pasted a smile on my face and walked into what had been a room filled with bookcases, boxes, and old furniture.

Boxes of books were neatly stacked against the inside wall next to the open door leading to the spare room.

Jennifer was vacuuming the rug, which shocked me. The bookcases had been moved against one wall and there was a queen-sized bed set up and pushed against the far wall. They had even found a box spring and mattress that looked to be in reasonably good condition, I remember that we had stored an extra bed that we were going use in a guest bedroom a while ago but it never happened, until now. The windows were larger on this side of the house; they were open to let in some fresh air, albeit cold air.

"You did a great job. How did you get everything done so fast?" I asked.

"Actually, you've been gone a little longer than you thought, Mom," said Rodney.

Old Bones

"We heard you come in and then nothing for a while. We had started and wanted to know where you wanted stuff, but since you didn't come down, we made executive decisions." He opened his arms wide with a grin splitting his handsome features. "What do you think? We can move…" His voice trailed off, evidently waiting for my response.

I tried not to laugh. "It looks good. Really good, actually." I nodded. "You've put the bookcases and bed exactly where we had decided to. Good job, everyone." From the corner of one eye I saw Tom nodding and grinning with pride.

"Tom, can you reach up and take those curtains down? I'm going to wash the set in the other room; I may as well do these too."

"Here, Oma, let me do it," interjected Kit, "I can reach it even better than Gramps, since now I'm taller than he is." Kit smiled at me and then at Tom.

I watched as Tom faked a scowl but he quickly gave up and punched Kit in the arm as he walked past to get to the window.

Boys, these were my boys. I was so proud of Rodney for the man and father he had become. And Kit was turning out just fine too under the guidance of Jennifer and Rodney. It was nice to see another generation of Rosses doing well.

Tom started coughing as Kit went past him since he was shaking out the dusty curtains in his direction.

"No, Kit, I don't think you want to do that," I said. "You'll have to vacuum and dust the bookshelves again. The next thing would be to put the books into the bookshelves." I pointed to the stack of boxes. "If you start with the box marked number one and put the contents on the first shelf on the left hand side and only put one box to a shelf, you will end up shelving a good portion of the books that go into those shelves."

We hadn't decided which of the spare rooms the books were going into, but these were my, or I should say our, research books. I'm glad we were getting them sorted out so I could bring down the ones that had migrated into my office and onto my bookshelves in the intervening years.

"Mom, do you know how anal that sounds?" said Rodney. "You guys have been in here for a while and you still remember how the bookshelves should be arranged?"

"Rodney, don't worry, I do have a life. These are research books—at least a good portion of them are—and I will be using them for upcoming projects from time to time. It will just be a whole lot easier when they're out on the shelves and sorted out so we'll be able to easily use them. Dad will use them too for his books."

I shifted my gaze to my husband. "Tom, I see we need to get a couple of lamps for this room," I said. "And there should be a dresser behind the furnace and I think I'd like to move the small loveseat from the family room in here, too."

Chapter Twenty-one
Pool Table

"But, Mom, if you do that, then there will be enough room in that large family room for a pool table," said Rodney with a twinkle in his eye.

"Yeah, honey, there will be lots of room in my dreams," joked Tom. "Don't worry, Rodney, we both know that your mother will just fill the extra room with bookshelves, but maybe one day."

"Yes, Tom, dreaming is always good. And you're right about the bookshelves; we do need another couple for your collections," I said as I grinned at him.

He had just gotten into collecting graphic novels and was grumbling about not having enough space. But once his office was done, I was going to get shelves put into the closet and proper file boxes. That would put a smile on his face.

Oh, dear. How do I get that boy to keep a secret? I made sure that I didn't look at Tom. I knew he really wanted a pool table; it was the one true thing that he had been yearning for, and looking at in the stores, for a good ten to twenty years. Where we'd lived before now, we hadn't had the room—but this house now had the room.

I had been saving for his pool table for the past two years. It was going to be a surprise for Tom's retirement. Rodney told me a month ago he and Jennifer had some money saved up for Tom's retirement, so with the family all pitching in, we had enough to get a good table and cues.

It was arriving tomorrow in the afternoon.

I had also found a wonderful old pool table light fixture that I bought that one of our friends from church was going to install for us. He was an electrician and he was going to come tomorrow morning and install the light.

"I don't know if it's quite big enough," I said. "I guess we'll have to measure the room to make sure, but then there is a matter of money, too." I spoke as grimly as possible. "I think if we were going to buy a pool table, it would take quite a while for us to save up. Besides, we want to travel and we have other priorities. Right Tom?"

"Yeah," said Tom, nodding, his lips forming a thin line and his eyes serious. "Nice idea, son, but Mom and I need to start saving for a car, and we're thinking of going to Hawaii for a holiday next January, so we have to save for that, too."

My heart skipped a beat. Tom looked so sad.

He was trying to sound happy, but I knew that he really wanted a pool table rather than a dumb old Hawaiian holiday. But I was going to do both and knew that he would have a couple of very pleasant surprises soon.

That's where this new book I had to finish in less than two weeks came in. It was a new series I was creating and had high hopes for.

"Come on, Tom, we have to go," I said. "Do you think you guys could give us a hand with this room?" I asked Rodney and Jennifer.

I felt awful that they were helping with the cleaning; they were guests, after all. No, I corrected myself, they were family. They were my family and I loved them.

Halfway up the stairs I heard the front doorbell ring and Buddy started to bark.

"Tom, are you expecting someone?"

"Just Marie and the kids," he said from behind me.

"Marie. I thought she was coming in next week and only staying for one week of spring vacation."

"Oh, I thought I told you," Tom said. "She called on Monday and said she'd decided to have a nice long visit with us. She explained she needed to get rooted in her family and community again."

I wondered what that meant and racked my brains trying to figure it out as I reached the top of the stairs. Tom was still talking to me although I couldn't really hear him. I waited for him. I'd have to ask him to repeat what he'd just said.

"I know you mentioned it to me that they were coming," I said as he came up the last stair and stood next to me.

"So they're coming today and staying for at least two weeks. It's going to be a full house," I said with a sigh. "But with that many people, I think it will be easier for me to do my writing if I wear ear plugs. Joy should be over soon and I'm going to work on the plot."

I opened the front door to let the cold wind and our daughter, Marie, and her two girls—Tracy, fourteen, and Morocco, who was twelve—into the warm entry.

"My girls, how are you? How was the trip?" I said as I moved back into the house and grabbed the little dog as quickly as I could. I didn't need him escaping again today.

"Let your father through so that he can get your cases. No, let's keep our little Buddy inside."

I dropped Buddy in the living room, then took their coats and got them to drop their shoes in our bedroom. Our small hall closet is fine for a few coats but we'd have to have another place to put everyone's. I then led them into the kitchen. I put the kettle on as we all talked at once, trying to catch up.

I looked at Marie. She had long, warm blonde hair and a dimple in her right cheek.

She had lost a lot of weight and the sparkle wasn't in her eyes like it used to be. I knew that she had gone through a hard time since her husband James died two years ago in a car accident.

When the others came upstairs, I pulled out a frozen lemon pound cake and a cherry strudel. I put them on a baking sheet to warm them up in the oven. The best thing was it would make the house smell of fresh-baked goodies.

We extended that table to accommodate eight people and Marie helped me set the table. I slipped my arm into her elbow and leaned toward her.

Her blue eyes looked into mine and I noticed her eyes were starting to fill with tears so I gently led her away to my office.

"Hi, darling. How are you doing?" I hadn't seen much of her since James died. They lived in Toronto, where his work was and his family lived. She had told me in private she hoped that someday they would move to the west coast since his company had an office in Vancouver too, but all their plans had changed.

I knew that it had been a very difficult two years for her. But she hadn't wanted to move the children from Toronto where they had their other grandparents, friends, and school.

I went to Toronto to help her as often as I could, but living here on the west coast, I could only do so much for her.

I wish I could take this terrible pain from her. I had hoped that over time the pain of loss would ease.

"I'm okay, Mom," she said. "Really. It is getting better all the time, but there isn't a day I don't think of him. I've decided my main responsibility is to the girls. I need to ensure they don't forget their father and his love for them. I do have something to tell you, though."

I saw her hesitate. She sucked in a deep breath, then locked eyes with me.

Her lips parted as she prepared to speak, then she hesitated. Finally she said, "Maybe we should call Dad in, too. I want to talk to the both of you, if it's okay?"

I nodded. I was growing increasingly nervous. What could be so important? When I was visiting Marie, I helped her with the funeral arrangements and also took a look at their wills and finances. I knew she was in good shape financially. The house would be paid off and his work had a good death benefit. The pension would not be that much since he had only worked for about fifteen years with his company, but the girls had a paid-up college fund, so that was another positive. Marie had a good job with the Bank of Nova Scotia in Toronto. She had worked there for fifteen years.

Marie disappeared into the kitchen.

My mind was going through all the terrible things it might be. Was she sick? Were the girls sick?

Marie, with Tom behind her, came back into my office. He had a worried expression on his face and moved to stand next to me.

"Mom, Dad, the girls and I are relocating to Vancouver."

Her eyes flitted between Tom and me, trying to judge our reaction.

"Um," I started and then just walked up and hugged her. I held back the tears. "I've missed you so much. I always wanted to do more to help you."

"You don't mind?" Marie asked.

"Oh, Marie, completely the opposite," said Tom, his voice thick with emotion. "No, it's marvelous."

"We're not going back," said Marie. "I've sold the house and I have some details to take care of. But if we can stay here with you for a while until we find a house in the neighborhood, it would be great. If that's okay with you guys?"

"Darling," I said, struggling to contain my excitement, "you and the girls can stay with us as long as you want or need to. Where will they be going to school? It will be our treat to have you and the girls here. You don't have to worry."

"The girls can go to Henderson elementary and John Oliver high school. We can register them tomorrow if you'd like," said Tom, wiping at his eyes with the back of his hand.

I hadn't realized how much Tom missed our daughter and our granddaughters until then. I had been lucky and had stayed on after the funeral with them for a couple of weeks, but Tom had had to go right back to work. And our timetables and vacations just didn't work for the last year at all. It had been a very long time since we'd had any quality time with Marie and the girls.

My head was going round with all the things that needed to be done. I stopped myself. I realized that it would all get done when it was meant to get done.

After all, we did have a guest room upstairs and Marie could stay there and the girls could share the other bedroom downstairs. It had a queen bed in it and they were both young so it should be fine for them to share until they had a place of their own.

I was so happy to hear Marie was thinking of staying in the neighborhood. If she could manage it, that would be wonderful.

"What about work?" I asked in a small voice. I didn't want to seem like those nosy mothers, but I was curious.

Marie nodded. "I've transferred to the branch at Forty-Ninth and Fraser. I start there after Easter. So we can have a nice relaxing holiday; I will start work right after. The best part is I can walk to work, right Mom?" Marie smiled at me.

I was so proud of her. She had taken care of all the essentials.

Old Bones

"And I have agreed to let the girls visit Mom and Dad Logan during the holidays. So they will have time with their other grandparents too. Kind of like a time-share for children, or more accurately, with children."

I was watching Tom. He hadn't said anything more. He was beaming. We would be talking about it in more detail when we were alone and out of earshot of our children. He was really a wonderful husband and father.

"Okay, well, that sounds like it's all settled then," Tom said as he opened my office door and led the way back to the kitchen. "Why don't we let the rest of the family in on the big news."

Funny, everyone quieted down when the four of us entered the kitchen. It was almost eerie, but our gathered family was exchanging smiles.

Marie went and stood next to Rodney and then everyone turned and looked at Tom and me. I had the distinct impression that they all knew something I didn't. I wanted to go into the bathroom and check my teeth to see if I had something green between them.

"Okay. Marie has something she'd like to share with everyone," Tom said solemnly, which even I knew was a put-on.

Rodney, Jennifer, Kit, and Marie laughed loudly. "We all know, Dad," Rodney said through the laughter. "But I don't think that you know our news," he said after glancing at Jennifer and Kit.

"Okay, what's the news?" I asked, feeling way, way out of the loop.

"You know that empty lot that they're building on down the street?" asked Jennifer.

Oh, Lord. I felt my excitement rise. It couldn't be. Could I really be getting my family back? I tried to calm myself and swallow my excitement, but my mouth had gone dry so I failed.

"Well, it's our house," finished off Kit with a grin.

"You're all coming home?" I asked as I found an empty chair and sat down.

Tom's eyes were shiny with tears. I picked up a napkin from the middle of the table and dabbed my eyes. I could see clearly again. And I started to laugh. We had been concerned that when we retired it would be so quiet with just the two of us rattling around in the old house. I guess we had gotten a bit of a reprieve from that.

"I've gotten a job at Langara College and I start in September. So that will give me some time to get myself ready for my first term at being a professor," said Rodney, looking very pleased with himself.

"You've finished your PhD," I asked, looking at him.

We had known that he had been working on it for a long time, but with Jennifer, the full-time job, and Christopher, well, I had stopped asking how it was going, knowing that if and when he had something to tell us, he would.

"Quick, Tom, get out the champagne from the downstairs refrigerator. I'll get the glasses. We have some non-alcoholic bubbly stuff in the cold room too; bring it all up. Tell us everything," I said looking at both of the families.

I realized we had missed so much with them living so far away and now we would have a chance to catch up.

"I've just graduated and the ceremonies are in May and I would like you both to be there," said Rodney.

I heard the doorbell ring and ignored it. I watched Kit get up to open it. Buddy only woofed once and followed Kit. He came back in a few minutes.

"Oma, Gramps," Kit said to me and Tom as he came through the basement stairs. "There are two policemen at the door for you," he said with a quivering voice, holding Buddy close to his chest.

Old Bones

I felt my heart start to pound hard. If it had been our police officers, they would have just come in and poured themselves a cup of coffee.

I looked at my watch and knew that it was something to do with Joy. Something had happened to her. I could feel it in my bones: something horrible had happened. Then I felt a wave of calm wash over me as I stood up.

"I'll go to the door, Tom; you stay here," I said, trying to deflect the others from getting involved.

I felt like there was a large lump of ice in my chest making it hard to breath. I felt cold and started to shiver.

I opened the front door and there were two uniformed officers standing on the stoop. One was an older, gray-haired officer with a dark, heavy mustache and thick eyebrows and the other a young, blond-haired man.

"Please, won't you come in?" I asked as I stood to one side.

They both came and took of their hats and held them in their hands.

"Hello, are you Mrs. Heather Ross?" said the older one to me.

I nodded and opened the door to the living room and went in. I motioned with my hand that they should sit down.

"No, thank you. Are you Mrs. Ross?" the officer asked again.

"Sorry. Yes, I am. How can I help you?" I asked, trying to keep my voice calm and myself from shivering.

"There was a car accident this morning, and a Mrs. Joy Kendal asked that you take care of her dog Kirby for them," said the officer.

I looked at them, puzzled with this request.

It didn't sound like they were dead.

"Are they, I mean is she…?" I couldn't say the words.

I had really only known Joy for such a short time, but it was like we had known each other for our entire lives.

"Oh, both Mr. and Mrs. Kendal are okay. They were in a car accident this morning and are in the hospital. Mr. Kendal will probably have to stay overnight and Mrs. Kendal wasn't sure what time she would be home. So Officers Ryan Falcon and Nigel Wallace asked us to come by your home and drop off the house key." With that the officer held out a brass house key.

I took the house key in my fingers that had been numb, but were now starting to warm up.

"Sure. Not a problem. You say that Joy is fine, but Mr. Kendal is in the hospital?"

"Yes, they were going to her place of work when a car ran right into them. They were T-boned and the driver fled the scene. It seems that the car was stolen. But they hit the driver's door with significant impact to buckle the door; another six inches and he wouldn't have been so lucky. Mr. Kendal seems fine but doctors want to keep him for observation," said the young officer.

I watched the older officer looking at the younger one. It seemed that he didn't approve of what the younger officer had told me. Which, I guess, was more than I should have known.

"Thank you, gentlemen. Do you know if Mrs. Kendal's cell phone is working? Don't worry about it, I will call her number and leave her a message. Thank you very much for letting me know," I said as I walked them out of the house.

They both nodded and put on their hats as they headed for the front door.

I glanced down the hall as I let the officers out and saw Tom watching me. I nodded and shrugged my shoulders to let him know that everything was all right; at least it wasn't too serious.

Old Bones

I really felt that my nerves were on edge. I had been counting on Joy to come over today and get the outline for the book down in print form.

I chided myself for being so selfish. I knew that no one was really hurt so my mind switched on to more mundane tasks.

The first thing I had to do was to go over and let Kirby outside and make sure that he had food and water. I'd take Buddy with me so they could play together for a while. I would normally just bring Kirby home with me, but with all the bodies in our little house right now and everything in an uproar, I thought that wouldn't be the best thing for anyone, especially Kirby.

Maybe I could bring him home this evening once I got people in their rooms and settled.

Chapter Twenty-two
Last visit to one who knows

Kɪʀʙʏ ᴡᴀs ᴅᴏɪɴɢ his best to pull my arm out of my shoulder socket. He was dragging me down the street, sniffing at every lamppost, tree, and blade of grass as he went.

It had gotten very cold last night, almost down to freezing. I couldn't believe it was March and almost Easter.

Fine; it wasn't freezing, but it was unseasonably cold. For people who were born and raised in Vancouver, or Lotus Land as some people called it, we just weren't used to it being this cold for this long. Yes, rainy or cloudy days we could handle, although we would grump about it to everyone, but not this cold.

I had contacted Joy that morning. She told me she would drop over to my house tonight. The hospital was going to keep Edgar overnight for observation since the car they had been in had been hit so hard, but she hadn't suffered any injuries. Edgar had been really jerked around but since he'd had his seatbelt on, it had kept him from anything too serious. He had been thrown against the steering wheel, striking his head hard. The doctors wanted to make sure he didn't have a concussion.

Edgar had been driving Joy to work; she had been dozing, trying to catch a few more minutes of sleep, so her head was back against the headrest and she was relaxed so the crash didn't really do much to her at all. But she wanted to sit by Edgar's side and make sure he was okay.

Old Bones

Joy did ask if I could walk Kirby. He was a wonderful dog; still, a puppy who needed obedience training, especially walking lessons. Tomorrow morning first thing I would go to the closest pet store and buy Joy a gift of a Halti, basically a horse halter for dogs. They are wonderful to control large, strong dogs like Kirby.

He kept surging ahead, then stopping short. Finally I instructed him in a stern tone to sit and stay as I approached his left side. I put his leash around the back of my waist and held it in my opposite hand. The hand next to Kirby's head was free and my body was taking most of the strain from his pulling.

We started off once again.

I looked at Kirby, who was really enjoying this walk training that we were doing. He started to watch me and follow me. As he let me lead him, I started to praise and give him treats. He was such a smart, funny dog.

Looking down at Kirby, I was very pleased as his progress.

I'd have to talk to Joy when she got home and let her know what I was doing with him. I find that everyone has a favorite training method, but the trick it to pick one and remain consistent.

"Hi there, what a beautiful dog you have," called a voice behind the fence.

"Oh, hello. It that you, Mister Rempel?" I asked as I approached the fence with Kirby beside me.

For his part, Kirby was panting heavily and his long, plumed tail was waving back and forth.

"It that you, Heather? Where is Buddy? He's okay, isn't he?" asked a worried Mr. Rempel.

I smiled weakly. It was too darned cold to be not moving. "Oh, Buddy is fine. He's at home helping the family settle in."

"Good, good. Please don't call me Mister Rempel, Heather, please call me Otto."

"Okay, I'll try." I hesitated. I had called him Mister Rempel forever, it seemed. I wasn't sure I would ever be able to change, but I assured him I'd try.

Regardless, the timing was perfect. I was hoping to talk to him in a couple of hours to ask him a few questions that Joy and I talked about, only now I had Kirby in my hands. I hadn't planned on running into him like this.

Joy and I both thought Otto had the information that we needed. But we also knew we had to be gentle with him and that anything we got, we would have to be sure we double and triple checked.

"Heather, why don't you and that handsome lad you've got there come into the house and join me in a cup of tea?" asked Mister Rempel in a hopeful tone of voice.

"That would be wonderful," I said, grateful to be getting out of this cold air. "Kirby is a really big handful, Mister…uh, I mean, Otto. Are you sure it would be okay?"

I could just see Kirby laying waste to the poor old dear's living room with his tail and leaving clumps of fur in his wake.

"No, please." He waved away my concerns. "I would love to have the two of you visit. I've always liked big dogs. We had shepherds in Germany, and we had big dogs when the children were growing up. Please, come in." He swung open the backyard gate to admit us.

It creaked as it swung open. I noted, from the chipped paint and gray wood, it must have been quite a while since the old wooden gate and fence had been painted.

I made Kirby wait until I had gone through the gate and then I turned and called for him to come. He followed me calmly. He was being a very good boy.

Old Bones

I was pleasantly surprised and very pleased with him.

"Please join me in a cup of tea, will you?" said Otto. "I enjoyed the party at your house the other day." He led the way up the back stairs into his warm, cozy kitchen.

The house was probably about sixty years old. It seems to me that most of the older homes in the area were built at about the same time.

According to what my parents said, all this area in Vancouver was pretty much undeveloped when they came here about sixty years ago.

The kitchen had wood veneer cupboards and a brown Formica countertop. The floor was covered by green tiles with a dark yellow grouting. I wasn't sure if the floor was really that color or if it needed a really good scrubbing, probably a bit of both.

Otto placed a steel kettle on an element of his old-fashioned electric stove and turned it on. I took a look around and it was a pretty standard kitchen for this style of house. I would say the house was about the same size as ours, so that would be about one thousand square feet on each floor, and there were two floors. The top one, where we were now, usually contained the kitchen, living room, dining room, two or three bedrooms, and a main bathroom.

The laundry room was usually downstairs. Then there was room for a family room, or what we used to call a rec room, short for recreation room, downstairs and quite often one or two additional bedrooms; and if the people were really lucky, an additional bathroom.

Otto's kitchen was painted with soft yellow walls while the appliances were plain white. The curtains framing the window overlooking the backyard were white with yellow daisy's. There was a round oak table that could seat four people in the middle of the kitchen, covered with a yellow-and-white checked tablecloth that fit exactly.

And something I thought clever was that someone had put glass on top of the table so that all you needed to do was wipe it down. It would always stay clean.

The kitchen had a nice sunny, airy feel about it.

Otto Rempel moved slowly, but steadily, around the kitchen making our tea. When he took the teapot out of the cupboard, I noticed the cupboard was filled with mugs and mismatched cups and saucers. A lot of the cups and saucers appeared to be cracked and chipped.

There were also a couple of stacks of empty yogurt and cottage cheese containers and a stack of unused Ziploc containers still in their original packaging.

I noticed his hands were shaking as he brought the teapot to the table and poured some barely steaming water from the kettle in the teapot to heat it.

"Mister Rempel…I mean Otto, how long have you lived here?" I sat down on one of the ladder back oak chairs at the table.

"Let's see," he said, his brow wrinkled in thought. "I've been in this home for about sixty…no, sixty-five years. It was one of the first of its kind built on this block. Elizabeth, my wife, had this house designed when we moved here from the East. We originally settled in Toronto." He chuckled softly at the memory. "We lasted two winters— and when I got my degrees updated, we moved to Vancouver."

"Oh," I said genuinely surprised. "I didn't know you had degrees."

He smirked and shook his head. "It's doesn't matter anymore. But I taught at UBC." He poured out the warm water from the teapot into the sink, then filled it with the now boiling water, then added tea bags.

"I enjoyed it. It was a good life," he said as he sat at the table across from me.

Old Bones

Now I knew, or hoped, that I would be able to lead this conversation where I needed it to go. But I also knew this was the same man who yelled at people and chased kids away from his front door.

"Before you were in Toronto, where did you come from?"

"Germany, just like almost everyone else in those days," he said, his eyes dropping to the table and his trembling hands wrapped around the mug. "Yes, we were the lucky ones. Our children were already older, but they were allowed to immigrate with us anyway. It seems that UBC needed a person with my credentials and I was the only one available on short notice, so they pushed through my paperwork. And the minute we were here long enough, we applied to become landed immigrants and then became Canadian citizens." He sighed. "But that was a long time ago."

"What did you teach at UBC?"

"I already told you," said Otto, his eyes flared with anger. I'd struck a nerve. I tried to calm him down.

"Yes, I'm sorry. I meant to say, did you like teaching?"

His eyes settled and his frail frame relaxed. "History was fine, but I didn't enjoy teaching journalism and having to work with the students on the school newspaper."

I watched him closely, worried I may have thrown a wrench into the works and gotten him agitated. I waited a few moments he seemed to have calmed down. "Would you like me to pour?" I asked.

Otto nodded and leaned back in his chair.

I could feel my excitement growing in the pit of my stomach. He would have known the students we needed to find out more about. It could be that Otto Rempel was the person who held the key to this whole mystery.

It occurred to me that I should wait for Joy; we really should talk to Mister Rempel together. I was afraid that if I did it myself and forgot any questions, he would clam up and not tell us anything.

But I was right here right now and I wasn't sure this opportunity would come again.

I had heard from various sources in the neighborhood that his memory wasn't very good. And I remember Angela telling me the same thing too. Sometimes his mind was as clear as a bell and at other times he'd forget the simplest things; then he would get mad, which was understandable.

It sounded like the early onset of Alzheimer's to me, but I wasn't a doctor.

"Get the cookies in the cupboard and a plate so we can have a proper tea," he said as he motioned to one of the cupboards next to the stove.

"Oh, thank you, Otto," I said as I got up and found the cookies in the cupboard he'd indicated. I brought a small plate with some cookies on it back to the table.

Kirby seemed to think the cookies were for him and decided to jump around my legs trying to steal one. So I had my hands full.

"Kirby, sit," said Otto in a firm, clear voice that had Kirby sitting within a second, his brown eyes watchful.

Kirby had his eyes focused on Otto, waiting to see if there were any other commands forthcoming.

"That's a good boy," said Otto. He grinned as he leaned over and gave Kirby a pat on the head.

"I see you have trained dogs before."

"Yes, it was always a joy of mine, our dogs," Otto said with a thread of joy in his voice.

Old Bones

"My family had German shepherds, and labs at one time too, but mostly shepherds. Dogs are wonderful, but I can't handle them any longer. I see you and your friends walking your dogs in the mornings. I used to enjoy the walks too." He hung his head, looking a little sad and wistful.

I poured our tea and we sat in silence, each nibbling a cookie and sipping our tea for what seemed like an eternity.

"Otto, would you like to come with us in the mornings sometimes? My little dog Buddy is a good little fellow. Maybe you can walk him, if you'd like? If you're not too busy."

I watched as he put out his hand and stroked Kirby's wide, honey-colored head. Kirby in turn put his head on Otto's lap and emitted a large sigh.

"Otto, would it be all right if I come back with Buddy and my friend Joy? I know Buddy would like to meet you. That way he'll know you a little bit when we go for our walk. What do you think?"

Otto nodded and shifted his gaze to look out the kitchen window.

"Sure, bring your little dog and your friend. I have enough tea and cookies," Otto said enthusiastically. "When?"

"Later today? Will you be home?"

"Yes, where else?" He chuckled brightly. I'd made his day.

I stood up, making sure Kirby's leash was still secured to his collar. I thanked Otto. I would be back soon with Joy and Buddy for some tea, cookies, and, most importantly, information.

***

"They killed my baby," wailed Joy as she entered my front door and collapsed into my arms.

252

My heart skipped a beat. My mind went instantly to a bunch of questions and the first one was why Joy didn't have any children, at least as far as I knew.

"Joy! Let me help you," I said as I half dragged and half carried her into the house.

"Are you okay, Joy?" asked Tom as he rushed to help me carry the upset woman. "What's this I hear about someone killing your baby?" he asked as he put his arm around Joy's waist in order to hold her up.

"It's dead," she uttered between sobs. "They say that it can't be repaired and they're going to scrap her."

"Joy, are you talking about your car?" I asked.

"Yes, Edgar drove my baby to work because his car was in the shop, so of course I told him to use mine. Now he's in the hospital for observation and I'm home without any car. I'm trapped inside the house. I can't get out!" Joy cried out in a loud voice.

I was shocked. What was she talking about?

"Joy, you're not trapped in your house. You're out right now. You're with us. You're fine." I spoke in a calm voice, trying to quiet her. She was hysterical. Maybe she should have stayed in the hospital with Edgar for observation too.

It was something I hadn't realized before, but some people are really close to their cars. I guess. I always looked at cars as an object that was for transportation only. You know, a necessity or convenience.

"Joy, I knew you liked your little car, but really, it wasn't alive."

Joy stopped crying on Tom's shoulder and looked at me, her blue eyes wide open, filled with tears.

"Oh, of course it wasn't alive. I know that," she said. "But Edgar really gave me a scare and I couldn't cry while we were in the car waiting for the ambulance or at the hospital.

He was watching me all the time. As long as I made a fuss about nothing he was convinced everything was fine. That he was fine."

I nodded. It almost made sense. If Edgar was really hurt, anyone's first reaction would be to make a fuss; but with Joy deflecting her worries to her car, she'd tricked him into thinking she was okay.

"How is Edgar?" asked Tom as he took Joy's coat and threw it onto our bed.

I opened the hall closet and pulled out a pair of cozy sheepskin slippers. I handed them to Joy; she wiggled her feet into them and smiled at me.

"Oh, these are nice."

We walked together down the hallway into the kitchen. I made a quick stop to retrieve my notebook from my office, then joined her at the kitchen table while Tom put the kettle on to boil.

"Tea or coffee?" I asked Joy.

"Cookies, sweets?" she answered with a question.

"You must be feeling better, Joy," I said as I opened up the cookie tin in the middle of the table. I made a mental note to fill the tin more often.

Joy nodded and then watched as Rodney, Jennifer, Kit, and Marie, Tracy, and Morocco wandered up into the kitchen looking for food.

I made introductions all round and, once they had treats for downstairs, they all wanted to claim chairs downstairs in the family room.

That left Tom, Joy, and me alone upstairs while they nosily clamored down the basement stairs.

"It wasn't an accident," said Joy, looking out the kitchen window. "Thanks for taking care of Kirby, by the way."

I followed her gaze and saw the large bare cherry tree that guarded our generous deck.

"What do you mean it wasn't an accident?" asked Tom, his eyes curious.

"It should have been me in the hospital, not Edgar," she said, her mouth a grim line. "Actually, I really believe they meant to T-bone us on purpose." She paused. "No, I take that back. I think they meant to kill me, since I was the one who always drove the car." She shook her head sadly. "Poor little Birdie."

I remained silent. What she was saying was nonsense, but maybe she was still a little shocked.

"We have an invitation to visit with Mr. Rempel later this afternoon," I said, glancing at the wall clock in the kitchen.

Then I shifted my gaze to the black cordless telephone next to the stove. The red light was blinking. Someone had left a message. I wondered if it was from the pool table company. I had to get red of Tom.

"Tom, could you go downstairs to the freezer and bring up a cherry coffee cake," I said as I looked at Joy.

"Sure Heather," he said and left the kitchen.

I pressed the playback button to retrieve it. It was a message from the pool table company saying they would be delivering the table this afternoon at 12:30, not Sunday as they had originally told me. If this was a problem to please call them and let them know.

My stomach growled and I realized it had been a long time since I had breakfast. I still had to get Tom out of the house in less than a half hour or he would be helping to move his surprise retirement present in himself.

Not quite what I had imagined.

We very seldom go downstairs, really only to watch a movie on the weekend, and I had planned to keep Tom busy. I wanted the pool table to really be a surprise.

Old Bones

"Joy, I'll be right back," I said as I took a deep breath and moved quickly to the basement door. I opened the door and flew down the stairs and into the family room.

The family's eyes were on me as I came to a halt. "Quick, on with your coats," I said to Rodney, Jennifer, Marie, and the kids. "You need to take Tom out for lunch right now. They're bringing the pool table over a day early. In half an hour, to be exact."

I was pleasantly surprised when Rodney assured me they had a great idea about where to take Tom for lunch. They soon had pulled, pushed, and dragged Tom out of the kitchen into his coat, hat, and shoes and were leaving the house.

I was relieved when the front door closed behind the group with a dull thud.

It was finally quiet.

I checked the clock and everything was looking good.

Joy looked worried. Normally her bright blue eyes were lively and interested in everything going on around her. Today her eyes were dull and she appeared stunned by recent events. I concluded she must be in shock. This was a Joy who had lost her energy.

"Joy," I said. "How's your tea?"

"I knew you wouldn't believe me, but really, I was supposed to be driving that car this morning, not Edgar," she said. "The other car is in the shop, so he was going to drop me off and then use it for the day."

I took in Joy's words, listening without making any comment. There was no point. She needed to feel safe right now and that someone was paying attention to her. I wasn't going to make judgments about her.

I waited for her to finish.

When she paused I finally made a suggestion. "I need something to eat before the pool table guys arrive. How about I make us a couple of sandwiches? Toasted cheese with a pickle on the side, how does that sound?" I stood up.

Joy sat at the kitchen table sipping her tea, staring blankly at the wall. Her eyes flitted back and forth so I could tell her mind was racing with conflicting thoughts and emotions.

"Why me and not you?" she finally said.

I followed her line of thought, or at least I thought I did. Nothing had happened to me, or our stuff. Our house hadn't been broken into. My car hadn't been keyed. But I had been tripped on the ferry and that could have been a really serious accident.

"I was tripped," I said.

"Yes, I know, but nothing before or since then has happened to you. Maybe you getting hurt scared the person who was or is behind all of this. But they don't have the same regard for me," said Joy, staring at me.

Joy sat at the table as I mulled her words over in my mind. The obvious thing would be if it was someone from the neighborhood, someone I knew and that like me, and someone that didn't know Joy or care about her.

When I put it all together, it didn't seem so strange after all. Maybe I was correct and someone was after something, or at the very least wanted something covered up or to stay covered up. These events must somehow go back to the Old Bones case.

"I saw Mister Rempel this afternoon when I walked Kirby," I said to her. "You and I have an invitation to have tea at his place."

"Fine. When do you want to go?" She lifted her mug and drained it.

Old Bones

"Joy, do you want to go home and change or rest or something first?"

She smiled at me and shook her head. "I'll just use your washroom, then I'll be right as rain."

She disappeared into the washroom and I waited for the inevitable. It started low at first, then gradually grew louder until I heard a soft scream coming from the washroom. The door opened and Joy came out with a towel over her face and only her eyes were showing. "I'm naked. I'm completely naked."

"I don't think so, but you might want to put a little makeup on your pale, pasty, white face," I said, trying to interject some humor into the day.

"My purse, where is my purse?" asked Joy. She dropped the towel and looked around the kitchen.

"I didn't see you with one," I said as brightly as possible. "Did you leave it at home? I have a nice new Este color you might want to try. At least it will get you to your house."

"Listen," she said sounding slightly frantic. "I had my purse."

"O…kay," I said slowly. "I took your coat at the door and put it in the bedroom. If you had a purse, it's there since it's not in the kitchen."

We walked into the bedroom, where I knew we wouldn't find Joy's purse. I was sure she hadn't had it with her when she came to my door. "Joy, let's go to your house and see if we can find it, okay?"

I was surprised how really spooked she was. But then I could talk; my car hadn't just been hit and my husband wasn't in the hospital and my house hadn't been broken into.

We had to solve this case quickly. Whoever was behind this was upping the stakes and the stakes had gotten way too high.

They were putting people's lives in danger. And especially people I cared about.

***

We arrived at Joy's house, where she decided to quickly shower and change into something I hoped would be more like Joy. I kept my eyes fixed on the front window, watching for the Pool Tables R Us delivery truck.

I was really hoping the delivery guys would be able to get the table into the house, set up, and be on their way before Tom came back from lunch with the family. After all, how hard could it be to put up a pool table?

"Joy, I've got to go. Meet me at my house," I called to her. "Let's just hope that this pool table setup will be a fast operation. There is still a huge bunch of stuff I need to do today. Once the pool table is in, we'll to go to Mister Rempel's house, okay?" No response. "What time do you want to go to the hospital to see Edgar?" I asked as I opened her front door.

I looked back down the hallway to see Joy in her bedroom pulling a lime green fleece sweater and hot pink scarf from a dresser. The knot of tension that had been building between my shoulders relaxed. Now this was more like the Joy I knew.

Even her posture was different: her back was straight and her head was high. She had on a lovely coral lip gloss and dark brown eyeliner. I hadn't realized until now she had been a shadow of herself—a pale shadow at that.

"Sure, we'll go and see Mister Rempel," Joy called cheerily, her voice echoing down the hall. "And we'll get the information we need. Then we will see Catherine. I think, between the two of them, they hold the key to our little mystery.

Old Bones

That is, of course, after we see Edgar and go to the Bay. They have a sale on linens right now and I was going to check to see if I could find something for the guest bedroom. So that's perfect," she said as she pulled on her dark navy jacket over her sweater.

I looked down at my navy jacket. I had gotten at least one of the colors correct. I smiled to myself. I knew I would never become a peacock, probably not even a peahen, but that was fine with me. I liked classic style and comfortable function.

I could hear Buddy barking next door and I looked again; one of the deliverymen was ringing the doorbell. I ran out the door and raced over to my house, calling him as I went.

"Don't forget your purse and notebook. I'll drop them in your office," called Joy as she walked over to my house with them in her hand.

Chapter Twenty-three
Delivery

I GOT HOME just as a short, stout man with a long dark mustache was walking away. "Hello. I'm Mrs. Ross," I said, taking a deep breath. "You have a pool table for us? How long will it take to install?"

He grinned. "Hi, there, I'm Jake. Of Jake's Pool and Billiards. Yes, we do indeed have a pool table for you. It will take at least two hours to install and make sure the table is level. We'll get on it right now if you want. Do you want upstairs or down?"

"That would be downstairs, please, in the rec room," I said.

My heart sank at the thought of the time it would take. Should I call Rodney or Marie and ask them to somehow delay coming home?

I opened the front door and Joy was coming out of the upstairs of our house. "Just dropped off your purse and notebook in your office."

"Thanks, Joy," I said as I walked to the large moving van that two men, plus Jake, were standing at the back of. Jake had unlocked and opened the massive metal door at the back of the truck and was climbing inside while the other movers stood waiting.

"Excuse me," I said. "Do you think it would be better if you just went into the alley, then into the basement door with the pool table, rather than coming upstairs and through the front door and then down the somewhat narrow stairs into the basement?"

"Lady," said Jake as he scowled at me, "It's up to you, but it is easier to move it straight into the basement, and if that's where it's going to go, that's better for us. Is it a wooden floor or slab cement?"

261

Old Bones

"I believe it's a wooden subfloor over cement. Is that a problem?"

He shook his head. "No worries as long as it's level." He looked up at his workers.

"I had it checked by someone from your company and he said it was solid and level. He said it would take the weight of the pool table easily." I wondered what he was on about.

"Good. That's a good thing," he nodded and his lips curved up; he seemed to approve.

That made me feel much better. I had been worried the floor wouldn't be strong enough for the table and then the balls would be rolling around all over the place and the table would be useless.

"I'll unlock the basement door and meet you there to show you where I'd like it set up," I said and hurried back into the house.

I decided to call one of the kids and have them sit with the deliverymen while Joy and I paid visits to Mister Rempel at his house, Edgar in the hospital, and a shop for linens. (To tell the truth, the linens could wait—but I needed to help my friend in her time of need.)

I had just gotten into the house and the phone was ringing. I sighed. I just couldn't get a break today. I was almost ready to crawl back into bed and pull the sheets over my head and start a do-over. But I didn't have time for a pity party so my bed would have to wait.

I picked up the phone. "Hello," I said cheerfully, making a happy face at the receiver.

Joy started to laugh. I glanced at her and smiled. I had momentarily forgotten about her. Then I remembered she had brought over my purse and notebook when I ran home after the delivery truck showed up.

"Mom?" It was Rodney on the phone.

"I'm coming home with Jennifer and Kit. Don't worry, Marie and the girls are taking Dad to show them a couple of places with her real estate agent so that should keep him busy for a while. He said no at first, but then she asked him for his help and he had to change his mind," said Rodney with a brief laugh.

"Great, get here as fast as you can," I said. "I need you to stay with the deliverymen while Joy and I go and do a couple of interviews and then go shopping."

Finally. Everything was getting back on track.

"Okay, while you wait for Rodney, I'll go home to get my file. I think it might be a good idea if I brought Kirby with us on this mission too. You said Mister Rempel really liked him, so Kirby might keep him distracted while he answers our questions," said Joy.

"Do you want me to bring Buddy too, or are two dogs too much?"

"I think that might be a little much. I'll be right back."

I looked at Buddy, who sat on the floor looking up at me, his brown eyes hopeful. I sighed. If the rest of the day was going to be as busy as the day had been so far, I doubt Buddy would be getting his long walk in today.

"Sorry, Buddy, I can't walk you today, but tell you what. Rodney and Kit are coming home; I'll see if Kit will go for a walk with you, okay?"

I went to the ally and backyard to speak to the pool table installers and let them know that I would have to leave but that Rodney would be home to help give them if they had any questions.

Joy made it to her house in record time and I got Buddy squared away with fresh water and a stuffed dog toy, then grabbed my notebook and a lemon pound cake as a gift.

I joined Joy and Kirby. Kirby was pulling at the leash and yapping at every leaf, cloud, and breeze that came our way.

Old Bones

"Do you really think it's a good idea to take him?" I asked, worried Kirby might be too hyper. I knew Mister Rempel was really looking forward to having a dog come to visit today.

"Yeah, he'll calm down in a little while," Joy said. "Do you have any recommendations or ideas how to train him?" she asked as she looked at Kirby. He was so glad to see me. His ears were flopping around, his tongue was hanging out, and his tail was wagging so hard I was surprised he wasn't airborne.

"Okay," I said. "I'll show you what I do for puppies and dogs that are really pulling on their leash. The trick is they need exercise and discipline—and affection, but he's getting plenty of that." I smiled at Joy.

"I'd recommend a puppy obedience class; it is great for training and socializing. PetMart on Marine Drive has one coming up soon. But right now it's not going to be any fun if he pulls you this hard. I start by wrapping the leash around my waist," I took the leash from her and showed how I did it. "In Kirby's case, I'm going to hold the end of the leash in my opposite hand and actually use my body to hold him in place. That will free up my left hand, the one closest to him, so I can do some quick corrections. It's a start, but as you work with him in the house and outside, he will learn what you want him to do."

I snapped the leash once hard to get his attention and put him into the correct position at my side and told him to sit.

He did as instructed.

Joy's mouth dropped open and she gaped at me her, eyes wide with surprise.

"How...?"

"I'll trade you dog obedience lessons for stories. That way we both win. You'll have an awesome dog and I'll have an awesome story."

Joy nodded. "I know, it's going to be hard work for both of us over the next couple of weeks. Let's get this mystery solved."

***

Joy and I sat in Mister Rempel's sunny bright kitchen and watched as he fussed around making tea. The sweet scent of vanilla candles reached my nostrils.

I watched him put his white, whistling kettle on one of the stove elements to heat and it soon started to whistle. I really enjoy the homey sound of a whistling kettle.

"Mister Rempel…I mean Otto, can I give you a hand?" I asked as I put the lemon pound cake I had brought with us on the kitchen table.

I didn't want to upset him because, from the look of his messy house, I don't think he receives guests very often.

"Sure, the tea cups are in the right hand cupboard and the small plates are in the cupboard next to it," he said as he opened the tea cupboard to reveal a common brand box of black tea.

I peeked over his shoulder, noticing he had quite a variety of tea and coffee, so maybe I was wrong about him not entertaining. I even saw a French press among the containers of coffee, and next to it was a small grinder. I was changing my mind by the moment; it seemed that Otto either entertained or he gave himself the treat of good coffee and tea. Both were good ideas.

I smiled at him as I got a small plate out for our cake and sliced it with an old but very sharp knife with a bone handle. It reminded me of the ones my parents used to have that my dad would sharpen and use for carving the Sunday roast.

Old Bones

I got side plates and mugs out too. The plates were from an old English set I think called Petit Point. One of my aunts collected this kind.

I sat down again and pulled out my notebook. I glanced at Joy, who had her notebook poised ready to go, too. My lips curled at the corners.

Joy opened her book and a photo slipped out to fall on the floor.

I picked it up and showed it to Joy. She nodded to me, but didn't say anything. It was the picture we had received from Catherine Braun of the two men and the two women. One of the women was Catherine and the other she said was her sister, or did she say friend? I would have to check, but it certainly looked like our missing girl from UBC.

Joy took the picture from my hand and slipped it back into the inside pocket of her notebook.

Otto brought the tea to the table and sat down.

"Mister Rempel, would it be all right to ask you some questions about your days at UBC, specifically about some of your students?" Joy asked as she signaled Kirby to a sit next to her chair close to Mister Rempel. I was pleased to see him do as instructed

Otto smiled and leaned over to pet Kirby, who responded with a big friendly lick of the old man's hand accompanied by the heavy thudding of his wagging tail striking the floor repeatedly.

"Nice, boy. Yes, you are a wonderful boy," Otto said as his attention focused on Kirby.

I wondered if we had made a mistake bringing the dog for this particular visit.

"Sure, ask," Otto said with a shrug. "If I know, I will help." He poured the tea for us and then passed the plate with the cake.

I quietly opened my notebook and put down the time, date, where we were, and who was at this meeting. Then I took a slice of cake and was ready to take a bite when there was a quick tap on the kitchen door. It opened and there stood Angela with a faltering smile on her face and her hands full of fresh cinnamon buns and a small loaf of bread from BreakTime Bakery.

I looked at her and smiled. "Would you like to join us for a cup of tea, Angela?' I asked. Otto agreed.

I almost laughed as I watched the shocked expression on Angela's face, but I didn't. I was getting beyond angry with Angela. If it turned out she had the answers to our questions, then there better be a really good reason that she hadn't shared the information with us and, by extension, the police.

My heart did a flip-flop at my next thought. What if she wasn't covering up for another person, what if she was the killer? What if she was the one that committed the murders all those years ago? Would she kill again to protect herself? Or was she protecting someone else?

Now what? Do we wait for her to leave before we ask Otto our questions or do we just ask with her there? I think it would be best for her to leave. We can always visit her later to conduct a follow-up interview.

"Angela, can I help you with some of your groceries?" I asked as I stood up and took the bags from her.

"Tea or coffee, Angela?" asked Otto with a smile on his wrinkled features.

I wondered when was the last time he had three females in his house all at the same time?

"Angela, you caught us at a bad time. We came to ask Otto about the old bones," said Joy, taking the lead of stirring the pot, "to find out what he knows about them. Maybe you could come back and visit later?" It made me feel a lot better Joy had made the suggestion we talk later with Angela.

"Yes, I'll give you a call later," I said, trying to quell my growing unease. "Maybe we'll have some follow-up questions for you, too."

I decide to press Angela little further. "I recall you saying you didn't know anything, but maybe the information we've gotten from other people will help you remember something important and you can help us fill in the blanks."

I didn't understand what was going on. Angela was one of my closest friends. How could she have kept me in the dark about all of this? Angela went to her car and brought more groceries to the front door. She gave me the two bags of groceries, smoothed her gray hair with her hands, and gave me a brittle smile. Her ice-blue eyes were cutting into me.

"Of course, Heather, I'd love to help you," she said, but her words rang hollow. "Like I said, if there is anything I can do to help, just let me know."

I wanted to shake her. Her sudden cooperation rang false and I knew it because I know her. How dare she lie to protect herself?

Angela looked at Otto standing in his foyer and then at Joy. Angela wouldn't or couldn't meet my eyes again. I wondered what was going on in her mind.

"Otto, are you all right?" she said. "I didn't realize you knew Heather and Joy." Angela's voice sounded stiff.

"Oh, sure I know Heather and the family. Joy is new, yeah, but she has such a nice dog," replied Otto as he leaned down and petted Kirby on the head.

The dog gave him another wet kiss on the hand and Otto looked up at Angela and grinned at her.

"Otto, Kirby certainly likes you," I said. "I think I'll wash up first before we eat our cake. Do you have a little towel?" I prayed he would join me and wash his hands too.

"Yes, of course." He got up and opened a small drawer and pulled out a white-and-blue tea towel.

I quickly washed up, leaving the water running so he could do the same. Meanwhile Angela was standing by the door, not moving. I watched as her hand went to the zipper of her dark gray fleece jacket and wondered if she was going to take if off and stay.

Otto saw her and went and opened the back door. "Angela, come in, come in," said Otto.

But instead it seemed she had made a decision and zipped up her zipper as far as if would go under her chin. She appeared nervous, her fingers trembling on the zipper clasp.

"Not today, Otto, you have guests. Have a nice tea," she said as she turned to leave. "I guess I'll be hearing from you later. Otto, I'll give you a call tomorrow to see if you need anything."

I could hear her footsteps on the back deck until I heard the sound of the gate being opened and closed.

Joy had gotten up and was looking out the window over the kitchen sink. Finally she shifted her gaze to look at me.

"We'll call her to see if we can talk to her this afternoon. I think she may be able to help us." Joy tucked a lock of hair that had fallen in front of her face behind her ear. "That's going to make for a very busy afternoon with shopping and visiting Edgar."

"Maybe we should talk to her now and get that done," I suggested. "She might be able to help Otto remember as well. Just as long as she doesn't interfere with what we're doing here. What do you think?"

Old Bones

Joy nodded her agreement.

I quickly stood moved to the front door and opened it. I spotted Angela on the sidewalk.

"Angela," I called to her. "I'm sorry, that was very rude of us. Would you please stay? I think it would help Otto remember if there was another friendly face around. You're right, he only knows me a little and Joy not at all." I quickly stepped back into the kitchen, leaving the outside door open.

Angela quickly came back up the stairs, stepped into the warm room, and closed the doors behind her. I took her jacket from her and hung it on the back of her chair as she sat down. Her eyes looked expectantly at us.

It might be a mistake having her here, but I was hoping we would get a little more conversation from Otto and her together rather than separately.

"Well, Otto, I guess we should get started before the tea gets cold," I said in what I hoped was a normal voice.

I poured us—Joy, Otto, and myself—a refill, and a fresh cup for Angela, then passed the cake around again. I was surprised to see I had already eaten my slice. I recall taking the first bite when Angela came in, but where had the rest gone? I looked at Kirby and got another round of tail thumps from him. No, he couldn't have eaten it.

There was definitely the taste of lemon on my tongue, so maybe I did eat it after all. I took a sip of my tea and then got my pen to take notes.

Joy had done the same. Excitement grew in the pit of my stomach. I expected we would have the answers to a good many of our questions today. And even if we didn't, Joy and I would put something together that would be an awesome story.

"Otto, I have a couple of photographs that I would like to show you." Joy flipped to one of the pouches in her notebook and took out two pictures and handed them to Otto. "If you know who these people are or if they bring back any memories, please tell us."

Angela was sitting next to Otto and leaned over to look at the photographs.

I watched their reactions carefully. Joy jotted something down in her notebook. I also noticed Angela look at Joy's notebook and then at mine. Her jaw clenched tight and I watched as she closed her eyes. I smiled at Joy as she gave me a small nod.

I wondered if Joy was thinking the same thing I was. I suspected that the break-in into her house and a few other things were an attempt to retrieve one of the notebooks. But I think they may have had the wrong notebook.

Joy passed Otto the copy of the newspaper article with the picture of the two girls and waited.

He leaned forward, squinting, then laid the picture on the table. He must want to see it again. He looked at it again because he picked it up with his thick, gnarly fingers that moved almost gracefully. He stood up and went to the far kitchen cupboards and opened the top drawer. He looked almost shy as he slipped on a pair of glasses.

"My eyes are getting old," he said with a grunt of indignation.

"Otto, have you ever seen the people in that picture before?" Joy asked softly.

"Ya, as it says underneath, this is a picture of the group that produced the UBC Workers' News at the University. They were my students, working for me. They won awards for their paper. They were good students."

He scanned our faces as he spoke. His voice was firm and his words were clear.

Old Bones

He seemed to be standing taller, his back straight, his head held high. I could see him as a teacher at UBC. He would have been formidable as well as challenging to his students.

Otto looked down at the photograph again. His shoulders suddenly drew together, his back hunched, and he sighed deeply.

"She never came back to school. No word, no note. June would not have done that. She wouldn't have just disappeared." His hands trembled slightly. "Is she the old bones that were found at the empty lot down the street?" he asked with a catch in his voice.

"Otto, you remember her name." Joy said, excitement in her voice. "June. June what?" asked Joy.

"June Baker. She's the one on the right. The beautiful blonde. See the bracelet that she's wearing, and the little gold ring on her right hand. That's how I can tell that girl is June and not Irene Martin, the girl next to her. They were cousins, you know. Although they looked like twins, but June was the best. She was the nicest and smartest."

"Otto, they were identical. Neither was smarter or nicer than the other," interrupted Angela firmly, her lips pressed into a thin line.

I watched as Otto and Angela shook their heads simultaneously and spoke sharply and rapidly in German. They spoke too fast. I couldn't follow what they were saying. I looked at Joy, who was writing in her notebook and hoped that she had a better understanding of German than I did.

"Okay, you disagree as to which was smarter or nicer," I said. "I think that's just a matter of taste. You say they were cousins?"

"Yes, first cousins," said Angela, glaring at me. She pursed her lips, obviously not happy at being made to give up this information.

Chapter Twenty-four
Memories

"THE MARTINS IMMIGRATED from Germany a long time ago and became citizens of Canada. Both their children, Irene and Luke, were born in Canada. Then their cousins in Germany thought it would be good for their daughter, June Baker, to come to university here to learn better English. June was very pretty and the Martin family was surprised when she arrived because June and Irene could have been twins. Irene wasn't very pleased because she was used to being the pretty girl and wasn't ready to share her popularity."

I watched Otto nod.

"Yes, Irene was pretty, but not very smart and not very nice," he said. "People soon saw through her and preferred June." He gently shook his head.

"Angela, Otto, there is another picture I need you to look at. Please tell me if you know who is in the picture. Okay?" I opened my purse, then pulled out the photograph we had gotten from Catherine Braun showing Catherine, Peter, and Peter's brother Arnold and a very pretty blonde woman who looked like one of the girls. I set it on the table. I also had a picture of the students involved with the newspaper from the archives.

Otto and Angela looked at each other and then I watched Angela take Otto's hand in hers and hold it. She looked at him with a very sad smile on her lips and sighed.

"I think that it's time, Otto."

"Ya, it is. It's time," he said sadly.

Angela shifted her gaze to lock eyes with me. "If you look in the picture from the student paper, you will see in the background a few other people that you may not know." She took the paper and placed it in front of her.

"In the background you will see the two girls." She pointed at the background of the image of the would-be twins. "Peter and Arnold Braun are there. Also, if you have a copy of the names of the rest of the students involved, you will see Beverly Frissell's name and a few others."

I looked at Angela and saw in her eyes she was remembering rather than reciting something she had heard and committed to memory.

"We were so young then," she said wistfully. I saw her hand tightened on Otto's, then let go.

"Otto was teaching European History and Journalism at UBC and was involved with the student paper. My husband, Ervine Kay, was finishing his degree at UBC and was helping Otto with the student paper. We really weren't involved except for the paper, which, as it turned out, was the eye of the storm, you might say. We were all swept into it."

"My two brothers, Peter and Arnold, always did compete at everything. As they got older Peter took it more to heart, he couldn't let Arnold win at anything. I don't know the entire story, but I will tell you what I know," Angela said, looking directly at me. Her eyes were open and honest. I wondered if I would finally believe her. "Arnold and June were in love, they wanted to get married. They did their best to keep it from Peter, but when Peter found out he became crazy with jealousy."

Kirby started to whine and got up from under the table. He padded to the back door, then looked at us expectantly.

I knew that look. It meant he had to go out to relieve himself.

"Joy, I'm sure he can use Otto's backyard this once. Otto?"

The old man shrugged. "Ya, sure, let him out. The backyard is completely fenced so he won't escape." He stood up, unclipped Kirby's collar, and opened the door for him. Kirby got the idea right away and ran down the steps to the backyard.

Otto came right back, but left the door slightly open.

"The best I know is the body was June's and the baby's body was Irene's baby," Angela began to explain, her voice taking on a slight German accent. "It was a stillbirth and June's death was an accident. But Peter used it to force Irene to change her name to Catherine in order to marry him. I was told he had a shovel in his hands and was digging a grave for the baby in the backyard when June came up to him and started attacking him. She thought he'd killed Irene's child. What happened next, you'll have to verify with Catherine / Irene. I wasn't there and neither was Otto, but we were told that when Peter's back was turned, June attached him, and he swung out with the shovel to defend himself and hit and killed June," Angela shifted her gaze to Otto, who nodded his agreement.

"Why didn't Catherine come forward and tell the police?" asked Joy.

"She couldn't," Angela said. "Peter told her if she did, they would hang him and her."

"Peter didn't love Irene but married her and made her promise not to tell anyone," said Otto. "He also told her that since they were married, she couldn't tell anyone what happened or testify against him in a court of law. I guess if he couldn't have June, he'd have Irene." Otto's forehead was wrinkled and his eyes reflected his frustration at the memory of those past events.

Old Bones

"Ya, I think that Irene went a little crazy after she lost the baby and June and lived in her own made up world," said Angela.

"But that's not true," said Joy. "But again, if you're afraid for your life, you'll believe anything."

"I told Irene she was being stupid. But whenever I tried to talk to her, she just started to shake and almost have a panic attack," said Angela.

"Why didn't you go to the police?" asked Joy.

Both Angela and Otto were weighing their answers, but most important, their body language said they were scared. Then a bark at the outside door broke the rising tension in the room. Angela smiled to herself.

"Coming, mother," said Joy as she got to her feet and opened the two doors wide.

Kirby bounded into the kitchen; his eyes were bright and his head was held high. His long, heavy, feathery tail was wagging hard and his mouth was open with his tongue hanging to one side. He looked like a very pleased and happy dog.

I continued to watch Angela and Otto. Finally he looked at her and nodded.

"Heather, just so that you understand," said Angela, "Otto and I have been seeing each other, as friends, for the last fifteen years. We worked at UBC all those years ago, but there was never really a spark between us then. Otto was married then and I got married while I worked there, but we were friends and were aware of some of the things that were going on around us.

"Also, my brothers were passionate and impetuous. When June died, we really didn't wish to ask too many questions."

Something was wrong with this picture. How could you not ask questions or talk to the police when someone is murdered?

I forced myself to keep my head still and concentrated on taking down my notes without saying anything.

"You should have gone to the police," said Joy. "What about the baby? How could Irene have hidden the fact that she was pregnant? And when the child was stillborn, what did Peter do, just dig a hole in the ground?"

"Look, why don't you start from the top," I said. "I have a little tape recorder, which I'll put on the kitchen table. That way you can both just talk about the things you remember in the order you remember it. Okay? Just as long as you know that the police are going to want to talk to you. Joy and I just want to see if there is enough information and if they can use it."

"Ya, I think that we should tell the girls and the police what we know and that way they can sort it out. People are gone now and the truth should come out. No one can get hurt now," said Otto, looking at Angela.

Angela's eyes flitted between Otto and me. Finally she nodded her head. Her eyes had filled with tears.

I pulled out my tape recorder, put it on the kitchen table, and turned it on.

"Stop," said Otto as he looked at Angela. "Please, get the police. This is too hard on Angela. If we have the police here, then we will only have to go through this one time."

I turned off the tape recorder. Actually, I had a sense of relief, in a way. I agreed with Otto: the police should be called in right now.

I wanted to be there when they questioned Otto and Angela, and also Catherine.

Joy nodded at me. We were still on the same wavelength.

"I have my cell phone on me," Joy said. "I'll call the police from here. I'm sure they have their own way of taking care of these things."

I finished taking my notes regarding our conversation.

Joy stood and put her hand on Otto's shoulder and then lightly touched Angela's, too.

"You have to understand that most of what I know and Otto knows is heresay," said Angela's voice broke and the words failed to come.

"Angela, it's time for it to come out," said Joy, her voice gentle. "It's been fifty years. Maybe Catherine will put this behind her, too. I gather that Janet Frissell knew as well? And that was one of the reasons you kept in touch with her all these years too. I saw the Christmas cards from you to Janet when we went to the home in Victoria."

I nodded, thinking of the cards I had found and given to Joy. That made sense. They'd kept in touch with each other not just because of friendship, but because of guilt as well.

"Heather, I am so sorry about Joy," said Angela as she fidgeted with her fingers.

"What do you mean?"

Joy was on her phone talking to Ryan to set up a time for them to come to Otto's house.

"Here's Otto, you can arrange a time with him. Would it be possible for Heather and me to witness the statements being taken? I see…" said Joy.

Joy handed the phone to Otto and shook her head. I understood it was time for the professionals to take the ball and run with it.

"Angela, was it you who keyed my car and broke into my house?" Joy softly asked Angela.

"Yes, it was me who keyed your car and the robbery, I live very close and after Pastor Jeffery waked me home I came back, broke into your house and tired to find the notebook with all the information you had. I took your jewelry to make it look like a burglary. I have it at home," Angela stopped and took a deep breath. " It was me, too, that tripped you, Heather," replied Angela. "I'm so sorry. I was just trying to scare you both off. I just wanted you to leave us alone."

I started to speak, but she held up her hand.

"What we were doing was making it bad again. Especially after that fall you took. I was so scared that you'd really been hurt. You're both right, the whole story needs to come out into the light." She stopped talking as tears began to roll down her cheeks. She hung her head.

"Joy? Shall we?" I asked as I heard the murmur of Otto in the background talking to the young detective on Joy's phone. She nodded. Otto gave the phone back to Joy and looked a me.

"What about Janet Frissell?" I asked.

"That was Ryan, he said the police checked out Janet Frissell and she wasn't murdered she had a heart attack and died of natural causes."

It was time to go. Joy came and stood next to me, and Kirby stood too, his tail wagging.

"Let's get together after dinner tonight. We have the story to complete," I said, after Joy accepted her phone from Otto.

"I have a house full of people and it will be just fine. I've written a book at super speed and I can do it again," I said as I picked up my notebook.

Old Bones

"Okay. Let's go visit Edgar, then go to Buy Rite in Richmond to get the linens and things. They have pretty much everything you were talking about on sale," said Joy.

"Perfect," I said. "Because I need to get typing. I am a writer and I have a story to tell.

About the Author

Rita lives in Vancouver, B.C. with Russ, her husband who is also a fiction writer.

She loves to read and paint in her spare time. She is learning to enjoy golf, and he is learning to enjoy gardening. They are kept company, and on track, by their two dogs and Glenn, their younger son.

She has written for years and is an alumni of the Oregon Writers Network and the Greater Vancouver Chapter, Romance Writers of America. To find out more about her and her work visit her website at http://www.ritacrossley.com

Also by Rita Schulz

Novels

Fire In Their Hearts (with Russ Crossley)
Old Bones

Collections

Ladies of the Jolly Roger with Russ Crossley
Ten Tempting Tales with R.S. Meger
The Fantastic Five with R.S. Meger
Unique Tales of the Fantastic
Tales of the Fantastic
Nightmares (coming soon)

Short Fiction

Blarney
Flower & Bird
Party Central
Once Upon a Time
The Scarlet Curse
Spoken Words
The Brownie's Holiday
A Little Old Fashioned
In The Land of Dragons
A Little Kitchen Magic
Silver Light
For Pete's Sake
Cleaning Up is Hard to Do
Confessions of a Bold Maiden
All for One
Lucky List
A Spark of Courage

Party Line
Spoken Words
One Day At A Time
Three Sisters

Another title from 53rd Street Publishing.

Nightmares come in many forms and from many places.

Blood thirsty vampires.
Flesh ripping werewolves.
Brain eating zombies.
Spirits of the dead who walk among us.
Monsters of unspeakable horror appearing from the darkness.

They attack us from the past.
They attack us from alternate realities,

They appear from the depths of unspeakable darkness thirsting on our fear.

These tales of terror are guaranteed to keep you awake at night with the lights on. So sit back keep the lights burning brightly and hope ther